LIKE

COURAGE

ON A

STARLESS

NIGHT

LIKE
COURAGE
ON A
STARLESS
NIGHT

STACY BAIR OGDEN

Cover design by Victoria McCombs
https://violet-night-designs.square.site/

Interior Formatting (Print) by Cheyenne van Langevelde
Interior Formatting (ebook) by Susan L. Markloff

Proofread by Cheyenne van Langevelde

Author photo by David Ross

ISBNs:
979-8-9890960-0-8 (paperback)
979-8-9890960-1-5 (ebook)

TABLE OF CONTENTS

Chapter One: Danger in a Simple Gaze..1
Chapter Two: An Extravagant Prison..4
Chapter Three: Shattered...7
Chapter Four: Reunion..11
Chapter Five: Worrisome Introductions..18
Chapter Six: The Deal..21
Chapter Seven: Enemy...28
Chapter Eight: Healthy Release..33
Chapter Nine: On Edge..38
Chapter Ten: Learning to Breathe...42
Chapter Eleven: The Weight of Loneliness..49
Chapter Twelve: Humbled..55
Chapter Thirteen: The Kindness of a Stranger......................................64
Chapter Fourteen: Forgiveness Extended...75
Chapter Fifteen: Songs and Summons..81
Chapter Sixteen: Interrogation..89
Chapter Seventeen: A Plot Uncovered...95
Chapter Eighteen: The Eternal Binding...101
Chapter Nineteen: Seeking Deceit..107
Chapter Twenty: A Feast of Lies...114
Chapter Twenty-One: Inky Guilt..120
Chapter Twenty-Two: No Such Thing as Coincidences.........................126
Chapter Twenty-Three: An Impulsive Plan...129
Chapter Twenty-Four: The Heckler...135
Chapter Twenty-Five: Found Out..138
Chapter Twenty-Six: Confession...140
Chapter Twenty-Seven: Consequences..143
Chapter Twenty-Eight: Menace at the Border.......................................148
Chapter Twenty-Nine: The Arrest...152
Chapter Thirty: A Reason to Celebrate...158
Chapter Thirty-One: A Milestone Reached...161

Chapter Thirty-Two: What the Darkness Hides....................................165
Chapter Thirty-Three: The Morning After....................................174
Chapter Thirty-Four: Beginning Anew....................................179
Epilogue....................................185
Acknowledgements....................................188
About the Author....................................189

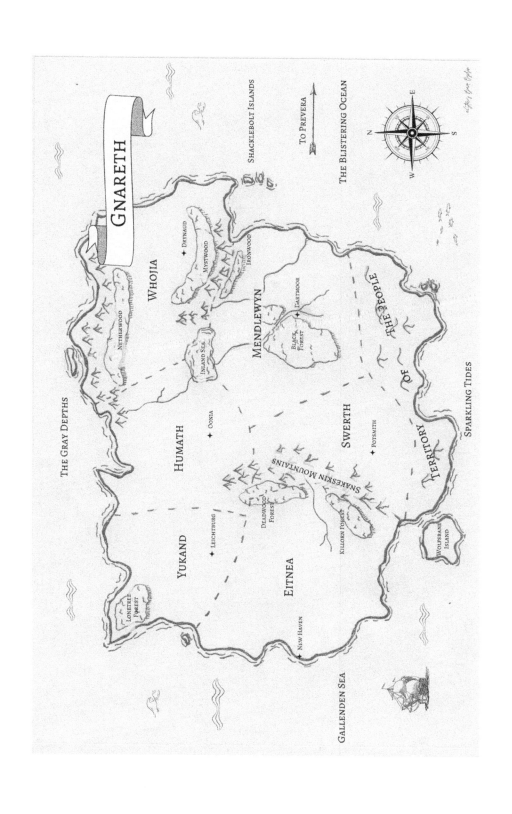

ꞸHAPTER ꞸNE
ꞸDANGER IN A ꞸSIMPLE ꞸGAZE

Naya

Middle of Thirdmonth, 1249 R.K
(Reign of Kings)

WHATEVER YOU DO, don't look them in the eyes.

That phrase had become my mantra over the years.

Don't look them in the eyes, don't look them in the eyes.

A faint rattling sound, almost too quiet to hear, tickled my consciousness.

The dishes on the tray I was holding were vibrating ever so slightly. The tray was shaking. No, not the tray. It was my hands that were trembling.

Stop that. My order changed nothing.

As smoothly as I could, I set the tray down to avoid a disaster. I stepped away quickly and barely caught the soft feminine voice as it whispered, "Thank you."

My face remained lowered, but even then, I refused to allow the cringe to show. The voice was kind. Gentle. And that made it so much worse, because if I ever did look into this woman's eyes—eyes that in my heart of hearts, I imagined would be just as soft as her voice—it would spell the end of my existence. After all I had done to get here, to this small realm of peace amid day-to-day chaos, that would shatter me.

I studied the floor and willed my hands to cease their quivering.

Whatever you do, don't look them in the eyes.

I could not leave the dining hall fast enough. Gripping the empty tray with hands now free from tremors, I turned in the direction of the kitchens, weaving through the line of servants entering the room behind me. I hurried until I found myself alone in the hallways, and then I leaned against the cool stone wall and simply breathed.

In.

Out.

In...

Out...

There never seemed to be enough air in the grand room where the royal family feasted— no matter that you could have fit my childhood home in there with ease. And the neighbor's home as well. All that openness and still to this day, it made my lungs constrict in my chest the second I entered its walls.

Footsteps echoed nearby and then my solitude was gone, as quick as it had come.

"Naya! What is this? You had better not be slacking, girl." A short rotund woman came down the hallway, a waddle in her step.

I straightened, hugging the tray to my chest. "Forgive me, Miss Sue," I murmured, never raising my gaze above her shoulders. "I just was taking a moment to..." I trailed off, unable to voice my latest disappointment.

Miss Sue huffed and glanced back toward the dining hall. A beat passed and then she held out a plump hand for the tray. "Never you mind, lass. Get on your way. You best skedaddle to the library. Quickly, quickly!" She hurried away, muttering something about how she should have known better than to assign me to serve the royals.

Tucking away the shame that bubbled up from my belly, I made my way to the library.

Pushing open the doors, I snatched up a feather duster that was resting on a nearby table and headed toward the far side of the room. Here, I was in control— in charge. When I first arrived here two years ago, it quickly became clear to my employers that, while I could work in the kitchens and among others, I needed solitude in my work days, and I was sent to the library. It was a spacious room, with dozens of shelves with even more trinkets sprinkled through them. It took a lot of work to maintain its pristine appearance but I did it with enthusiasm.

An hour or so later, I drew aside the floor-to-ceiling drapes in the corner, blinded momentarily by the brightness of the glaring sun. My eyes adjusted and I slipped into the circular den. Comfortable in size, three large windows took up the far wall, and a well-worn chair nestled under the right window. In my opinion, this was the best view in the whole castle.

My first impression of Mendlewyn, my adopted country, was the color green. Rich, vibrant green. It was as if the Being who created this place wanted the eye of the viewer to drown in the hue.

Below the windows, Dartmoor, the capital, sprawled all the way to the edge of the towering forest, miles away. Movement was rampant: children skipping, farmers herding livestock through cramped streets, and guardsmen patrolling from the battlements of the castle wall, watching over it all.

Taking it all in, I allowed my shoulders to relax. Here, I did not have to glance over my shoulder, buzzing with tension. Here, in this castle, in this country, I was secure.

In this safe haven, I was free.

CHAPTER TWO
AN EXTRAVAGANT PRISON

Benjamin

DARTMOOR. I HADN'T laid eyes on it in years, but as far as I cared to remember, nothing much had changed. The city was just as chaotic as I recalled. The roads leading to it were uneven and muddy from a recent rain. Castle Dartmoor still loomed, perched on the hill in the distance.

To the casual observer, Castle Dartmoor was all that was upright and beautiful: soaring, embattled towers, heraldic flags that fluttered in the breeze, polished stone without a visible flaw covering every surface. It was as if a fairy-tale book came to life.

Me? I saw it for what it truly was: an extravagant prison. That was all it was, all it ever would be.

If it were possible to mentally set something on fire, that building would be smoldering. But alas, I lacked the fearsome powers of a vengeful god of old. Instead, I would have to do this the hard way. The I-will-make-my-stay-here-so-impossibly-tortuous-they-will-wish-for-a-fire plan. Perhaps it was childish. But in a world that had suddenly gone upside-down and inside-out, childish was all I had—my only plan. Nothing about the last few weeks had been my choice. *Go here, son. Pack up your things. Do this. Don't do that.* It was as if they were whittling me down, stripping away every part of who I am to the bare bones in an effort to fit me into their perfect little world.

Well, I'd show them. And it wasn't going to be pretty.

"Benjamin!"

Torn from my dark musings, I glanced over my shoulder to find the captain of the half-dozen men escorting me to my prison—*ahem*, new home. Dressed in black armor with navy accents—the colors of my father's house—Gregor reined in his stallion within shouting distance. His eyes pierced mine like the edge of a freshly sharpened spear. Aside from the sharp look, I could read nothing from his expression. Not that I cared to know his thoughts on his newest task.

"We are almost within the city limits. Let us ride in formation, sir," Gregor called.

I held his gaze, despite the fact that looking into his mottled eyes made me feel as though cold water was dribbling down my spine. I kept my eyes on his, made a show of thinking it over, and then responded, "I think not. You all have made it clear whose side you're on, and the last thing I am going to do is ride in there in formation, like we are *brothers*." I handled that last word as if it was something too sour to ingest.

With that, I spun my mount around and urged him into a trot. Brothers. That's what those men had been, up until three weeks ago. But I couldn't think about that, not without my anger welling and oozing like a vast tar pit inside my soul. Yet, try as I might, I couldn't get out from under the weight of that ooze. Just like an actual tar pit, I often got sucked down into that hot black mass and I would get trapped in that anger. Which was unfortunate for the inhabitants of my uncle's castle.

A short while later, I started up the slope to the castle. Too quickly, I entered the courtyard, and then I handed the reins off to a waiting groom. I slowly took in a deep breath, squared my shoulders, and raised my gaze to the regal-looking couple waiting midway up the broad stairs. Those stairs led to the over-sized double doors, which were agape, as if the castle were a living thing eager to devour me whole.

There was silence as all three of us stared at one another. It soon became awkward. But I refused to be bothered by it. I would let one of them speak first.

Sure enough, it was my uncle that broke first. He cleared his throat. "Benjamin."

I paused a beat before I spoke. "Uncle," I drawled. "Aunt." I nodded at them both.

The only reaction from either of them was a slight tightening of my uncle's jaw. I knew I was being beyond rude. No bow or effort to address them by their official titles, when servants and townspeople were here to witness this spectacle I was making. Already, I saw some servants passing with startled or disapproving looks upon their faces. Good. Let them gossip. I didn't care one bit.

I had stopped caring three weeks ago.

After exchanging the expected inquiries of my travels, I followed the king and queen into the castle. There they paused, and another long, drawn-out silence began, which I also refused to break. This time, Aunt Ahmelia was the one to pipe up, which surprised me, as I had never remembered her being particularly vocal.

"A servant will show you to your chamber. Dinner is in one hour. I hope to see you there, Benjamin." A tentative but no less beautiful smile crept up her cheeks.

I saw it for what it was: an olive branch. An attempt to mend ruffled feathers for the way I had been cast off and betrayed.

I sniffed. "Actually, I am feeling rather tired from my journey. Send a tray up to my room, if you will."

The smile wilted.

With that, I turned and left. Somehow, that first victory didn't feel quite as good as I had imagined it would.

Chapter Three

Shattered

Naya

"I HEARD HE left them gaping in the grand foyer, jaws scraping the floor."

"I can do you one better. I heard he snubbed the king and queen, and refused to join them for dinner last night," Betsy, my roommate, added.

Several gasps echoed that comment.

"He snubbed the king and queen?" someone whispered, voice edging between amazement and disgust.

"Yes, and he ate from a tray that I brought up to him myself."

Along with the others at our table in the servant's dining room, I leaned toward Betsy at this new information. I usually did not pay any attention to the latest gossip, but this time I could not help myself. I had only gotten the briefest of looks at this newcomer and that was on his way up to his room. The way he had moved through the castle had made everyone apprehensive. How was that possible?

"You brought the tray up? So that means you interacted with him! What did he do? What did he say?"

Several others shot questions at her as well and Betsy shushed everyone at our breakfast table. Once everyone had quieted, she continued, "I wouldn't truly call it an interaction; I believe that involves more than one person talking. In truth, it was more of an announcement. I knocked, waited until he opened the door, and then I declared that I had his dinner tray."

"Did anything else happen?"

Betsy shrugged. "He nodded and shut the door. That was it. No 'thank you', but it could have been worse; I could've been cursed to Holda."

The other girls dove into that bit of gossip, tearing it apart and analyzing it to death. I returned to my meal and listened, never extending my own opinions or further slander.

Soon, I had cleaned my plate and I left the table, leaving my used dishes on top of the pile near the door. Behind me, the girls were still gossiping, and I focused until I could no longer hear their giggles and whispers. Eventually, the regular sounds of the castle replaced the eager, idle talk, and for that I was grateful.

Several hours later, I swiped one last time with the cloth I held, stepped back from the trinket, and eyed the piece for any spots of dust that I may have missed. I did not see anything, and I smiled. I looked over the library as a whole, and felt my smile widen into a grin. I knew it was not always the best to take pride in your own accomplishments, but I could not help it.

Miss Sue called what I was able to do a 'miracle'; I simply referred to it as a talent.

With very little effort, since I was a child, I have had an above-average ability to remember things. I would not call my memory perfect, but it was as close as it could be. It had come in handy many times over the years, including here in Dartmoor.

Within a few weeks of arriving at the castle, a mishap happened in the grand library. Servants had taken down all the various and expensive trinkets to clean around them. They had then been called away to deal with a laundry emergency and had left everything in disarray.   Miss Sue, who could usually be counted on to remain calm, was almost in hysterics when she had found the mess, and in her fit, she failed to notice when I had started to put each trinket back in its proper spot. When she finally noticed, she could not believe it. She immediately demanded to know how I could do it. Embarrassed and expecting a punishment, I hesitantly told her that I had slipped in early one morning to take it all in, going row by row until I had studied the entire library.

"And now I know where everything goes," I had ended quietly, eyes down.

Miss Sue, after a long and awkward silence, said something about a miracle and declared me to be in charge of the organization and cleaning of the library from that moment on. She wouldn't take no for an answer, even when I had begged for her to choose someone else, stating that I was too young, that I could not handle it. In a tone that had brooked no further arguments, she had proclaimed, "You'll thank me later, lass."

She was right. I almost chuckled now to think of all the bellyaching Miss Sue had endured from me.

After two years of sole management of the cleaning of the library, I felt myself returning to a place of peace and health. In short, the library was my oasis. In the library, after helping with the chaos of meal preparation and distribution, I could finally *breathe*. Here, I was in control, and I was trusted with the care of this room. And by far, the best thing was that there was not anyone lurking above me, eager to rudely point out my flaws or mistakes.

I smiled at the thought, then raised my eyes to the water-clock on the mantel. I sucked air in through my teeth. *I'm behind schedule!* I thought with concern. Muttering to myself about the dangers of getting lost in my thoughts, I hurried to the next area and task on my mental list and soon, I was back in my rhythm, lost now in the monotony and order, secure amid those two old friends.

Moving smoothly, I climbed a teetering ladder near the entrance to the library, where I cautiously brought a delicate figurine down to ground level. I carried it with near reverence, making sure the cleaning cloth was a barrier between my bare fingers and the glossy surface. Taking careful steps to ensure I didn't trip or bump into anything, I headed for one of the many tables in the room, where several other items had already been dusted and waited like soldiers at attention, according to size and where they went in the room.

I was barely three steps from the table when, from directly behind me, there was a thundering crash. Startled, I instinctively brought my hands up and over my head and face. Too late, I remembered the figurine and scrambled to try to catch it.

I was not fast enough. Curse it all, I was too slow!

Another crash, followed by the tinkling of glass, echoed into the sudden stillness.

Frozen for all of two seconds before reality set in, I frantically began to sweep the fragments toward me with my hands. I ignored the sharp stings as my flesh met jagged glass and kept sweeping, inwardly berating myself over my foolishness. *Stupid, stupid, oh, what am I to do? How am I going to fix this?* I cringed to even think of how Miss Sue would react. Would she be furious? Would I be let go? I banished that thought immediately.

A white piece of fabric fluttered in front of my face. I ignored it.

"Take it. You're bleeding."

Again, I did nothing, said nothing, my whole focus on the disaster right in front of me. I had more pressing concerns than me bleeding.

There were a few choice words muttered before a large pair of hands came into my field of vision, reaching for my own. I shrank back and snapped, "No! Leave me alone!"

"I am trying to help you!"

My own anger flared, fueled by my anxiety. "I didn't ask for your help!"

"Fine, then!"

Turning to get the last word in, to really let him have it, I filled my lungs to prepare to match his volume and raised my eyes to the face of the king's nephew.

I felt the words clog in my throat and I shut my eyes, tucking my chin to my chest. I scrambled back and in the next second was on my feet, executing a shaky curtsy, eyes fixed on the ground.

"I apologize, sir," I gasped, "I-I didn't know who you were, that it was you, that—" I cut myself off, mid-ramble.

As I waited for his reprimand, I thought back, frantically searching my memory. Did I look into his eyes? And if I did, was I too late? Not this. *Anything* but this. Before I could reassure myself that I hadn't made that grave error, a new voice rang out.

"What in the name of the holy saints happened here?"

Miss Sue. The clog in my throat was back.

"And your hands, Naya! What did you do to them? I certainly hope you have a good explanation for this, lassie!"

Hesitantly, I lifted my face and glanced at Miss Sue.

"I am so sorry, Miss Sue. I can explain, I promise."

I quickly explained how one of the priceless pieces was now a pile of debris, apologizing again and again until Miss Sue demanded that I stop. She surprised me then by stepping close to me, lifting one hand and pressing a clean rag into it. I sucked in a breath, but remained perfectly still. She inspected the other hand and then clucked her tongue in disapproval.

"It almost looks like you took a cheese grater to your skin, dearie." She secured the cloth with a tidy knot. Soon the other hand had a similar make-shift bandage as well. "I tell you what: you are going to the physician for these hands, and in the meantime, I will clean this all up. Once you're finished getting tended to, come back and I'll get a few other girls to assist you in putting everything back."

"No, Miss Sue, this is my fault. I will clean everything up, I swear."

She let out a snort. "Go to the physician, lass. Don't make me order you to do it; you know it'll be no skin off my nose for me to do it."

I opened my mouth to argue, then shut it and nodded mutely. I shuffled toward the entrance of the library, then stopped. I pivoted back, glancing around the room. Miss Sue, already reaching for a broom leaning against a bookshelf, was the only other person in the room. In my worry over getting punished, I had nearly forgotten the king's nephew in this whole debacle. But he was gone. He must have slipped out when Miss Sue had come in.

He had barged in like a rushing windstorm and, just as quickly, swept out again. Causing chaos in his wake and leaving me to face Miss Sue on my own.

"Who are you looking for, lass?" Miss Sue asked.

I flicked my gaze around once more. "No one," I responded. "I'm not looking for anyone, Miss Sue."

Chapter Four
Reunion

Benjamin

"BENJAMIN!"

THE VOICE echoing down the hallway behind me gave me the incentive to turn my hurried walk into a jog. That voice, angry and gravelly, belonged to Rasmussen, second-in-command to Gregor, and one of the least likable people that I had ever had the displeasure of meeting. If my uncle had truly wanted me to meet with him, he should have sicced someone else on me. But I supposed I was the only one to blame for finding myself feeling like a hunted fox.

I had been in my uncle's castle for three days and, aside from the uncomfortable interaction on the front steps, I hadn't seen him once, not even at mealtimes; I had eaten alone in my chambers. I had made it my mission to avoid him, and I had been quite successful—although I could see that my streak of success was probably coming to an end, and an abrupt one at that.

The first morning here had dawned bright and early with a gangly servant looming over my bed, politely informing me that my uncle requested me in his study immediately. I had pretended to be agreeable, shooed him away to dress, and had slipped out of my room to the stables. My grand plan had been to saddle up Joker and high-tail it as far away as possible, fleeing my prison and my past, and just start over. How I would have survived on my own and where I would have gone were secondary issues to take care of at a later time.

I had gotten three steps into the stables before the lead groom had hesitantly stammered out that my horse was off limits to me, and that it would be in my best interest to return to the castle before he summoned the closest guards.

Now *that* had pushed me over the edge. I had already been frustrated with the early wake up call, but to deny me access to my horse was beyond the pale. Seething, I had told him, quite forcefully, where he could take himself off to, and had marched back inside, directly into the library, which had been a mistake due to the chaos that my entrance caused. I still winced at the memory of the servant girl's frantic movements and the injuries that had followed, as well as the fiasco of the horrible conversation afterward. That whole situation had been a dung pile lit on fire from beginning to end.

"Confound it all, where is that miscreant?"

That jerked me out of my musings over how I had dodged two more meetings isince that first day. Rasmussen's voice, to my surprise, was up ahead of me and closer than I liked. Switching directions quickly, I darted back down the hall in the direction I had come. Voices ahead stopped me in my tracks. I recognized what they were doing, the tactic a classic one: they were flushing me out! Biting out a word that would have had my grandmother—may she rest in peace—hyperventilating, I escaped the only way I could, down a hall to my right. Too soon, I drew up short at a dead end. There was only one door and I had no choice but to slip inside, cursing my luck.

Shutting the door, I leaned against it, ear at the crack. I quieted my breathing and listened to the growing pandemonium outside.

Someone cleared their throat behind me. I whirled around.

Twisted around in a hard-backed chair was a young man. Pale, with limp blond hair askew, and the remnants of a previous meal in the corners of his mouth, he was quite a sight. He blinked owlishly at me.

"Can I help you?" he asked in a voice that made it clear he hadn't spoken aloud in quite some time.

"Er, hello," I responded, caught off-guard. "Didn't see you there. Don't mind me, I am just popping in—wait a minute, do I know you?"

Eyes widening, he broke into a grin. "Benjamin, is that you?" The voice, though deeper than it had been, was familiar.

"Fitzy!"

Just then, someone began to pound on the door, setting off a ringing in my ears. Raising a finger to my lips, I crossed the cluttered room to him.

"Please, Fitzy, I am not here. I was never here."

A moment passed while Fitzy and I locked eyes; I could see his mind turning over, processing everything. Another set of knocks rang out, firmer and more insistent this time. For a moment, I thought it was all over, and then he nodded firmly.

"Hold on, hold on, let me get decent!" he cried out, hastily shoving his arms through the sleeves of a robe as he rose to his feet, scraping his chair over the rough stone floor. Silently, he beckoned me under his desk and I clasped my hands together in front of my chest to express my gratitude. As quietly as possible, I shimmied under the desk.

Fitzy scooted the chair so it blocked most of my body, then tossed a blanket that had been lying in a crumpled heap on the floor over the chair and added a high stack of thick books on the seat for good measure. I could still peer into the room through a small crack between the books and the armrest. I was fairly well hidden, from one angle. If these guards, and Rasmussen, were trained well—and I knew they were, for my father had trained them himself—they would search the room thoroughly. I was still in deep trouble. I hissed as much to Fitzroy, who waved dismissively at me from behind his back.

"You may enter now," he called, and in rushed Rasmussen and three other guards.

Only four men? I'm insulted, I thought bitterly. After having a sword thrust into my hand almost before I started walking and learning almost everything there was about being a soldier since then, I would have expected a minimum of seven, and one of them a giant.

The one in the lead straightened, and then gave a stiff bow to Fitzy. "Your highness, forgive the intrusion. We need to know if someone has recently entered this room."

Stepping to the side to further block my hiding place, and my limited view, Fitzy made a sound of pondering. "Can't say that I've seen anyone. Who did you say you were looking for?"

"We didn't say, your highness. Apologies. The boy we are looking for is your cousin, Benjamin Lamar."

"You don't say! I had forgotten he was coming. When did he get here? And why are you looking for him?"

"He arrived three days ago, your highness. He has had several meetings scheduled with your father that he has failed to attend, and we have orders to find and escort him to your father's study at once."

"Interesting, indeed. Well, I will keep you posted if I ever do see him."

Someone cleared their throat awkwardly. Then, "I am afraid we have to search this room before we leave, to ensure he isn't here."

I tensed. I had known this would happen.

"Fine, fine." Fitzy sighed."But make it quick, captain. You have interrupted me in the height of my philosophical contemplation, when all earthly needs become secondary and absolute concentration is paramount."

"Of course, your highness."

There was an odd, almost mocking undertone to his words. I squinted as I assessed that information, but pushed the thought away for a later time. I had more pressing concerns at the moment.

Footsteps thudded as the men started fanning out; I didn't need to see them to know what they were doing. It was a small room, with limited spaces to hide. What hope I had had to begin with faded. I mentally started counting down the seconds until my freedom was no more.

I closed my eyes to better listen, and I clenched my fists as I heard someone drawing closer to my hiding place.

"Wait!" Fitzy yelled.

A long, drawn out moment. "What is it, your highness?"

"My cat, Mimsy, naps there, under my desk. If you could, I would appreciate it if you didn't disturb her. You have no idea the headache she'll cause me if her nap is disturbed; I still have the scar from the last time I woke her."

An exasperated breath escaped someone. "I believe we have no further reason to tarry. Wouldn't you agree, Polk?"

"Aye, captain," Rasmussen grumbled. "Let's move on before he slips even further away."

In short order, the room emptied. I waited a solid minute after the door was shut before I slowly came out from my hiding place. I stood to my full height, and studied my cousin, who had his hands on his hips and seemed to be a million miles away mentally.

Two years older than me, Fitzroy had finally passed me in height. Raised in the lap of luxury, his features were plump; he looked as if he spent more time behind a desk than out on the sparring mat. He had broad shoulders and he wore no shoes.

Brushing off the last remnants of tension from being hunted, I smirked. "You know, Fitzy, the first memory that comes to mind when I think of you was that time I rescued you from that unfortunate swim."

Torn from his thoughts, he let out a laugh and I joined in. It had been a good bonding experience, that memory.

Many years before, a bunch of local boys had ganged up on Fitzy and were in the middle of roughing him up. They had been taunting him with the knowledge that he'd soon be swimming in the moat, where the servants had just emptied all the castle's chamber pots. I had sized up the enemy, rushed in, and had gone straight for the ringleader, giving him a walloping that had left him crying. He and his posse had soon scattered after that.

"Ah, good times," I mused.

"Not for those boys, it wasn't!"

We both laughed again until we were interrupted by a disgruntled mewl from behind me. I turned to see a fat tabby slink out from behind a thick curtain. It arched its back lazily, letting out another irritated howl as it did so.

"The infamous Mimsy, I presume?"

"Yes, this is she."

"I honestly thought you were shamming about the cat."

"I wasn't, though I did fib on her favorite napping spot. She loves to sun herself on the window sill."

I stepped forward, extending a hand. "That saved my behind. Thank you, Fitzy."

"You're welcome. For the record, I find this whole situation—the reason you're here—entirely ludicrous. An overreaction on your father's part."

I tensed again. "I'd rather not discuss it. But thanks for the support."

He nodded once, and then moved back to his desk. He nudged Mimsy aside and sat back down. I shuffled over, not quite wanting to leave, yet unsure of my welcome. So, like every other interaction I'd had since arriving here, I decided to bluff my way through it, pretending I didn't care if I belonged or not. I peered over his shoulder, reading the document he had on the desk before him. *A Comprehensive Overview of The Alliance: Is it truly gone?* was written in blocky handwriting at the top of the page. He quickly covered the page with a book and started up a conversation.

Taking his words as an indication that I was welcome in his untidy little study room, I settled in. Quite suddenly, this quiet corner of Castle Dartmoor was the only place I felt most at home.

I yawned, covering it with a fist and bounced the thick rubber ball against the wall of Fitzy's study, and watched it hurtle back toward my face. I caught it and repeated the action. The only sound in the small room was the sound of the ball striking wall and floor and Fitzy's occasional mumbles as he reread his own writing back to himself. He was sitting at his desk, idly scratching Mimsy and flipping through another thick book.

He had actually put his studies on hold yesterday evening to sit on the floor with me and talk. We had caught up on one another's lives since we had last seen each other and reminisced on our early childhoods, the long adventure-filled summer days and boyish mischief. Soon the town clock had struck midnight, and we had parted ways, with him extending an offer to come back the next day. I had slunk up to my chambers and fallen asleep quickly. The next morning, before any servant could come in to summon me to my uncle's beck-and-call, I had hurried to his study, where I had found him hard at work. We had eaten breakfast together and settled into our current arrangement.

I was growing restless. I was unfamiliar with sitting around and not doing anything. Fitzy had offered a book or two for me to read, but I had never been one to read for pleasure. That had been close to torture for me as a child, and as soon as I had been able to leave the schoolroom, I had never looked back. Weapons training and the rigorous lifestyle of a soldier appealed to me; books and studying did not. That had always been Fitzy's preference.

"I need to move," I declared. "I need to get up, need to stab something."

"Hm?"

I rolled my eyes. That was one thing I hadn't missed about my cousin. He had a tendency to get completely lost in his books and studies. He also had an annoying habit of getting distracted during conversations with people. What was he distracted by? You guessed it: thoughts of his books and studies. But he had always endured my presence, so I did likewise. He wasn't all that bad. Just an intellectual.

I snatched the ball, switched targets, and nailed Fitzy in the back of the head. He jerked in surprise, which startled Mimsy; the cat promptly scrambled across his desk and up the curtains. I snickered as she hollered unhappily from her position, claws sunk deep in the fabric.

Fitzy rubbed the back of his head, stood and reorganized the papers that the disgruntled feline had disturbed, muttering as he did so. He faced me, glowering, and then scolded, "My mother is going to tan my hide for any damage done to these curtains, Benjamin. Mimsy absolutely destroyed the last set. Both my mother and I—as well as the innocent curtains— would appreciate it if you refrained from throwing things in Mimsy's general vicinity." He busied himself coaxing her down, unhooking her from the drapes. "There. Now, using words like a grown-up boy, would you please repeat what you said?"

"I need to stab something."

"Remind me to be grateful it was only the ball that you threw."

I laughed once. "Enough of just sitting here. I need to do something active."

"And I thought Mimsy was high maintenance."

I made a face. "Har har. Very funny."

He snatched up two books from a stack. "All right, let's get out of here for a bit. Follow me."

We locked up, cautiously made our way to the main hallway and to the right. The few servants we passed nodded and moved out of Fitzy's path respectfully. They directed curious looks in my direction, which I ignored. I just hoped one didn't tattle on my whereabouts to my uncle. After a few more turns, our surroundings were becoming more familiar and I finally spoke.

"Where are we going?"

"You'll see."

I halted. "We're going to the library, aren't we?"

He lifted the books and waved the other hand. "I thought that much would be obvious."

I sighed, my mind rushing back to the poor startled servant girl and bloody hands. That hadn't been my finest moment. I clenched my fists, fighting the urge to insist we return to his study. But I never ran from confrontation—something my father no doubt cursed me for. No, I wouldn't run. I would calmly walk in there and hope that she wasn't there. We kept moving until we reached the library.

Descending a ladder in the front section of the room, hands wrapped in bright bandages, was the servant girl from two days previous.

Of course, my luck had decided to hastily pack up and desert me.

Fitzy called a hello to her and waved her over. He knew the library girl. Great.

In the chaos of our first interaction, I hadn't gotten a good look at her. I did so now as she came toward us. Long black hair in a braid over one shoulder, she was on the shorter side with an unexceptional figure. She was neither ugly, nor beautiful. Her body language showed wariness in its movements. Then her eyes flicked in my direction.

That wariness in her posture turned to tension. She evidently remembered me. I inwardly sighed. I knew enough about dealings with women—my mother mostly—to know I needed to be a man and apologize.

I just hoped I didn't bungle this next conversation with this girl as much as I had the first time.

If only that blasted luck of mine hadn't hightailed it.

CHAPTER FIVE
WORRISOME INTRODUCTIONS

Naya

HE WAS BACK. The boy from two days ago.

The bringer of chaos into my little oasis.

He was also the king's nephew. I curtsied to him, not as low as the one I directed at Prince Fitzroy, but no one could find fault in the depth of it. I rose from the curtsy after waiting the appropriate amount of time, folded my hands carefully in front of me—as best I could with bandaged hands. I kept my chin angled down and murmured a proper greeting as I fought to keep the disquiet in my heart and mind from rising further.

Why has he returned? I thought with unease.

After the visit with the court physician, I had returned to my duties, directing the new girls in the library with a shaking voice, shoulders tense. I had been waiting for the condemnation to rain down on me, half expecting Miss Sue to return and at last punish me. I had also bounced on the balls of my feet, ears attuned to the slightest noise at the double doors leading into the library. What I had been waiting for, I do not know. I just knew I had to remain alert for another invasion, for more bedlam and blaring sounds.

The day had passed by uneventfully, the following day as well. Things were going so well that this morning, I had found the courage to persuade Miss Sue that I was perfectly able to oversee the library on my own again. She had made sure I was confident, and then let the girls that had come to help me know that they were free to go back to their former chores.

I had calmed down enough to cease tensing at every entrance into this room. I had begun to breathe again, and a contented smile had returned to my face.

I should have known it was too good to be true.

"Benjamin, this is Naya Gavi," I heard Prince Fitzroy announce. Then to me, he stated, "Naya, this is my cousin, Benjamin Lamar. He will be staying here for the foreseeable future."

My mind caught on the name, filing it away as I did all others, grasping onto it in an effort to remain in control of this foreign situation. I was being introduced? To a *noble*? I dimly wondered if I had tripped while untangling myself from my blanket this morning and cracked my skull on the way down. I could even now wake to find myself in the physician's quarters again, bleary-eyed with a raging headache. That would be far less strange than this current conversation.

In all my years of servitude, I had never, not once, been introduced formally to someone of such high rank. Not in my Nanni Venna's home, nor the skill-building school. Definitely never within the walls of the bawdy tavern. I was so out of my element that I fiddled with my fingers carefully, unsure as to what to do.

Voices of patrons within the library became more obvious as silence descended. It was not my place to break it, so I waited, head down. My spine stiffened with each passing second until someone cleared their throat.

"Well, I'd best return these books and let you back to your tasks, Naya. It was nice to see you," Prince Fitzroy said. I watched his feet move from my line of vision.

I dipped another curtsy. "Thank you, sire," I mumbled to the carpeted floor as his footsteps padded away.

I never quite knew what to think of the youngest prince. He was odd, but not unkind. He went out of his way to speak with me, and he often asked me questions as I worked if he was perusing the shelves in my vicinity. Kindness aside, I never let my guard down around him. It would be too cruel to open myself up only to have his mask fall, to have him dart in and skewer my soul with slicing words.

"How are your hands?"

I jumped. So absorbed was I in my musings of the prince that I had not noticed his cousin had remained behind. I tucked my hands, still bandaged, behind me and thought furiously. What was I supposed to say?

"They are healing, my lord," I responded. Surely a quick, truthful answer was the best approach.

"I just wanted to say that I am sorry for surprising you the other day. For making you drop the statue and for the damage it caused."

It took everything in me to keep my mouth from popping open. First, I was introduced to a high ranking noble, the king's nephew of all people, and now said noble was apologizing to me, a nobody. I was beginning to truly believe I was recovering in the physician's rooms with a severe head wound, one that was making me hallucinate vividly.

A low curse caused me to tense, shaking myself from my whirling thoughts. *Can't you ever pull yourself out of your own mind long enough to answer me? It is a simple question, girl.* Nanni Venna's impatient voice echoed across nine years, ringing in intensity and cutting anew. One of my greatest failings was thinking.

She had constantly berated me for thinking.

I curtsied, blurting out an apology. I risked a glance up. I was alone in the entrance to the library. A quick look over my right shoulder showed the prince's cousin stomping around a corner.

Who was this boy who appeared and disappeared with no warning? The only entity I knew of who could do that was the trickster god, Glofi. I shuddered, drawing three fingers across my chest in the sign to ward off evil.

The last thing I needed in my life was a rogue trickster god running amok in the castle.

CHAPTER SIX

THE DEAL

Benjamin

GET IT OVER with, Benjamin, says Fitzy, I jeered to myself as I marched up the corridor to my uncle's study. *Don't draw it out any longer, says Fitzy. I ought to show Fitzy where he can—.*

I cut my thoughts off, knowing if I continued that line of thought, I might not be able to help myself from acting them out and then my grandmother truly would be pirouetting in her coffin. If only my father could see me now, see me halting my thoughts—and therefore my actions—before they could explode into life. I didn't need to break like an untamed, ill-bred horse. I had no need of my uncle's training and lectures. I'd show them all.

Reaching the solid oak door, I sucked in a breath and threw it open, marching into the antechamber of my uncle's study. A lanky secretary jerked in his seat across the room, the motion causing papers to sprout wings and take to the air all around his balding head. The man hurried to gather the papers as I strode across the small room past his desk and reached for the doorknob.

"Excuse me! Do you have an appointment?" the frazzled man squawked at me, scrambling up from his chair.

I snorted out loud and made a grand show of slamming the door to the office closed behind me. The room was empty, and part of me was glad for it. The other part of me wanted to get this over with as soon as possible. I crossed to the windows behind the imposing desk and tossed open the curtains. It was an impressive view and I scowled for having admitted that to myself. I folded my arms over my chest and watched the people milling in the courtyard below, quickly losing focus on the movements.

I could not seem to help myself from revisiting the awkward and frustrating interaction with the library girl yesterday. I spun my mind in search of the name she had given upon being introduced and I could not think of it no matter how hard I tried. My mother was always playfully scolding me for never retaining the names of those around me. I always told her in response that I had better things to remember. I tried once more to recall the name of the silent girl from the day before but I eventually just shrugged and moved on. Library Girl it was, then.

After the stilted introduction and Fitzy wandering away to return the books he had with him, I had asked over her hands, which she had promptly hidden behind her back. As if that would have made the bandages and the damage beneath cease to exist. She had mumbled something about them healing, directly to the floor. That carpet must have had the secrets of the universe scrawled across it because she never once looked up from it after I had entered the library. Odd.

It only had gotten worse after I had attempted what I had thought was an acceptable—if not downright flawless—apology to her over my role in her injury. Her only response was to crumple her eyebrows and stay completely silent. My apology was left to flop and jerk at our feet like a dying fish on dry land. I was willing to give her the benefit of the doubt after a few seconds, but after thirty seconds passed, I had realized that she was going to refuse to even acknowledge my apology. What a strange mixture of bashfulness and self-importance! She couldn't look me in the face, yet she couldn't deign to forgive me. I had finally cursed under my breath and had left her studying her enchanting carpet. Let her think on that.

Muttering to myself about how I wished to have never left the familiar confines of home, I shook myself from those thoughts and instead began to wander around my uncle's office. I picked up a paperweight in the shape of a seated bear and began tossing it from hand to hand as I let my gaze wander across the space as a whole. This room was tidy, organized in a way that communicated the owner's desire to control. I grimaced. My father was like that as well.

Pushing that lovely musing away, I moved in front of the bookcase that stretched across one wall. Well-worn books peered out from the shelves, everything from political science to land management. *Yawn.* The only thing that caught my attention was several volumes on the topic of battle tactics and strategies. It wasn't enough to tempt me, but at least there was some sanity on the shelves.

Switching from tossing the paperweight to rolling it back and forth across my palms, I paused as I heard voices outside the door, drawing closer. I recognized my uncle's voice as one of them and I faced away from the entrance. The door cracked open, letting in the conversation like a needy dog.

"Is this the first of such reports? Or have there been others?" My uncle's voice.

"As far as I know, this is the first, although I find myself surprised, sire. Unrest at the southern border is something I would have thought to be a greater concern, and reported quickly and directly to you."

A long sigh stretched out. "Thank you, McMannon. Keep me abreast of further reports."

I had heard nothing of unrest in the south, something that piqued my interest. But I had more important matters to think about at the moment. Like being the biggest pain I could be to a certain monarch. I heard the door creak open further and then a grunt of surprise.

"I was about to tell you, sire, that your nephew was waiting for you in your office. Apologies, sire."

My uncle murmured something to his secretary, and then I heard him close the door. I finally faced him, keeping my face neutral. Hands on hips, he stared back. The similarities between him and my father nearly made me want to drop my gaze. I refused the urge, instead continuing to stare him down.

"Since I was unaware of this meeting," he began, his tone of voice clearly conveying the dry edge of his statement, "if you will take a seat, I have a few things to finish before I will be able to speak with you." He waved a hand toward the two seats situated in front of his desk.

Instead of stepping in line like a good little soldier, I plopped down on the trunk to the right of the chairs, stretching my legs out in front of me, watching him for his reaction. His shoulders rose and fell as he breathed deeply. Then he crossed to his desk, stepping over my legs with kingly finesse. That was disappointing. I crossed my arms over my chest again, glaring at the opposite wall, listening to a quill being scratched across parchment.

The silence stretched out, and with every second, I felt my anger rise, along with a tremor starting in my toes, slowly trickling up my legs until I was tossing the paperweight I still held from hand to hand again. I already regretted this. This was not going the way I had wanted it to. Stupid Fitzroy for tickling my pride and all but manipulating me into coming here. Apparently I hadn't hit him hard enough with that ball yesterday—a mistake I wouldn't make again. I had a feeling more curtains were going to be thoroughly abused before I left here.

If I ever left here, that is.

My uncle sat behind his desk, furiously finishing up a treatise or sonnet or the slavery-of-nephews act or whatever kings wrote about. His eyes looked bruised with dark smudges beneath them; I briefly wondered if he was taking care of himself. Then I sniffed at my traitorous thoughts. He wasn't my friend here. The more accurate word might be *jailer*.

At last, he set the quill down and looked me full in the eye. "Benjamin, thank you for coming here today."

I waited a beat, expecting more. I anticipated him throwing out the fact that I hadn't made it to the other appointments he had set up. My father would have done that—*had* done that on many occasions. I also couldn't fathom how he had made it seem as though he had planned this whole encounter, when he had just admitted he hadn't been expecting me.

I raised my fingers to my brow and saluted him. "My pleasure," I drawled, then stood, moving to lean over his desk, right into his face. "Now let's skip the niceties and get this over with. What do I have to do to get out of here?"

Uncle James watched my face, saying nothing for several seconds. Then he shook his head and muttered to himself, "That plan is out. Plan B it is."

Plan B? What was he blabbering about? What was Plan A? It took nearly everything in me to not blurt out those questions. I actually had to clamp my lips to keep them back. I watched, confused, as he pushed his chair back, setting it to screeching along the wooden floor. He brushed past without looking at me, opened his door with such vigor it crashed against the opposite wall, and strode through the antechamber and out into the main hallway, disappearing out of sight.

I stood frozen, unsure as to what had just happened. I cursed out loud. Nothing was going according to plan. I shifted my weight, then released a growl. I turned quickly to place the paperweight back on the desk and hurried in my uncle's wake. Briefly, I saw the secretary collecting his papers again and a grin surfaced; it seemed I wasn't the only one who could get under the man's skin.

Glancing both ways when I reached the hall, I saw a flash of emerald vanishing around a corner down the passageway. Cursing unpredictable monarchs, I moved in that direction, refusing to go faster than a controlled walk. As I turned several more corners, I came to the conclusion my uncle was strolling at just the perfect pace for me to see him take the next turn. That blasted man. He knew exactly what he was doing. My father, when I was a boy, tried to help me see how my curiosity could get me into trouble one day. I listened to his speech long enough to agree with him on one point: my curiosity *would* get me into trouble. I had done nothing to curb that curiosity, instead, feeding it every chance I got.

Eventually, I turned the corner to see the king entering a room up ahead. I reached the door, grunted and opened it, startled to walk into a large training room. I felt a sense of relief, of calm familiarity wash over me. If there was one place that was a second home to me, it was a training room. From the time I could hold a sword, I was in a room very similar to this one for hours on end, day after day, learning the basics of the sword, dagger, and spear. The smell of lye, used to clean up after bloody noses or cuts, tickled my nose, and the echoic quality to the air brought back dozens of memories, both good and bad, ones of triumph and others of humiliating defeat. I had passed what felt like lifetimes in a place like this.

I tensed, on edge immediately. I had to keep my wits about me. No mawkishness allowed, not when my uncle had so thoroughly thrown me off balance. I eyed him as he stripped off his outer jacket, leaving him standing in a simple linen shirt and breeches. He motioned for me to do the same and I did reluctantly. Uncle James walked over to where dozens of weapons, wooden and metal, leaned against the wall, selected two practice swords and returned to me, tossing one at my head. I caught it and began to see where he was going with this. He confirmed it when he spoke next.

"Let us try to break one each other's defenses and whoever wins gets to control the conversation. Shall we?"

I raised my sword in answer, feeling out the grip of the weapon as I sank into a fighting stance. He nodded. He matched my pose, then began to shuffle sideways, eyes suddenly shrewd and calculating. I felt a smile twitch my lips against my wishes. I was in my element now. He'd regret challenging me. He'd be surprised when I won and then strutted out of here, leaving him to gape after me.

I feigned a thrust and he danced back, more adroitly than I would have expected of a man who led a country from behind a desk. Scowling in concentration, I circled to the left, feet facing continually forward, never crossing.

Suddenly, in a burst of energy, he sprang forward and I quickly parried his strike, shocked at the force. I felt the first inkling of incredulity. He could fight! I ducked my chin, gritting my teeth.

Several more exchanges passed with no clear victor, and I skipped away, shaking out my sword arm. His blows rang up my arms. I was grudgingly impressed. I had had no idea he could fight.

Time passed and soon we were both panting from the exertion. Finally, he got within my defenses and jabbed me in the chest. I grimaced, both at the loss and the sharp pain that faded when I rubbed at it. He had won, fair and square, which surprised me to no end. I moved forward, extending a hand. He took it and shook it firmly. Then, tip of the practice sword resting on the floor, hands on the pommel, he raised his eyebrows in query. I nodded wearily. He could begin his scolding.

"What is your understanding of why you are here, Benjamin?"

I pursed my lips, tasting sweat. "My father has decided I need to be fixed. I am an embarrassment, a mistake, and everyone knows it."

"My understanding is a little different. You have trouble controlling your temper. Am I correct?"

I ground my teeth. "Yes." My defenses were rising again. I had heard this, or variations of this upcoming speech, over and over in the last month. I was heartily tired of hearing it.

"You're here because your father believed I could help you control the fire within you. But I am not going to 'fix' you. I know it doesn't seem like it, but you're not a screw-up."

Turning away, I swung the sword I held in wide arcs around me, feeling the surface of the tar pit within me start to agitate. Uncle James was patronizing me, trying to make me feel as if he *understood* me. It was making me angry. He was just like everyone else, trying to reason with me without being too close, as if the tar inside me would fly out and burn them too.

Before he could continue, I spun on him and snarled, "You don't know anything! So please, for the saints' sake, stop trying to sound as if you do. If everyone would just leave me alone, I wouldn't be so angry!"

I threw the sword across the room and turned to leave. Before I could go far, Uncle James spoke again.

"Did you know that, when I was about your age, I nearly started a war with Eitnea?"

I froze, and looked back over my shoulder. "No," I drew the word out, watching him. "That isn't one of the stories my father has shared with me."

He cracked a smile, coming toward me. "My father allowed me, the crown prince, to join him in a delegation involving the Eitnean royal family. It was an honor. About halfway through the meal, the king of Eitnea at the time blatantly insulted our country, among other things. Being my usual fiery self, I shot to my feet and threatened to knock the arrogant king's head off if he didn't take his words back. It had taken three men to restrain me when the man had the gall to laugh in my face and I was dragged from the room. My father told me later how close I had come to starting a war with our western neighbors. He scolded me up and down, told me he had had enough of my devilry, and added in no uncertain terms that I had to shape up and control my temper."

That sounded all too familiar.

"You see," he continued, "I too have a problem with my temper. But I refused, after that day, to let it be the one in control. I have spent the years since learning how to keep the reins of my mind and heart in my hands, rather than in the grasp of my old friend, Anger. So I do understand what it is you're going through. I understand it perfectly. I know the struggles, the triumphs. I can teach you to come out on top of this, if you'd let me."

I stayed silent, stewing over everything he had said. I was yet again stunned. The truth was, I did have a temper. I hadn't seen it as a problem before three weeks ago, just something to watch out for, like a skittish horse. But deep down, I had to admit it was far more out of control than I had even realized. Even worse, I admitted to the depths of my soul that I *did* need help. How I hated it, but it was true.

Uncle James cut into my contemplation with a challenge: "Try it for three months, Benjamin. If my advice isn't helping, if you haven't seen any differences whatsoever, then you can leave. Go home and face your father. I'll even write a letter for you to take to him to make sure he doesn't argue with me. I can make it a royal order."

I stared at the scarred wooden floor beneath me, thinking furiously. What did I have to lose? Aside from my hopes and dreams, nothing. In order to finally be free of my father, to find my place within the army of Mendlewyn, I had to overcome my anger, to beat it.

"Do we have a deal?"

I made eye contact and nodded once firmly. "We do. Three months to try it your way, Uncle."

He grinned, then tossed his sword at me. "Fantastic. We start tomorrow morning, before the birds start their calling. Clean up in here then, would you?"

CHAPTER SEVEN

ENEMY

Naya

REALITY SWEPT INTO my dreams, an abrupt transition. One moment I was floating away from any and all waking worries, and then in the next, tugged into alertness. I waited briefly, wanting to nestle back into the warm cocoon of nothingness and waste the day away. But that was not an option. Resignedly, I stretched, let out a yawn, and then sat up, brushing the worn blanket to the side as I glanced across the room.

A faint candle's glow was the only source of light, as the sun had yet to rise. Movement in the dimness prompted me to get up, dancing a little on bare feet that rested on cool stones. Spring ruled the world, its sister season still several months away with its long, muggy days.

Another glance confirmed that Betsy, my roommate of nearly two years, was almost dressed; she had only her long white-blonde hair to braid away from her face and then she would be ready for the day. She must have felt my gaze on her because she glanced over her shoulder as she ran a brush through her tangles. I smiled at her, and her smile, while not a full grin, was friendly. I sighed, relieved to see it. It had not always been a ready thing.

When I had arrived at Dartmoor Castle almost two years ago, I had been shuffled from room to room in the sleeping quarters until I finally settled in Betsy's room, the one we shared now. She had been one of the lucky few who had somehow bargained for a room to herself. To say that she was upset at having her space invaded was an understatement. She had protested quite loudly to Mrs. Cox, the head housekeeper, insisting I could not stay. Mrs. Cox had finally had to shut down her attempts to get me out of her space permanently by threatening to dock her pay, as I had arrived at the beginning of a rush of new hires and there was no other place for me. Betsy had settled down after that, but I had consciously steered clear of her, pretending to be asleep if I arrived at night before her and being especially silent if she had beaten me to the room and was quiet in her corner. It had been exhausting, tiptoeing around my new roommate.

The ice from the first few weeks of sharing a living space eventually thawed as I had taken great pains to keep my side of the room pristine, which was no trouble at all since I had arrived with little more than what was on my person. One day, she had surprised me by suddenly thanking me for the cleanliness, that she had appreciated my efforts. In the following conversation, I had discovered a little more about my roommate; she was the oldest of four children and I had decided that if her family had been anything like mine—all the children occupying one sleeping space, with little privacy—then I could understand her resistance to someone coming into her little corner of the castle. After that conversation, things had gotten much better. I no longer felt as though I had to sneak about.

Now whenever I encountered her in the halls, I got a small smile. We had not yet reached the point where I had a standing invite to sit by her at mealtimes—and I was too timid to ask—but I had felt the first stirrings of excitement in my stomach as those smiles had become more and more frequent of late. I had the feeling I was on the verge of having a friend. I tried not to let myself become giddy over it, but sometimes I kept smiling all the way down the hall to my destination. Having a friend meant I belonged, that I was not so easily dismissed or forgotten. Having a friend meant I was one step closer to having a true home, that I was accepted, seen, and heard.

I wished for that more than anything else, yearned for it in the moments of quiet. It was no longer a seemingly unattainable dream, but something I could nearly take hold of, and I could not wait for it to reach me.

"Thank you," I whispered to a servant who had helped to serve lunch later that day. I got a nod in return as they hurried back to cleaning up after the meal.

Leaving the dining hall behind me, I began to weave my way back to the library, humming a little ditty I had picked up over the years. I rounded a corner a few turns away from the library and took note of a man and girl up ahead, blocking the way in both directions. My humming came to a stop as I braced myself to quietly ask for them to move out of the path when I drew even with them.

As I got closer, I sensed more was at play then a simple conversation. The air fairly buzzed with tension. My chest tightened as I observed the situation. The girl, small and quite pretty, was trying to shrink into herself, eyes betraying the depth of her unease as she tried to find a way to escape the man's suffocating presence. She tried to move away, but the man matched her stride for stride, not letting her leave. I had seen this too many times to count in my previous job at the tavern to be truly surprised by it, but that did not make it any less scary to watch or—heaven forbid—to live it.

My heart started pounding as I darted looks in all directions. *Please,* I silently begged, *please let there be someone else, someone tall and menacing, to handle this.* The hall was empty save for the small maid, the towering bully, and myself. I swallowed heavily, wiping hands on my skirts as I moved forward on watery knees. There was no one but me to help. *Good heavens.*

As I drew near, I ignored the part of my mind that screamed at me to run in the opposite direction, to hold my tongue, and sorted through the dozens of faces of those who lived and worked in the castle at rapid pace until I found the girl's. Penelope. Her name was Penelope.

"Penelope, darling," I stated, coming to a halt within a few feet of the pair. "There you are. Miss Sue sent me to fetch you. She needs an extra set of hands in the laundry."

Penelope's eyes flew to mine, a desperate light in them. Hope began to rise in in their depths as she flicked a look up at the man's face. Her coloring dropped a touch as she stammered out, "Y-yes, miss. Right away."

She curtsied shakily and then side-stepped around the man. Before she could move, a large hand snaked out and gripped her upper arm.

"Hold it," said a raspy voice. "I didn't dismiss you. We hadn't finished our conversation."

Mutely, Penelope turned her eyes to mine and begged for me to do something. Hands shaking, I intertwined them before bowing my head in submission.

"Pardon me, sir, but I truly must insist we be on our way. Our mistress can be most impatient when someone offsets her schedule and I fear we may already be late." I prayed he could not detect the quavering hint to my words.

A pause and then the hand released Penelope's arm slowly, deliberately. She continued forward, and I could see it took everything in her to not run. I took hold of her hand as she reached my side and she clutched onto it as if she were inches away from a precipice and I was her sole lifeline. I squeezed it in return and turned my back on the danger, though everything inside me wailed to not do so. We started back in the direction I had come from.

"Halt."

Our feet stilled automatically at the commanding tone.

"Face me, new girl, and tell me your name."

I shut my eyes, breathed in and then let it out. *In. Out.* Then I swiveled back, dropping into a shaky curtsy, head lowered.

"Your name." His prompting told me he was not a patient man.

"Naya," I breathed. "My name is Naya."

"Louder. And look me in the face this time, you little chit."

Summoning every ounce of courage within me, I hazarded a glance up at his face, so far above mine. I quickly settled my eyes on his stern mouth, but I had seen enough of his face to forever remember it: sallow skin, thick eyebrows arching over a sickly, skinny face. I was thankful I had not looked into his eyes, for I was sure they would have frozen me solid.

"Naya, sir."

"Know this, Naya: I do not take kindly to those who get in my way. And I never forget a face."

On that ominous note, he spun and stalked away.

I stood as still as a pine, focusing on my breathing for several seconds, shutting my eyes. *I never forget a face*, clanged dully through my mind. I did not appreciate the common link I had with the lecher.

"Thank you, oh thank you! I don't know what I would have done if you hadn't been here to save me."

I opened my eyes and focused on Penelope at my side, still gripping my hand. I nodded, smiling weakly. I could not bring myself to force any more words through my swollen throat. My courage had seeped out through my feet to sink into the stone floor beneath me.

I do not take kindly to those who get in my way.

Miss Sue was in a tizzy as soon as we stumbled into the kitchen and shared the disturbing story. If I looked anything like Penelope, then we both looked as though we had seen a specter. Miss Sue paced back and forth, hands waving as she muttered to herself after we told our story. To my utter shock, I realized that she was not angry with Penelope or I, but at the bounder who had made us so pale.

Not long after that, with orders to sit until we felt whole again, mugs filled with milk thrust into our hands, she had marched away, throwing down her towel and calling over her shoulder that "that no-good, dirty, flea-infested, stinking maggot" would soon know the wrath of Susanna Killjoy and it would not be a pretty sight. Miss Sue had a habit of describing the qualities of maggots when she was angry. The angrier she got, the longer the list of complaints about said maggots became.

"That's the longest one I've heard yet!" Penelope whispered in awe. "She must be steaming."

She returned less than an hour later, even redder in the face. She reported that the captain of the guard had dismissed her story, as the man in question—Rasmussen Polk—was technically not a member of the guard. He had transferred to the castle as part of the convoy escorting the prince's cousin and thus could not be punished. Miss Sue told us exactly what she thought of that announcement and in words that made me blush.

"Penny, you are on your own in your room in the west wing, correct?" Miss Sue finally said, interrupting her own rant.

Swallowing heavily, Penelope nodded. "Yes, ma'am."

"Not anymore, you aren't. As of this moment, I demand you move into Betsy and Naya's room. There is safety in numbers, dearie, and I will rest better knowing you are not by yourself at night."

Remembering Betsy's pique over gaining a single occupant to her rooms, I nearly spoke up in protest. But seeing the relief in Penelope's face and not wanting to get Miss Sue in another dither, I shut my mouth, sipping once more at the milk in my mug. No matter what she thought of it, Betsy was about to get yet another new roommate.

Chapter Eight

Healthy Release

Benjamin

UNCLE JAMES WAS true to his word. The sun hadn't even fully decided if it was going to resurface when I heard a soft knock on my door. Struggling to put my other boot on, I hopped on one foot across the room, and called for whoever it was to enter.

My uncle waltzed in, perfectly groomed and dressed casually. He grinned, rubbing his hands together. I had already had my doubts about agreeing to this whole idea—and had dwelled on them throughout the night as well—but the look of eagerness that filled his eyes made me even more wary.

"Are you ready, Benjamin?" he asked, clapping his hands together.

I eyed him as I tugged my coat on. "That depends."

"On what?"

"On whether or not you decide to stop looking so blasted cheerful when it is so ridiculously early." I paused, then asked, "What exactly do you have in mind for me today?"

"You'll have to find that out for yourself. Follow me."

With that directive, he spun on his heel and strode out the door. I groaned, but once again, I couldn't help myself from following after him. At least this time, he waited just outside the door. No trailing after the man as he slipped around bends in the castle's passageways. I tried to get him to answer a few other questions, but his abbreviated replies didn't encourage conversation. We walked on in silence. My curiosity expanded as we entered the stables and I almost broke the silence when I saw my mount, Joker, saddled and ready to ride. Ready to ride where? There was no explanation and I held back my questions, following my uncle in stony silence.

We rode for perhaps twenty minutes, until we were cloaked by the darkness of the forest beyond Dartmoor. We turned off the main road and my uncle reined in his horse a few minutes later. He dismounted, tied the lead around a low hanging branch by the side of the road and I followed, watching him as he removed his jacket. I didn't take mine off, just simply stood by my mount.

He breathed in deeply, looking in both directions, then spoke. "All right, Benjamin. Our first lesson is the lesson of healthy direction."

I made a face. "What sort of rubbish is that?"

"Listen. We are going to run, all the way up this road and back down to our horses."

Disgusted, I paced away from him. "You have got to be joking," I spat. "I just came from training like this. I have spent countless hours running. How is doing the same thing supposed to help me?"

"Hear me out. Those runs were to get your body ready to keep up with the rigors of the life of a soldier. This is to train your mind, Benjamin."

"Train my mind?" I didn't keep the disdain and disbelief out of my voice.

"Yes. A huge component of maintaining control over your anger is giving yourself healthy ways to vent it, to get rid of it. Similar to giving a boiling teapot a vent to release the steam. That way, you don't explode on people who don't deserve your rage."

Unbidden came memories of the faces of my mother and next oldest sister, Mary, twisting in shock, or in sadness at various outbursts during my youth—or even more recently. I shrugged mentally, pushing them away as I refocused on my uncle and his explanation.

"There are many different approaches to healthy venting. You can get in a few rounds with a punching bag, or practice your defenses with a sword or staff. Another way to do this is going for a run when you're angry. You can push your anger into your strides to make yourself go faster or run longer. But," he said, raising a finger in warning, "don't abuse yourself. Remember, this is to be a *healthy* release. Don't run until you can't move or punch a bag until your hands are raw and bleeding. Be smart about it as you let those emotions release. Now, are you angry right now?"

"I think this a load of cow dung. Is that close enough?"

"We'll make do with that. Now, I'd suggest you remove your jacket. There you go. Now, let's start out at an easy pace."

He broke into a jog, with an even stride and near perfect form.

Rolling my eyes, I quickly fell in step with him, finding my rhythm in the cool early morning. We stayed matched even as my uncle slowly increased the speed. The path began to wind, and it rose and fell in gentle slopes. Soon birdsong began, creating a pleasant background to the monotonous thumping of our feet and the steady chugging of our lungs. I started out internally grumbling about the ridiculousness of this whole venture, a low buzzing irritation. Eventually, all I could focus on was my breathing as the minutes stretched out and the sun gained altitude in the sky. Keeping up with my uncle became my sole goal. He never broke his pace, his breathing remaining steady and sure.

We reached the end of the road, which stopped at an area where hunters skinned their kill; a horizontal beam was tied between two closely situated trees. We paused to breathe and rest before returning to our mounts. Now the spring sun shone down, warming the air around us. We didn't speak. Uncle James, breath sufficiently caught, began again, heading back down the path. By now I didn't even feel the burn; I had reached the point where there was no beginning or end to this run, just one step after the next.

We came around the bend where we could see our horses small in the distance, and without warning, Uncle James pushed from a run into a full-out sprint. Growling, I tucked my chin and pumped my limbs, rushing to catch up to him. Greenery flashed by on either side, wind whistling in my ears. Seconds later, I edged past my uncle until I was one stride, two strides, three strides ahead of him! I didn't let the thrill of being in the lead distract me from maintaining it, though it sure did feel good. After the harsh treatment I had received in the wake of the incident, being made a prisoner in my own home, then the transfer to my uncle's home, I had thrust back feelings of frustration and discouragement. It was rewarding to finally be moving, to be victorious in a world that seemed suddenly so against me.

The momentum of my sprint carried me past our steeds and only then did I pull back, jogging and skidding to a stop. Though my body begged me to drop to the ground, I remained on my feet with Uncle James, who sucked in deep breaths, shirt soaked with sweat. As his breathing eased, he raised his hands behind his head and walked a few paces away. He retrieved two water skins from a saddle bag and tossed one to me. I practically drank the whole thing in one go. I felt like I could drink ten more and still be thirsty.

Once our sweat started drying and we no longer gasped for air, Uncle James motioned to remount and we began the ride back to the castle. For several minutes, the only sounds were the dull thudding of our horses and the birdsong. Then my uncle spoke into the silence.

"How was that? Did you notice any difference?"

I had. The pressure of the irritation resting on my shoulders had eased. Now that the run was over, my mind felt clearer. But it had to be a fluke, a one time thing. I told my uncle this, and his response was that I had to make a habit of it. I groaned inwardly, but nodded to him.

When we broke through the treeline and Dartmoor was in sight, I finally asked the question I had been wondering about ever since yesterday.

"Uncle James, what was Plan A?"

Torn from his inner musings, he glanced over at me. He processed the question and a wry grin split his face. He faced forward, urging his horse into a trot. I glared at his back.

"Seriously?" I called at his back. "You're not going to tell me?"
He only laughed.
I scowled deeply.

As we entered the castle, a messenger immediately pounced on my uncle, as if he had been lying in wait, poised to spring upon him as soon as he walked in. Uncle James—now well and truly King James, monarch of Mendlewyn—pulled the young man to the side of the entrance hall and stepped in close. The young man spoke softly, but I could still hear his message. How could I be blamed when the foyer had such excellent acoustics?

"There has been trouble brewing below-stairs, sire. Two servant girls became distressed by the actions of a man that recently came from your brother's home. Their overseer, Miss Sue, has been raising quite the fuss and wouldn't let me leave without promising that I report directly to you." The man sounded rather put out at this tidbit.

"'Distressed'?" Uncle James repeated, sounding uneasy. "What does that mean?"

Exactly what I was thinking, I agreed as I leaned forward, careful to keep my eyes elsewhere as I strained to listen.

"Well, sire, from what I have gathered, the man in question was inhibiting the first girl's ability to leave to finish her chores, and was making her quite, as I said before, uncomfortable. And when the second girl interfered, the man became more hostile and threatened her."

"Threatened, you said?"

The messenger confirmed that particular detail and they continued to converse. My mind had caught on that last part, as well as the clue about the man being from Uncle James's brother's house, meaning my own home. Digesting the information, I felt my lips curl in contempt. Only one man could be responsible for such awful behavior: Rasmussen Polk.

The man—and I always used that word *very* lightly when referencing this particular creature—was, in short, a nuisance. A boil. A pestilence in human form. How he had reached the rank of captain was beyond me, but he did know how to put on a good show, a convincing mask. I was unsurprised in the least to hear that he had been up to no good, spreading his diseased presence wherever he went. Whoever the poor girls were, I felt ill for them.

All at once, the foyer was silent and I glanced around, making direct eye contact with Uncle James. In one look I knew that he was aware that I had heard the majority of the message. He raised an eyebrow at me. It was a face that I had seen my father employ countless amounts of time: he was expecting me to apologize for eavesdropping.

The moon would have to roll over and cough up all its spots before *that* happened.

Chapter Nine
On Edge

Naya

"WHERE DOES THIS one go, Naya?" Penny asked, hefting a smooth globe after she had finished wiping it down.

"On this bookshelf, the third shelf from the top, near the middle. Be careful it does not slip out of your hand as you climb the ladder."

She made a sound of acknowledgment as she began to step carefully up the ladder. I watched her for a few moments, naturally a little guarded since I had accidentally broken one of the priceless treasures. But Penny—as I had found out she preferred over Penelope—was nimble and quite cautious in her movements, so I hadn't needed to watch her progress so closely. It was simply an old habit that was hard to break. I had been told I held on too tightly to things that fell under my care. I was trying to loosen up, to become more flexible but clearly I needed more practice.

Nearly a week had passed since Penny had moved into the room Betsy and I shared. True to my prediction, Betsy did get upset over the extra cot and belongings that began appearing that afternoon, but to my surprise, she had only sucked in a breath and left the room. Whether or not she went to Miss Sue, I did not know, but she had not reacted the way she did before, immediately demanding to know why I was in her room and for me to leave as soon as possible. Perhaps she knew she could not win against Miss Sue. Or maybe she had heard about the reason why Penny was moving into our space. Either way, it made me grateful that she had not reacted with such volatility this time. I felt I could breathe, and I hoped this meant there would not be a return to treading on dried leaves.

As Penny descended the ladder, I heard the library doors open and a male voice. Penny heard it too and froze halfway down the ladder, shooting a worried glance at me. I made a gesture for her to stay where she was, then moved on silent feet to the edge of the aisle, peering with one eye toward the entrance to the library. Immediately, I let out a tense breath. It was the prince and his cousin,

Benjamin. They presented a different sort of challenge, but one far better than we had been fearing.

I turned back to Penny and whispered that it was not *him*. She closed her eyes in relief and hurried down the ladder.

We had not seen Rasmussen again after that fateful day in the corridor, but we had both remained on edge since that confrontation. Penny had found reasons to stay close to me, finishing her regular chores each morning with an urgency, and then joining me in the library in the afternoons. As if I presented much of a challenge if the scoundrel chose to come back to enact his threat. Nevertheless, I had enjoyed the company, as Miss Sue's declaration of there being 'safety in numbers' was still rattling around in my mind. It was comforting to have another pair of eyes to watch the shadows in the corners of the library, another person to have their ears attuned to the slightest change in the air around us.

The voice grew louder, and soon the pair passed by our aisle. Prince Fitzroy, who was in the middle of speaking, did not seem to notice us, but his cousin did. He nodded in our direction. Penny and I slipped into curtsies and then the moment was over; the cousins kept moving and the voice quieted until I could not hear it anymore. I sighed, turning back to the small table that still held a few trinkets that needed to return to their original perches among the many tomes. I reached for one, found its spot with my eyes and pushed the ladder along the rail toward the desired location.

On the way back down, I glanced in Penny's direction, surprised to see her partway in the path between the shelves, head turned in the direction the nobles had gone.

"Penny? Are you all right?"

She started, spinning back to me. A blush crept up her neck. "I'm fine!" she blurted.

I narrowed an eye at her. She blushed deeper. Stepping down, I cocked my head, moved my eyes to the right, as if I could still see the prince and his cousin, and then returned my gaze to Penny. *Aha*, I thought with triumph. Fighting a smile, I nodded slowly.

"I see," I murmured.

"Oh no, it's not like that," she hurriedly said. "It's nothing. Nothing at all."

"Of course. Nothing at all."

This time she was the one who narrowed one eye. "Are you funning me?"

"Funning?" I repeated the unfamiliar word.

"Teasing," she clarified. "Are you teasing me?"

I could not keep the smile at bay anymore and I let it free. She glared at me, but there was no malice behind it. She stuck out her tongue at me, a gesture I had not seen since my early childhood, and a laugh spilled from my chest. I clapped a hand over my mouth, embarrassed. Penny giggled at my reaction and the sound was so contagious that I could not keep my laugh from returning to join hers. Our twin laughs echoed up between the shelves and it took quite some time before we could control ourselves. Fighting down one last titter, I hurried to the end of the aisle, peeked around the corner and breathed a sigh of relief that our outburst hadn't been noticed by the aristocratic guests who had disappeared into the depths of the library.

Facing Penny once more, I smiled. "I will admit that I was teasing you, but in my defense, you made it too easy."

She pulled another face, but there was enough humor in the way her eyes sparkled that I could tell she was not offended. "Well then, I suppose I can say 'you're welcome' for providing you with such effortless entertainment."

"Yes, thank you, Penny, for making the time pass with the delightful distraction."

She curtsied prettily. I laughed once more, then weighed pressing her about her earlier captivation. Deciding to speak up, I caught her eye and tilted my head to one side.

"Back to the scene from before, who was it that so caught your eye?"

She spun away, most likely to hide a blush, and shrugged one shoulder. "The prince's cousin is…"

She paused to think of the right way to phrase whatever it was in her mind. Unconsciously, I filled in the space her sentence had created. *Unpredictable? Chaotic? Or better yet, the epitome of pandemonium?*

"…simply dashing," Penny finished.

I blinked. Clearly she had never spoken to the young man, and the rumors of his behavior had yet to penetrate her mind. Dear girl. I called up a smile and nodded, to show her I was listening if she decided to go on; Penny did not need anymore encouragement. For the next several minutes, she rambled on in a quiet voice about the newest and most mysterious addition to the castle. She complimented everything from the shade of his curly red hair to the way he walked. I had no doubt in my mind: she was twitterpated. I had never heard so many words flow free from a mouth that seemingly needed no air, as she barely paused for breath as we moved along the rows.

Penny was still going when we finished the section that was due for cleaning today. Half listening to her endless stream of a very much one-sided conversation, I glanced back at the work we had completed and crossed my arms over my chest. A glance at the clock on a nearby mantle told me that we had finished much earlier than expected. I nodded in triumph, feeling the pleasure of a job well done.

"Oh," Penny suddenly exclaimed. "Are we finished already?"

I nodded, and motioned for her to follow me. She caught sight of the clock and her eyes widened.

"Was I talking for *that* long?"

"Yes, you were," I replied over my shoulder as we headed back through the maze that made up the rows and rows of books.

"I didn't even notice time was going by so quickly!"

"Perhaps I will bring up a certain handsome nobleman up in conversation tomorrow so the work will go by just as fast."

She gasped, then snorted. "Naya! How horrible you are!"

I grinned in response, then faced forward again. In this particular aisle, we had more room to walk side-by-side, as the shelves were further apart. We had just started another conversation when I suddenly halted. Ignoring Penny's questions about why I had stopped, I furrowed my brow, then thought back, mentally going through my running memories for the last minute of our walk. There. I retraced my steps, handing my rag to Penny as I went. Twenty paces back, I reached for the item that I had not seen in my daily sweep for rubbish: an envelope.

It was standard size, with a blank face. I made a sound of pondering, then turned it over. In the bottom right corner of the backside was a small circular emblem. Inside the circle was a vague outline of a rearing snake. One fang gleamed red, the coloring a stark contrast to the white of the envelope.

"Who is it addressed to?"

Keeping my eyes on the envelope, I shook my head. "There is no name."

"Interesting. In that case, just put it back. That reminds me, the daily mail is due any minute. Let's be quick in putting our cleaning things away and try to beat the boy to the dining hall. I've been waiting ever so long for my grandparents to write me back; I hope today I hear from them."

As we left the library, Penny continued on, explaining how excited she was to hear from her grandparents, who were avid beekeepers and kept Penny abreast on their adventures as they prepared their hives for the coming year. It was truly a fascinating topic.

Shortly before we turned down the hall to the dining hall, I felt the most peculiar sensation that there were eyes on me. Without stopping, I glanced over my shoulder and felt my knees go weak. A tall, dark figure peered back at me from down the hall.

Facing forward, I drew a breath in to call for Penny to start running, intending to start fleeing as well. A second glance over my shoulder showed an empty hallway. But there was no comfort in it, for I knew what I had seen.

Rasmussen had been watching and then, like a flash of lightning, he was gone.

CHAPTER TEN

LEARNING TO BREATHE

Benjamin

IT WAS THE seventh sneeze that broke my patience, which had been legendary up until this point. Pulling myself up from the ridiculously small fainting couch, I glanced over in the direction I had last seen Fitzy and couldn't bring myself to feel surprise at the sight. He hadn't budged from his hunched position next to a precarious stack of thick, ancient books that looked ready to topple onto his head at any moment. There was a shifting plume of dust stirring around his face from the book he had just opened. I rolled my eyes.

"Fitzy," I called. He didn't even twitch. "Fitzy!"

Yanked from his concentration, he startled and glanced up at me, blinking red eyes.

"What did you say?"

"You missed it, the belching pig that ran through this section a few minutes ago. You should have seen it. It was huge!"

He simply looked at me for a moment, then rubbed his eyes. "Very funny. What did you need?"

"I need you to do something other than staring at old books and sneezing. Let's get out of here. We've been here for hours."

With a deep sigh, he glanced at his stack of books, then to the shorter stack on his other side. "I am nowhere near done, Benjamin. I think I'll be here for some time yet. I honestly didn't know you were still here. I figured you had reached your limit and left a long time ago."

Throwing out my hands in front of me, I said in exasperation, "You mean to tell me I could have left and you wouldn't have minded at all?"

He shrugged, a smile at my expense tugging at his mouth. "Yes, that is what I am saying. I'm surprised you're still here. I thought you would have imploded by now."

I shook my head in disgust. "I don't deserve this sort of treatment. A man can only take so much silence and endless rows of books before he commits rash decisions."

"Like what?"

"Like hurling a chair through the closest window and following it down."

"That is quite rash. Why not use the main doors like a normal human?"

"It doesn't quite drive home my point, now does it?"

"Fair," he agreed, stretching his neck. He twisted from side to side in his seat, and groaned; I could hear the popping from where I was standing. He reoriented himself in the chair, then made eye contact. "Go," he said, waving a hand as if he were shooing away his cat, Mimsy. "Leave me to my research."

I shook my head, bid him farewell, and hurried away. I couldn't reach the main entrance of the library fast enough. Soon I was careening down the hallway in the direction of my bed chambers, determined to change into looser clothing on my way to the training room. I needed to train, even if it meant by myself.

No sooner had I rounded the corner down from my rooms, I spotted a messenger coming toward me. In the same instant, I realized I was due in my uncle's office for yet another of his lectures. I cursed softly. I could officially scratch stabbing things off my to-do list for today. We'd only ever crossed swords on that first afternoon, never since then. It had been a week since I had first agreed to this hare-brained plan, a week of daily treks outside the city limits, feet beating a path beneath the ceiling of pine boughs from dawn until the sun was high. Always running, running, running. I was entirely sick of running.

I was tempted to dart back the way I had come, but it was already too late; the messenger had increased his pace, eyes fixed on me. I sighed and continued forward. I nodded once in response to his summons and dismissed the man, foregoing the stop in my personal chambers, turning instead toward my uncle's office. This would be the first time Uncle James had requested my presence after our daily runs. It couldn't be for anything good.

Too quickly, I pushed the door open to the antechamber, dreading what was to come.

"Good morning, sir," said the secretary, rising to his feet swiftly. "If you wouldn't mind taking a seat, his majesty is currently in a meeting and will be with you when said meeting has concluded." With a polite smile, the little man gestured to several chairs lined up against the wall opposite the door to the office.

I considered ignoring him as I had done on my first visit to my uncle's office, but I thought better of it. The man had spoken as though he had rehearsed the short request many times over in front of a looking glass. Might as well take pity on the poor soul. Nodding, I pivoted and moved toward the chairs, smirking when I heard a relieved sigh from behind me.

Several minutes dragged by and I decided I was through with sitting, shooting to my feet. The secretary mirrored my action, warily eyeing me. Watching out of the corner of my vision, I started to pace, directly toward the door to my uncle's study. The man's chest filled as he prepared to protest, and right before he spoke, I spun on my heel and paced the other direction. After a few more circuits of the little antechamber, the secretary slowly lowered himself back into his chair, plucked a quill from the desktop and dipped it in the inkwell. Soon the only sounds were the rhythmic sound of my boots on wooden floors and the whispering skitters of a quill being run over parchment. If I concentrated hard enough as I drew closer to the closed door, I thought I could make out the muted sound of conversation in the next room.

I varied from pacing, to studying the landscape painting on the wall next to the bookshelf. Eventually, after an undefinable amount of time, the door to Uncle James's office swung open and a man stepped into the antechamber, closing the door behind him.

Clothes unkempt and dusty from recent travel, the man nodded at the secretary and moved in the direction of the exit. I started to turn away, dismissing him as a courier, and a sloppy one at that, with overlong hair. As he drew closer to where I stood, though, our gazes locked and my muscles tensed instinctively. Eyes as dark as mud peered back, searching and calculating. I instantly reevaluated the man, thinking back on my earlier glimpse. A stocky build, erect posture and a smooth, almost predatory way of moving told me this was no mere messenger. The gruesome scar marring his right cheek, just below the piercing eye, added to my suspicions.

His head swiveled as he passed, keeping our eyes locked. Only when he crossed the threshold did he break eye contact. He strutted away without glancing back, a total dismissal. It should have felt like a victory, having a man break a stare and turn his back on me, but it didn't. It felt far more like a beast that has brushed you off, its stomach full, having no desire to maul or feast.

Staring at the door, I clenched and unclenched my hands. "Who was that?"

Several moments of silence greeted me. I turned to look at the secretary, who made a great effort to appear absorbed in his pile of papers. Too absorbed.

"Who was that?" I repeated, putting in a tone that demanded answers.

"I have no idea what you're talking about."

That answer spoke volumes about the stranger who had just left.

Torn between following the stranger and thoroughly interrogating the secretary, I turned to the assistant after a few seconds of pondering. Of the two of them, I presumed the little office minion was the one who would crack first. But before I could open my mouth to start my line of questioning, the door to Uncle James's office sprang open again and he peered out, eyes roving the small space. Spotting me, he waved me toward him, then disappeared from the doorway.

Sighing, I followed after him. If I couldn't interrogate the secretary—what was the man's name, had I even learned it—perhaps I could get some information from Uncle himself. I figured it was worth it to at least try.

As I sank into the chair across from him, I casually asked, "Who was that man?"

Uncle James paused briefly in the act of stacking some loose papers, eyes flicking up to meet mine for a moment. Then he dropped his gaze to focus on his task. "Who?"

"The man who I saw leaving your study not thirty ticks ago."

His motions slowed again and I held my breath. Would he too deny not knowing the man, as his secretary had done? If he did, I would pounce on it, demand who the man was and why they were treating him as if he were invisible.

"Oh, right, him. He was simply delivering a message."

At least he had acknowledged the mystery man's existence.

"He seemed a bit too…rugged to be a messenger."

Uncle James, everything about his person completely unconcerned now, lifted a shoulder and replied, "Did he now? I hadn't noticed." He cleared his throat and clasped his hands together on top of the desk. "Now, onto the reason I asked you to meet with me after our usual run. It has been a week since we started our morning routine. Have you noticed any difference? Any change at all?"

Unbelievable. I knew now what this was. A heart-to-heart to discover how his loony mind-training experiments were going. I leaned back in the chair and folded my arms, slouching in a way that would make my mother's eyebrows climb towards her hairline.

"Well?"

"Well what?" I tossed back. "What do you want me to say? I'm cured? That you're a genius?"

He took in a deep breath. "Have you noticed any change in the levels of your anger? Is it constantly on the brink of spilling over, or has it mellowed at all?"

The serious look on his face told me he'd keep asking until I actually put some thought into it. Blowing out a rough breath, I searched my mind, going through the events of the past week. Reluctantly, I had to admit that right after the daily runs, I felt better. Lighter. But as the day went on, I forgot about the effects of the run, and, in dealing with those around me and left to my own devices, the tar field had begun to churn again, slowly but surely.

Smugly, I shook my head. "No, Uncle. I haven't noticed any difference. Seems to me this whole thing is a sham."

I waited, watching his face for the way he'd react to my baiting words. Instead, to my disappointment, he nodded.

"I thought as much. A week is too early to tell if we're making lasting progress."

"Then what was the point of even asking?"

"I wanted to make you stop and think about it, to review everything that has happened since we started."

"Oh no," I moaned, rolling my head back until the nape of my neck rested on the top of the chair, eyes directed at the ceiling. "You sound like my tutors. I left the schoolroom years ago. I would rather not return."

"You say that as though thinking is abhorrent."

I refocused on him, uncrossing my arms and raising both hands, palms toward him. "You said it, not me."

"Benjamin, when you leave my home, free to pursue the rest of your life, what is your next step?"

"Enlist in the army, of course."

"Of course," he agreed. He leaned back, matching my posture, slumping in his chair. I almost laughed. A king slumping. I had never dreamed it possible. Was the world coming to an end?

"Say you enlist in the army," he continued, "and you make it through the basic training, start to rise in the ranks. You become a captain. Do you think a captain is free from thinking? Or let's say you're second-in-command and, in the midst of a battle, your commander suddenly falls to the ground, dead. Now you're expected to step into his place, to lead your remaining men to victory or death. Does that not require thinking?"

I shifted in my spot. He had me there. Yet I couldn't resist saying, "So we've established that thinking is important. Again, what is the point of this?"

He lifted a finger. "I was getting to that. The point is that the ability to think is paramount to your success here, Benjamin. You cannot expect yourself to succeed in reining in your temper if you don't have control of your mind."

"Are you insinuating that I am stupid? Mad?" I couldn't help the bite that entered my tone.

"Not at all. You're an intelligent, sane young man. You just haven't been taught to control your mind, your thoughts, your moods."

"And you're going to teach me?"

"Yes."

I huffed, resuming my earlier posture with my head resting on the back of the chair. I hoped he could read my skepticism in the silence I gave him.

He let the pause stretch on, then he suddenly spoke again. "Benjamin, what does an approaching rainstorm smell like?"

Screwing my face up, I lifted my head. "What nonsense are you spewing now, Uncle?"

"This goes along with the next trick I have to teach you." He then raised his eyebrows, waiting.

I shook my head, then pondered his question. Did a rainstorm even have a smell? I shut my eyes, thinking back to the first spring storm of this year, which I had experienced while traveling to Dartmoor. We had seen the rolling clouds on the horizon on the open road and had sped up, hoping to reach the tree line in the distance before the dark clouds could unleash their fury on us. We had pulled off the road, dismounting under the thick branches of the forest, with only minutes to spare. The wind had stirred, then intensified, bringing with it a hint of freshness. Like freshly turned soil or simply the sense of *cleanliness*. Then the rain had come, soaking us through in minutes, despite our shelter.

I opened my eyes. "An approaching rainstorm smells fresh. Clean."

He nodded. "Yes! Brilliant descriptor. It smells like something is about to change, that the world, so filthy and aged, is about to be reborn."

"Is this the start of poetry lessons? If so, please put me out of my misery and beat me over the head with that paperweight. A few hefty thumps should do it."

Ignoring me completely, he sat forward, leaning across his desk. "I am going to teach you a tool for you to use when you feel the anger fighting to get free. What makes you angry?"

Besides pointless exercises like this one? I thought tartly. Instead, I said out loud, "When people belittle me. When I'm patronized."

"Excellent. The next time someone belittles you or patronizes you, I want you to use this tool I am about to teach you."

"What is it?"

"Back to the rainstorm. You can smell it coming, right? I want you to imagine that when you are feeling patronized or belittled, or anything that makes you start to become frustrated, that your anger is like a rainstorm coming towards you. When you start to get provoked, I want you to take in a deep, slow breath through your nose. Smell the rainstorm. Really try to fill your lungs as much as possible. And then I want you to breathe out through your mouth, blow it out gradually. In through your nose, out through the mouth, like you are blowing the clouds away. Try it. Sit up."

I did so, but I couldn't help grumbling, "You can't blow away a storm with your breath."

"Breathe in through the nose," he ordered, pausing until I had done so. He did it with me. "Breathe out through your mouth. Good. Again."

I inhaled deeply through my nose, pulling in air at the same rate as my uncle. After a moment, we breathed out together. We did this over and over.

Soon he switched his mantra to, "Smell the rainstorm, then blow it away."

Smell the rainstorm. Blow it away.

Smell the rainstorm.

Blow it away.

I let my eyes fall shut, focusing only on the steady timbre of my uncle's voice. I could feel a battle begin to wage inside my mind, dual voices rising and swirling around one another like a cyclone. *This is an utter waste of time! Just swing a sword and you'll get over it!*

Yet another, opposing voice cried, *You gave your word. You may be many things, but a liar is not one of them! See it through.*

On and on they went, until it took everything in me to remain seated. I finally had to shut off my mind entirely, to simply tune into the breathing.

Eventually, Uncle was through demonstrating the breathing exercise, and he went on to talk about the benefits of said technique. I did my best to focus on his words, but the twin voices had come to stay.

CHAPTER ELEVEN

THE WEIGHT OF LONELINESS

Naya

I KNEW SOMETHING was wrong the moment Miss Sue crooked a finger at me from the doorway of her small personal room, a serious look on her wrinkled face. Although my stomach clenched with worry, I abandoned my route to the library, wringing my apron between suddenly sweaty hands. She stepped to the side, revealing Penny perched in one of the chairs in front of the desk. I swallowed heavily at her nervous expression, took a seat, and waited for Miss Sue to waddle behind her desk.

She wasted no time, thank goodness, getting right to what she needed to discuss with us.

"I wanted you two to know the information immediately," she said quickly. "I just received word from a messenger that his majesty has heard of that dirty rotten maggot's behavior and has punished him."

I held my breath, and Penny snatched my hand, squeezing it. We waited.

"Rasmussen's pay has been docked and he has latrine cleaning duty for the next three months, with a warning that if he so much as puts a toe out of line again, he'll be dismissed immediately."

Penny grinned, releasing my hand to clap hers together. It took her a few seconds to realize that she was the only one celebrating. Her vibrant smile faded as she looked between Miss Sue and I.

"I seem to be missing something. Why aren't you two happy with me about this? What's going on?"

Miss Sue looked like she had taken a huge bite of something sour. She also did not look inclined to speak at the moment, so I turned to Penny, trying to think of how to inform her of what we expected to happen now.

"Rasmussen has been punished, yes, but in a way that is more demeaning and frustrating than anything else. In my experience, when bullies are humiliated instead of humbled, it only serves to make them even more of a nuisance."

"My thoughts exactly," Miss Sue declared, slapping her palm on the desk. "This punishment will make the man as irritable as a kicked hog."

Penny, whose shoulders had sagged, picked at the hem of her apron nervously. "You mean that even though he's been punished, things are not going to get better?"

I met Miss Sue's eyes and then shook my head alongside her. Penny shrank into herself, eyes going blank. She began to ramble.

"I was holding on until he was properly reprimanded. I told myself that all would be well once that happened, that I wouldn't have to be wound tighter than a weaver's bobbin. But it won't! What do you think will happen now? No, don't answer that. I don't want to know. Oh, Naya, what are we going to do? What can we do?" Her voice rose to a wail and tears began to fall.

Sighing, Miss Sue opened a drawer, plucked a crisp handkerchief from within and handed it to me, motioning with her chin in Penny's direction.

I placed the cloth into Penny's grasp, then pushed her hand up toward her face. She finally buried her mouth and nose into it, shoulders heaving. I patted and rubbed her back, all while trying to keep the searing anxiety within my own chest at bay.

Miss Sue began to softly explain her plans to have more people coming in and out of the library at random times, so we would not be alone in there. She expressed a hope that she could appeal to the captain of the guard to perhaps have more men in the area too.

"If that pig-headed man won't listen, then I'll just go around him and talk to the king again. It worked this last time. That'll show him." She laughed.

The morning's passing felt excruciatingly long; it dragged on like a nasty headache. Penny had been my shadow as we had gone through our morning routine in the library, eyes flitting from place to place, hardly resting on one thing before darting to the next. She remained pale, her freckles standing out like paint flicked across a blank canvas.

I was not much better than her internally, though I did my best to hide all hint of the anxiety that threatened to burst free from me any moment. Unlike Penny, I had had endless practice hiding feelings that could be used against me. If only burying the emotions got rid of them entirely, but alas, such was not the case. They simply stewed and brewed.

I glanced at the waterclock in the corner and sighed, relief tickling my worn nerves. It was time to break for lunch. I called to Penny, who set down the rag and jar of wood polish with enthusiasm. I could smile at that. The polish was pungent—and since the library was nearly all wood, all I could smell was the overpowering scent. I knew from experience that it would linger the rest of the day. Thank heavens we only had to polish twice a month.

As we exited the library, Penny let loose a mighty sneeze, which echoed down the near empty corridor. Reddening, she covered her nose and mouth with her hands, then grimaced and yanked them away hurriedly.

"Ugh," she moaned. "Is polishing day *always* this miserable?"

I nodded sympathetically. "Unfortunately."

She muttered under her breath the whole way to the servants' dining hall, where she was quickly summoned by several girls closer to her age. She waved back, turned to me and flattened her lips, eyebrows furrowing in concern. I could read the question in her eyes. Smiling as best I could, I assured her that she could join her friends, that I would be fine. She still hesitated until I lightly pushed her in the direction of the waiting group. She then thanked me profusely and skipped toward the girls, who all embraced her with obvious affection. She fused into the mix seamlessly.

I tore my eyes away from the sight, moved in the direction of the line, and shuffled in behind the last person in the queue. I did all this unseeingly, mind reviewing the welcome Penny had received moments before. As I shuffled forward, I wrapped my arms around myself, acutely aware of my loneliness. Loneliness in an overcrowded room, a soul-deep pain I would not wish on anyone. It was times just like these that made me crave for acceptance. For belonging.

Unbidden, countless memories seeped up from the depths of my mind, flooding to the forefront like a river overflowing its banks. They pelted me, coming faster and faster.

The illness, slowly consuming each and every one of my immediate family until I was the sole survivor, the last to fall ill.

An endless road stretching out into the unknown.

Family, only in the barest hint of the word, and a new roof over my head.

Shunned.

Lost.

So, so, alone.

Sucking in a deep breath, I squeezed my arms until my fingers shook and the flesh caught in my grasp begged for release. Reeling back from the storm within, I blinked away tears. This was no place to dissolve. A few more breaths should do it. And just in time too, as I had reached the front of the line. I took a tray of food and wiped my eyes with my sleeve.

A low snicker met my ears. I raised my gaze and cringed before I could stop myself. Peering over their shoulders ahead of me were two girls, of equal height and build, both of whom had willowy frames. One covered her mouth with a hand to hold back further giggles, while the other made a slow perusal of my person, from head to toe and back again. Her nose crinkled as if she had just gotten a whiff of a pigsty.

I dropped my eyes, wishing myself away from the cruel gazes. They had clearly seen me on the brink of tears.

"Say, Lucinda," the one on the left drawled, loud enough for me to hear, "have you ever had the misfortune of seeing such a repugnant pair of eyes? Why, there's hardly any hue at all! Gray is *such* a bland color."

Lucinda tittered in response, then agreed wholeheartedly. She went on to say, "And those boots? I do believe I've seen rubbish heaps in better repair than those. What? Can't afford to purchase a new pair from a drifter?"

I drew my shoulders up to my ears, eyes fixed on the offending footwear. My repugnant eyes on tattered boots. No wonder they scorned me. A chorus of high-pitched laughter went up and I tried to ignore it.

"Well at least those gray eyes you speak of are shining with intelligence, unlike *some*," a voice declared from behind me. I spun around, finding Betsy, who had come out of nowhere, giving the girl who had first spoken a haughty look. She closed in, getting in the bullies' faces. "Why I've seen deer with brighter eyes than yours, Hattie." She set her contemptuous gaze on the second girl. "And Lucinda, don't get above yourself, dear. You're just as poor as the rest of us."

Shocked and disgusted gasps echoed from my tormentors.

Over her shoulder, she said to me, "Naya, come and sit at my table. There is a spot next to me that's begging for you to claim it. And don't pay any heed to these she-pigs anymore." She then spun away from the girls, flipped her sleek braid over her shoulder—striking Hattie in the cheek with the end, for good measure—and strode away.

For several seconds, I remained where I was, stock-still, unsure what to do or say. Betsy's defense had been as thorough as it had been unexpected; I was as stunned as my former tormentors, who looked frozen in shock. Then I processed Betsy's invitation and hurried away, following in my roommate's wake before the girls could recover their nastiness.

Betsy led me to a corner table, slipping into a spot on the bench beside a young man and across from a young woman. Hesitating, I looked from face to face. Neither of them appeared dismayed at my presence, so I took in a deep breath and sat. Betsy introduced me to her companions and I nodded, smiling shyly. I left the fact unsaid that I had already memorized their names and faces, along with every other occupant in Dartmoor Castle. No need to advertise my strangeness. It was better to stay quiet and hope they could endure my proximity.

Shortly after I had sat down, the young woman, Cherie, began to list the day's current gossip. Who was sneaking away with whom, the antics of various members of the nobility, and the like. She went on to mention the arrival of a new servant, one that had all the women belowstairs whispering and speculating. Assuming it was more of the same unimportant content, I tuned her out, unconcerned about rumors. I was simply pleased to not go back to passing a lunch hour on my own.

I was surprised when Betsy drew me into the conversation, asking my opinions. The other two included me as well and in a short time, we were finished with our meal. After returning our trays, Betsy touched my shoulder and stopped walking. She waved her friends on, and they bid us farewell.

She faced me, serious. "I hope you don't listen to what those girls were saying, Naya. It was all mean-spirited and false."

I shrugged a shoulder. "It was not the first time I have heard something similar, and I am sure it will not be the last time either."

Betsy's face turned fierce. "No, Naya," she ordered. "Don't talk like that."

Amazed at her vehemence, I rushed to say, "All right, I will not listen to what they said."

"You had better not. They were wrong."

"Is that why you stepped in? Because they were wrong?"

She made a sound of pondering. "Something like that. Perhaps I simply don't like bullies."

Penny appeared at my side, smiling a greeting at Betsy, who returned it and quickly left. Penny and I made our way to the library, Penny dominating the conversation. I felt immense relief to hear her jabbering like her usual self; she had been quieter since the meeting in Miss Sue's office that morning. Perhaps she had forgotten momentarily about our situation in being with her friends. I wished I was that fortunate. I continually scanned up and down the corridors as we walked.

"Do you think I should start worrying?" Penny asked unexpectedly.

I blinked. "Worrying about what? I apologize; I was woolgathering."

"No need to apologize. I was simply asking if you thought I should worry about the fact that my grandparents still haven't written me back. It has been weeks! It's not like them or my parents."

I hurried to reassure her, comforting her with the assumption that they were simply caught up in their daily chores. She seemed to accept this and moved on to other subjects.

We reached the library and Penny sighed heavily, retrieving the rag and jar of polish from where she had set them down. I laughed.

"If it makes you feel better, with your help, we should finish in a few hours," I called to her. "It usually takes me a day and a half to do all of this by myself. You have shortened this torture significantly."

"Hooray," she intoned, about as enthusiastic as a cat receiving a bath.

I laughed again, scraping some polish onto the rag in my hand and bending over an end table. With one hand, I reached for a vase and lifted it to set it on the ground. I paused at the whisper of a sound, glancing around. The sound had been faint, nearly out of my perception entirely. I waited a beat, then dismissed it. I shifted my arm that held the vase, angling to set it down at my feet, and again I heard the noise, a small rustle. It had emanated from inside the container. Frowning, I tilted it to the side until I could peer down into it. I spotted a flash of something off-white. I set the rag on the table and reached the now free hand inside.

It was an envelope. Plain and unaddressed, with that odd snake symbol in the corner on the front, the same as before.

I waffled, debating on what to do. Would it be better to put it back in the vase—and what a strange place to find an envelope—or to open it and find out who the intended recipient was? I bit my lip and turned it over, opening it. The message was brief, written in a barely legible script.

A wild bird was never meant to be caged. Remember your purpose. It would be a shame to see her wings clipped.

It was unsigned and there was no recipient name. I flipped it over, checking the back, and then reread it, feeling a peculiar sensation creep down my spine. The tone of the letter was ominous, its meaning vague. I returned it to the envelope and the envelope to the vase.

Whatever it was meant to imply or who it was intended for, I wanted nothing to do with it. If only I could dismiss the words from my mind so easily, but alas, I had wished for that many times over my life and it had never come true.

CHAPTER TWELVE

HUMBLED

Benjamin

FOUR AND A half weeks. I had been in the capital for just over a month, and I had finally received some correspondence from my family. Preoccupied all of yesterday, I had failed to notice the stack of envelopes until I was leaving for my usual morning run.

It's about time, I thought to myself. *I was beginning to wonder if they remembered me.* I scooped up the pile, returned to my bed, and lit a candle. Uncle James could wait a few minutes; I had letters to read.

The topmost envelope bore Mother's handwriting. I broke the seal and devoured its contents. She expressed her apologies for the way things had ended before I came to the capital, and her worry for my comfort while so far away from home. Her motherly concern was natural, I supposed, despite the fact that I was seventeen—nearly a man—and Dartmoor was only a day's ride from Graystone Manor, the family seat. She asked me about my stay so far, and nearly a dozen other questions. She expressed her love tenderly in the closing of the letter. I reread the last part a handful of times before folding the paper and tucking it under my pillow for later.

Next was a letter from Mary, the sister just above me. She started out in her usual way, completely forgoing a proper greeting, jumping straight into stating very bluntly that our father had truly and officially lost his mind. She rambled a bit about the injustice of it all, and I agreed with everything she had written. Then she had cut herself off, going on to state how much she had missed me in the past weeks. She also threw in that our nieces, Yulia and Ada, longed for my company and asked after me every time they came over for family dinners, demanding to know when I would be back. Mary also reported that Albert, our nephew, who had been a month old when I had been sent here, was growing like a weed. She expressed her excitement at the prospect of becoming a mother in the future, and then gushed about her new husband for the rest of the letter.

In a quick post script, she told me that Gertrude, the oldest of us siblings, had breezily told her to tell me hello. I raised an eyebrow at that, surprised that I had even gotten a greeting from her. Miracles could happen, apparently.

The last letter caused me to pause. I recognized the heavy, no-nonsense script on the front; my father's handwriting. I clenched my teeth, feeling the scalding tar pit in my chest bubble once. My hand automatically moved in the direction of the candle, but I hesitated. Scowling, I tore open the letter in jerky movements and began to read:

Son,

I write to you to reiterate the terms of your banishment. Yes, my mind has not been swayed in this matter. I have let your unruly ways go unpunished for long enough, assuming you would learn as manhood approached how to control yourself and your temper. Unfortunately, it seems that will not happen of its own accord, something that disappoints me to no end. That is why I have sent you to my brother.

You have until your eighteenth birthday—the end of the year—to prove to me you have the ability to rein in your choler and only until then. I demand to see marked improvement in your handling of your ire, and hopefully your defiant nature as well.

To provide further incentive, I have reached out to my fellow generals and expressed my desire that should you fail me in this, you will be barred from enlisting under any of their banners. Do not test me, Benjamin, and do not throw away everything we have worked for.

I expect to hear from you.
Damian Lamar

Seething, I read it again, then crumpled the parchment in my fist. Shooting to my feet, I cast the wad of paper across the room. That failed to release the rage building inside me, so I picked up a vase and pitched it across the room. The resulting crash only seemed to fuel my anger and I began to pace. My lungs felt like a blacksmith's bellows; huge amounts of air rushed in and out of them, getting louder and louder. I hunted for something else to throw or rip up or strike out at.

Hissing out a curse, I snuffed the candle, and stomped out of the room. Everything in there was in danger. For the first time, I *needed* the upcoming run. I would outpace my uncle with all this tension threatening to eat me alive.

Once outside of the castle, I headed in the direction of the stables, hands in fists at my sides. I entered the structure, marching in the direction of Joker, who shuffled as I drew closer. I rubbed his nose, and glanced around. Two other horses, saddled and ready, waited nearby. In my anger, I didn't find that odd until two unfamiliar figures strolled in through the double doors. Dressed in informal guard's attire, they came to a stop next to the mounts.

One saluted me smartly, and the other quickly followed suit. The one who had first saluted was taller than me by a few inches, with close-cropped blond hair and a muscular build. He appeared to be several years my senior.

The second was shorter than me, and I would guess his age fell closer to mine. He had red hair that held a bit of a curl to it and he lacked the confidence of the older one.

They held the salutes and waited. I watched them, unsure what they wanted from me. I eventually motioned for them to relax.

"Who are you?" I said abruptly. I was too frustrated to be polite.

"My name is Clark Lively," the older one stated. "This is my brother, Anthony. You must be Benjamin Lamar."

I nodded once. "Why are you here?"

The one called Clark shifted and peered at his brother. "We're here to escort you on your run, as per orders from the king."

I frowned, glancing back and forth between the two. I studied the pair of horses closer this time. Neither were my uncle's steed, and it clicked in my brain. Uncle James wasn't coming.

"Why isn't he coming?" I demanded, voice tight.

"He has business to attend to, said it was urgent. He sent us in his place so you wouldn't be alone on your run."

Business? Wasn't *I* his business? Another thought occurred to me: how much did these two strangers know? Tar pit beginning to roil again, I growled at the idea of these people knowing the how and why of my being here in Dartmoor. My pulse ratcheted up a notch, then another as my thoughts darted back and forth. The depth of the feeling of betrayal at my uncle's blithe actions stunned me. I scoffed. Why was I surprised? It was the people closest to you that could drive the knife of treachery deepest into your soul.

Spinning around, I mounted Joker, steadying him with a hand when he snuffled and threw his head. Without another word to the brothers, I urged my horse into a trot, heading for the open doors. I didn't react to the shout for me to wait, guiding Joker through the small crowd of groundskeepers. As soon as I was free of the gate, I nudged him into a gallop.

The bruising ride did little to calm my fury. By the time I reached the spot where Uncle James and I would usually tie our horses up, I was ready to run. If I wasn't careful, I might just keep on running and never stop until I was far away from this infernal kingdom, in a land where I knew no one and no one knew me. The temptation was high, the idea appealing in my agitated state.

I heard the faint sound of hooves galloping behind me. They had managed to stay on my tail after all. Unless Uncle also provided the directions to our running place. I cursed loudly, ripped my jacket off and threw it onto a branch, not waiting to see if it stuck. Without another thought, I started into a sprint. The landscape became a blur, my focus on the dirt track ahead.

My breaths stung and ripped at my chest and throat, but I didn't care. I poured everything I had into my leg muscles, reaching my top speed. A shooting ache soon developed in my side, reminding me I was still alive. I ignored it, hissing in pain, but pushing myself harder.

The point of turning back appeared in my line of sight quicker than it had ever had before. I stumbled to a jog, and then a walk. My whole body vibrated with the energy coursing through me; my chest heaved and my head felt faint. Instinct told me I had to remain standing or risk never returning to my feet. Instead, I leaned over, hands on thighs. With the motion, my stomach rebelled and I dry-heaved. Thank goodness I never had breakfast before these runs.

Once the fit had passed, I straightened again, putting my hands behind my head, opening my chest and began to pace back and forth. As my breathing and heart rate calmed, I became more aware of the aches and pains in my body; the back of my right thigh started to protest each time I put my weight on it. *Fantastic*, I thought bitterly. *That will be horrendous on the return run. Not to mention the ride back to the castle.*

I suddenly heard rapidly approaching footsteps. Begrudgingly, I was impressed by he two young men. I had set an arduous pace. Ten seconds later, the brothers turned the corner, matching one another step for step. Both looked winded, with the younger one's face red to his hairline, but they didn't stop until they were level with me. *I guess these palace boys can keep up after all*, I thought to myself. I watched them out of the corner of my eye, debating on taking off as I'd had enough time to recapture my wind. But I dismissed it. I wanted to see these two in action on the return trip, which was always an effort as the run was slightly uphill most of the way.

"Don't you dare throw up, Clark," the red-head suddenly gasped out from where he was bent over, head close to the ground. "You've got to keep it all down, let it marinate."

The older one, who had his hands clasped behind his head, lifted a leg and shoved his brother with his foot. Laughing, the younger brother hit the ground, but rolled with the movement, getting back to his feet in one smooth motion. He made a face, a particularly unflattering one.

"Is that the face you use to woo all the women, Anthony? No wonder they run as fast as they can in the opposite direction."

"At least their toes are safe with me when out on the dance floor!"

"That was *one time!*"

"You looked like a drunk mule out there. And you couldn't remember your lefts from your rights!" His laugh sounded odd, as he was still trying to catch his breath.

Scooping up a clump of dirt, the blond one chucked the projectile at the red-head. Chuckling harder now, the younger one ducked the missile, but didn't see it for what it was: a distraction. The tall one—Clark, I think—rushed at his opponent while Anthony's head was down as he covered to avoid being hit, and tackled him. They squirmed and rolled, each trying to get the upper hand and were fairly evenly matched, for now.

As I watched them tussle, I felt a lump in my throat begin to form and harden. Without my permission, my mind flew back to similar childhood romps with a scrawny, freckled boy, my fellow mischief-maker. My best friend. *My brother.* I remembered pranks, both elaborate and simple, races and mud fights. Endless summer days, laughter echoing against a leafy ceiling.

Blinking rapidly, I forced the thoughts to stop before it went too far down the road of recollection. I turned away, trying to block out the playful taunts and grunts of the pair. All the anger from Father's abrupt, demanding letter had abandoned me. All that was left was an emptiness, a hollow space in my chest cavity. It threatened to expand until I, Benjamin Lamar, was no more. No matter how hard I tried, that hole remained. I couldn't fill it, seal it up, or bury it deeper. It was always there, waiting for a moment of weakness, for me to stumble and fall into its grief-stained clutches.

Without glancing back, I pushed myself through the pain, both physical and mental, and started the run that would take me to my waiting horse.

Fortunately, my rage was sizzling again by the time I swung down from Joker's back within the royal stables. Disregarding the calls of farewells from my escorts, I stomped inside, trying my best to hide the limp that dogged my every stride. My blasted thigh was refusing to cooperate and had stiffened up on the ride back.

Every soul that crossed paths with me wisely steered out of my way, plastering themselves to the walls and trying to fade into the background. Whether it was from the warpath I was creating or the way my face was screwed up in defiance, I didn't know. It was probably a combination of both.

I reached the door that would lead me into my uncle's antechamber and took in a deep breath. I threw open the door, barely hearing the secretary's call for me to halt, that my uncle was not receiving visitors at the moment. I paused to glare the little man into silence before I wrenched open the second door, briefly acknowledging the slamming of another door in the close confines.

Uncle James's lips flattened as he took in the look on my face. He sighed and opened his mouth but I rushed to speak first, to vent the ire swirling inside of me.

"How could you?" I bellowed. "How much did you tell them? Do they know everything? Is that what you're doing now, just airing my business to anyone? Leaving it to strangers to babysit me? Hm? Answer me!" I slammed my palm down on his desk so forcefully it stung, reverberating up into my shoulder.

"Enough," Uncle James ordered. His voice, level and calm, bespoke of years of being in charge and of being obeyed without question. It wasn't my father's bark or holler, yet it got my attention. I straightened automatically, spine stiffening. My eyes locked on his.

"You seem to have forgotten just who you are addressing. You will treat me with respect, not only because I am your uncle, but because I am also your monarch. Do I make myself clear?"

I swallowed. "Yes, sir," I muttered.

"Good," he responded, "and while I have your attention, allow me to be blunt: I am not your enemy, Benjamin. I am not your warden, so you can stop marching around my home like the world is against you. Trust me, it's not, but if you keep spitting in everyone's eye and lashing out like this, that could be your reality soon. I'm trying to help you. Take a step back and realize that, and things will go much smoother from here on out."

He didn't yell, but his words smashed into me nonetheless, taking the power from my anger with each hit. He spoke the truth, and the truth seared my consciousness. With the surge of emotion fading, I realized how blind I had been while in my fit of temper, how foolish, and I barely recognized myself.

Uncle James was the one who finally spoke again, gesturing toward the chair and inviting me to sit. I limped forward, straightened the chair and sank into it, chewing on the inside of my cheek. My anger had been snuffed out and I felt strangely empty.

"For the record, I didn't tell the Lively brothers anything."

I slowly brought my head up, watching him. I didn't speak.

"It's true," he continued. "I only told them that I made a habit of running everyday with you and that I couldn't make it myself this morning. Their only order was to accompany you on your run. Nothing more, nothing less."

"Thank you," I murmured.

How wrong I had been; I despised being wrong. I clenched my fists, then relaxed them, wanting to get up to pace, but forcing myself to stay seated.

"You were in quite a state when you barged in here, Benjamin. I have a feeling there is more to the story than just having strangers escort you on your run when you didn't expect it. Tell me what's going on."

I shifted in my seat, wincing slightly as it tweaked my sore thigh. I didn't want to speak aloud the words Father had written, didn't want to bring it up at all. I wanted to shove it down, burn it from my mind, anything but talk about it.

I was saved by a quick set of raps on the door. Uncle blew out a frustrated breath, speared me with a look that said *we aren't through with this topic of conversation*, and called for whoever it was to enter, rising to his feet. Turning in my chair to see my rescuer, I spotted the office minion clutching several letters.

"News from the situation in the south," he said, pitching his voice low, holding up first one letter, then another. "And this is from the goings on in the west."

Accepting the letters with a quick thanks, Uncle James began to turn away, then stopped and stepped in closer to his secretary. Their brief whispered exchange was far too quiet for me to catch anything, though I did try.

I faced forward again, pondering on the conversation I had been able to understand. Situations in the south and in the west? This came as a surprise to me, as I knew for a fact that we almost never had problems with the People to the south and with Swerth to the west. The kingdom of Swerth had been our allies for decades, firmly sealed because of the marriage between Uncle James and Aunt Ahmelia, daughter to the previous king, and sister to the current one. As for the southerners, the People, they were dead-set on their isolation, and rarely came so far north.

I had heard nothing about any tensions while at home, not that Father kept me informed with news. Perhaps they were newly developing and had yet to become well known. I mused on the tidbit as Uncle sat down, shifting between the two envelopes in his grasp as he read the names on the front. I hoped he would read them immediately and I could make my escape, but he set them down and looked up at me, serious and focused.

I cleared my throat. "What is happening in the west and south?"

His lips twitched but didn't form a full smile. "Nice try. I believe you were just about to explain what is truly bothering you." He made a circling motion with his hand, encouraging me to go on.

Grumbling under my breath, I debated refusing further, but Uncle James's posture declared that he would wait for as long as it took for me to speak, even if he had to wait until he was old and decrepit.

Thumping my fist on the arm rest, I avoided looking at him as I laid it all bare for him, quoting from the letter as best as I could. After I had finished, it was quiet enough that I fancied I could hear the scratching of his secretary's quill through the wall that separated us from him. I fidgeted with a loose thread in the fabric of the chair as I waited for Uncle James to speak.

"That must have been a discouraging letter to receive," he finally murmured.

I laughed humorlessly. "That is an understatement."

"Benjamin... I'm not excusing what my brother said, but I do want to give you a bit of wisdom, wisdom that was never told to me when I was your age."

I raised an eyebrow when he paused. "Do go on. I'm positively dying to hear what it is you have to say." As soon as the words were out, I grasped how rude they were. Remembering his earlier lecture, I quickly added, "Sorry."

He nodded in acknowledgment of my hasty apology and threaded his fingers together on top of his desk. "The unfortunate reality is that people mosey their way into your business, inserting their thoughts and opinions whether you asked for it or not. That's how life is. Mothers want to plan your wedding down to a meticulous level and will push you out; strangers will tell you how you're messing up and how they think you could do better. And some people will hold you to unattainable expectations. You can't control what people do or say, but what you can control is how you internalize and respond to the words and actions of those around you. You have the power to choose how you react."

I slumped in my chair, taking in his advice. As much as it galled me, it did make sense. I had seen Uncle's advice in action as he had dealt with my outburst today. He didn't explode in return at my accusations, but firmly put me in my place. He had remained neutral, using the tone of his voice to make me listen rather than the volume to batter me into submission.

I had never been good at letting things roll off of me. It had always been too easy for Gertie to get under my skin, for example, and get me to burst out in a fit of temper; perhaps it was because of my lifelong training to react to attacks that didn't allow me to brush things off.

"What is wrong with your right leg?"

Not expecting the question, I blinked. "Pardon me?"

"Your right leg. You were limping when you came in and I can see it still hurts you as you're sitting here. What happened?"

"I hurt it when running today. It's nothing."

He gave me a knowing look. "You pushed yourself too hard, didn't you?"

I rolled my eyes. "Yes," I admitted unwillingly. "I did."

"These runs are meant to be a *healthy* release, Benjamin."

I nodded reluctantly as another knock rang out in the small space. I heard the door slide open. I didn't bother looking, expecting it to be the little minion again, but at the soft look that stole over my uncle's face, I had to turn around. Aunt Ahmelia hovered in the doorway, returning her husband's smile. She crossed the room, moving gracefully. She stopped next to my chair. She held a medium-sized jar in both of her hands.

"Good morning," she greeted us. "I brought my ointment, as you requested. Where are you hurting, love?"

"It isn't for me, but for Benjamin here."

I instantly felt awkward. I hadn't spoken much to my aunt since my arrival, and that interaction was not one of my finer moments. I cringed internally as I recalled the brusque way I had rejected her innocent invitation to dine with the family my first night, rejecting not only the invite to the meal, but the olive branch she had extended. A deep inner voice had urged me to apologize since then, but I hadn't known how. I had done my best to avoid her since and I deliberately kept my eyes away from her now. Learning that the ointment was for me, would she turn around and leave just to spite me? I wouldn't blame her if she did. It would only be fair.

I felt a hand lightly grip my shoulder. I glanced to the right, seeing my aunt bend to try and look me full in the face.

"Where are you hurt, Benjamin? Are you all right?" she asked in a melodic voice, with just a hint of a Swerthian accent. I saw concern in the way her brow crinkled.

"I'm fine, Aunt. Just a sore muscle, that's all."

She offered me the jar and I took it. She squeezed my shoulder, instructing me to apply the cream at least three times a day and to rub until it dissolved into my skin. She told me to return it to her rooms when I had healed, then left the office after pecking her husband on the cheek.

She had not treated me with scorn and dismissal, and I found myself pleasantly surprised.

CHAPTER THIRTEEN
THE KINDNESS OF A STRANGER
Naya

TAKING IN A deep breath, I took a step forward, rolled my neck, and raised my hand to knock on the solid wooden door. I mouthed the simple sentence as footsteps approached from within the room. *Having to practice an uncomplicated sentence before speaking it,* hissed a brutal voice in my mind. *Pathetic.* As always, it was Nanni Venna's voice.

I poured my attention into the words, doing my best to expel the voice as the door opened. A quick glance up showed a face lined with exhaustion, shoulders rounded with responsibility.

I dropped into a curtsy, eyes lowered again. "Good day, Lord Donovan," I stated, beginning the practiced string of words. "I have come to retrieve any books you may have finished with and bring them back to the library."

Wordlessly, he left the doorway, returning quickly with a tiny stack of books. He placed them in my outstretched arms, gave an almost muted 'thank you' and shut the door. I stared at the wood for several moments, breathing in heavily, then turned and headed for the next room.

Rapping quickly, I repeated the phrase over in my mind again, as I had done at every door. No one answered this time and I closed my eyes in relief, enjoying the respite. The next interaction was just as abbreviated as it had been with Lord Donovan, which was what I preferred.

Arms full, I retraced my steps to the top of the servants' staircase, where I deposited the books on top of one of the tall stacks. I shook my arms out, feeling the burn of carrying dozens of volumes from the fourth and fifth floors of the castle—where the living quarters and personal offices for the advisors of the king were located respectively—down to the second level. The service of offering the busy lords a way to get their borrowed books back to the library was a biweekly occurrence; it was another of the less enjoyable duties I had to attend to as the main servant in charge of the maintenance and running of the library.

"Are you displeased with me, Naya?"

Startled, I nearly caused a rather precarious stack to topple over before Penny, who had reappeared through the door of the servants' staircase, righted it.

"What do you mean?" I asked, concerned. While I awaited her answer, I frantically sifted through all of my interactions with Penny leading up to this moment, analyzing them for anything I had done wrong. I picked apart my words, my actions, every single one.

"Work like this—going up and down the stairs over and over with a heavy load—is usually reserved for someone who has displeased the one in charge. So are you mad at me?"

"No!" I cried out, "Of course not! Here, switch me places and I will—" I cut myself off as Penny began to laugh.

"I'm kidding, Naya! I'm not complaining, I was just poking fun at you. I don't actually think you're upset with me."

Embarrassed, I pivoted to straighten a pillar of books, wanting to do something with my hands. Penny's laughter faded and I could sense her close the distance between us.

"Naya, are you all right?"

"Of course!" I replied, too quickly and cheerfully.

"I'm sorry for teasing you," Penny said after a moment. I could tell she meant the apology, but she was also concerned at my reaction.

"You are forgiven. No need to worry about it any longer."

She smiled hesitantly, then scooped up another armful and trotted down the stairs. After she was out of sight, I dropped my smile, covering my face with my hands. I let out a soft groan, wishing I could reverse time and counsel my past self to react differently. *It was just a harmless joke, Naya*, I told myself. *Calm down!* The last thought was easier said than done. For too long I had been without a light environment, where playful teasing had been a regular occurrence. I let out a tense breath and continued on my route.

Five doors from the end, I once again prepared myself to raise my fist and knock. This next door gave me the most anxiety—or I should say, the occupant inside made me quite nervous. The next door was Prince Fitzroy's personal study, tucked away at the end of a lonely hallway. I could rarely say my rote phrase, pick up the books, and leave. The prince often got to chatting, asking me questions or talking about the books as he handed them to me. It caused me to have mixed emotions; on one hand, it put me behind schedule, which filled me with anxiety. On the other, his conversations stoked the need deep within me for companionship, even from someone so far above me in station.

Luckily, I would have a moment to breathe, as the prince usually did not hear the first rap or two. Or so I thought. The door sprang open within a few seconds, startling me into stumbling through the introduction.

"Good day, your highness. I have come to retrieve any books you may—"

I cut myself off, as I knew immediately something was different. The feet in the threshold wore a pair of sturdy boots. Every time I did these runs, the prince was either barefoot or in house slippers. Never boots. I ran my eyes up to the waistline and spotted another oddity: a knife in a sheath. I had never, ever seen Prince Fitzroy arm himself with weapons before. This was not him. The question was, who was it?

"May I help you?"

I knew the moment the voice rang out in the awkward silence who it belonged to. The person standing in the doorway was Benjamin Lamar, the prince's cousin.

Completely taken off-guard, I mumbled, "I have come to retrieve any books his highness may have finished and return them to the library."

He hemmed for a moment. "Fitzy isn't here at the moment and…I don't know what books he may or may not be done with."

I stood still, thinking quickly. Prince Fitzy had always been in when I had come before. I didn't know what to do. Then I remembered that the prince would throw his door open wide as he went to grab the books he needed returned, allowing me to see the spot where he placed the ones he had read all the way through. He always kept them in a pile to the left of his desk. If there was a stack in that designated spot, then I would know it was meant for me.

Clearing my throat, which was suddenly dry, I said, "May I come in? I will know which ones he intends to return."

"Do as you please."

He stepped to the side, waving me in. I passed him, eyes going to the left of the desk and, just as I had predicted, there was a tower of books waiting for me. I crossed to them, crouched and began to fill my arms.

"That's a lot of books. Are you sure you can get them all by yourself?"

I nodded. "It might take me two trips, but I should be able to manage it. Thank you."

I rose carefully, balancing the books as they swayed. They nearly reached my chin. My arms, already tired from the full morning of lugging tomes, trembled a bit at the strain. The majority of the pile were volumes that were several inches thick. I had almost made it to the hallway when the prince's cousin blocked my path. He lifted his hands palm out and then pointed at my burden.

"Those are mighty heavy books and the library is two floors down. Allow me to assist you."

My heart flew to my throat. "Oh no, of course not!" I protested. "I can manage it."

"Your arms are shaking."

Perhaps if you got out of my way, I would be able to set them down faster! I muttered waspishly to myself. I would never say it aloud, but I let myself think such rebellious thoughts.

"Truly, thank you, but I will be fine."

"Look," he said, a bit of an edge to his tone. "I have two empty hands and I need to do *something*. I don't know when my cousin will be back and I'm starting to go mad. Just let me help you."

I could not believe I was considering it. Letting a member of the nobility assist me in my chores, in menial work? My natural instincts urged me to walk around him, tell him no, anything to avoid letting him help. Instead, I found myself quietly agreeing.

He reached out, took half of the armload, and stepped around me. I watched over my shoulder as he bent and hefted the rest of the books off the ground. He straightened with ease and I felt my arm muscles weep at the sight of him carrying his burden so effortlessly. He gestured with his chin for me to start moving. I faced forward and left the room. His long legs ate up the distance between us, until he was walking by my side. It was not right. I was meant to be behind him, not at his side as if we were equals.

The only sound for several minutes was that of our feet thumping on the stone floor as we walked down the hall. My ineptness grew with each passing moment.

Out of the blue, he asked, in a calm but grave tone, "Why is it that you hate me?"

I screeched to a halt. "What?" I gasped.

"Why do you hate me?"

"I-I do not hate you, my lord," I stammered, my mind swirling as violently as a tornado. Where had that question come from? What was I to do? What could I do? Panic swelled. I could see my stay in the castle—this refuge—dwindling.

"You have been quite standoffish ever since that day we met, when you snapped at me. It would have been understandable had that been the one and only time; you had just been startled and your hands were hurt. Yet each time I've interacted with you since, you have been so cold. So again, I ask, why do you despise me?"

I floundered for a few seconds before I began to ramble. "My lord, I do not know what to say, except that I know my place and I also know yours. What you have interpreted as dislike or hatred must be my observance to the proper way of treating someone so above me in rank. Please believe that I have no negative feelings toward you." I bit my lip to silence myself. That last part was a bit of a fib, as I was quite concerned for my livelihood in that moment.

It took him a moment to ponder my words. "Well, good," he responded. "At least I know now why you've been behaving so oddly."

"I am sorry, my lord. So very sorry."

He made a sound of annoyance. "I'd rather you not call me that."

"'My lord?'"

"Yes, it makes me sound old and stuffy. Call me Benjamin."

"I cannot call you by your first name!"

"Considering the other option is to call me by my surname, I would rather you call me Benjamin. Don't make me order you to."

I bit my tongue. I wanted to snap at him again, but restrained myself. It would never do to speak in such a way to someone so far above me.

"Remind me again what your name is," he requested. "Don't worry, it's not you. I'm terrible with names."

"Naya, sir."

"Naya," he repeated, but with a complaint in his voice. "'Sir' is nearly as bad as 'my lord.'"

He sounded so much like a grumpy toddler that it made my lips twitch unexpectedly and I sucked them in to stop a smile from forming fully. We rounded a corner to the hall that held the servants' staircase and Benjamin halted at the sight of the numerous heaps of books. I could see the difference Penny had made in my absence, but even with that, there was still a lot left.

"You could start your own library with this! How long have you been doing this today?"

"Three, possibly four hours."

"No wonder your arms were shaking."

We set our loads down, and I resisted the urge to stretch out my aching limbs. I slipped into a curtsy, tucking my chin.

"Thank you," I said humbly, then added in a quieter voice, "Benjamin."

"There we go. That wasn't so hard, was it?"

Before I could think of something to respond to his absurd question, the door leading to the staircase swung open and Penny emerged. She was in the middle of letting out a tired moan when she caught sight of Benjamin and the moan turned into a startled squeak. The effect was as though a tiny creature had first been sat upon, then kicked. Penny looked as though she was debating if she should bolt back down the stairs or not. She hurried instead to curtsy and mumble a greeting. Her face was rapidly turning scarlet.

"Hello," Benjamin said, bowing to her and I heard what sounded like a sigh from Penny.

Remembering that introductions had not happened yet, I swept a hand in the direction of my friend. "Benjamin, this is Penelope Manwaring. Penelope, this is Benjamin Lamar, nephew to the king."

"Please, call me Penny," she blurted, her eyes fixed on his face. Her embarrassment was rapidly changing into awe.

"Penny it is, then."

She continued to stare at him, a sappy smile on her face, and I nearly rolled my eyes. I pivoted back to him, laying a hand on the closest stack.

"Thank you for your help."

"You're welcome, but this project is only just getting started, it looks like. Why would I quit when there's so much to do?"

It was a relief that Penny also instantly started to protest with me; I was pleased that her crush had not completely stolen her wits. We might as well have been trying to convince a river to reverse its current, for all the success we had. Benjamin was proving to be rather stubborn. In defeat, Penny and I glanced at one another, then shrugged. If he wanted to spend the rest of a morning hauling things to and fro, who were we to stop him? We grabbed some tomes and led the way down the cramped, dusty stairs.

Eventually, Penny's natural friendliness broke free from her deference of Benjamin's station and she began a conversation with the king's nephew as we tromped back and forth, up and down between levels. While he was not as enthusiastic in conversing as Penny, he did respond politely to her questions. I listened, and as I did so, I realized that I had been wrong in my first impression of the young man who had so forcefully barged his way into the library weeks ago. Oh, he was still abrupt and opinionated, to be sure, yet he was also softened with a level of civility and did not brush off young Penny, but listened as she spoke endlessly. I was pleasantly surprised. Not enough to wholly lower my guard, however. One thing I had learned early in life was that people had many faces and ways of acting for different situations and for dealing with those they were obligated to interact with. I was loath to expose myself, quietly listening and observing until I knew all of them.

Some time later, Benjamin rolled his shoulders before taking up another load. He led the way down this time, and I followed, with Penny on my heels.

"There has got to be a more efficient way of shuttling these between floors," he declared to no one in particular. "This seems unnecessarily inefficient."

"Naya has thought the very same thing for years," Penny chimed in from the rear of our little troop. "She has thought of wagons for each floor, but that doesn't solve the problem of moving the books up and down the stairs. She has a brilliant idea for—"

"Penny," I chided. "That is enough."

Sometimes Penny tended to overshare, and I thought it best to curb the flow now, especially with this topic.

"She has a brilliant idea for what?" he prompted. "Do tell."

I attempted to change the subject. "We are almost done. Thank you for help once again."

"You're welcome, but I'm not giving in to your desire to change the subject that easily. Continue, Penny."

Penny took up the conversation with vigor. "Naya thinks that if we could somehow create a system of ropes and pulleys that went between floors, all we would have to do is fill a box of some sort full of books and then raise and lower the contraption, which would save us a lot of time."

I pursed my lips, waiting for his mocking laughter. Why had I ever told Penny about my idea? It had been a mistake. Now the inevitable ridicule would come. Thinking always had gotten me into trouble as a child.

"Where would these pulleys be set up? It's far too cramped in this stairwell to even consider it."

I nearly missed a step, shocked that he had not instantly dismissed the idea but actually seemed to be pondering it. What was more, that had been the exact conclusion I had come to myself.

They were both silent and I quickly realized that they were waiting for me to respond. I swallowed, then tried to answer but my tongue suddenly had stage fright. I cleared my throat and willed myself to speak.

"I-I had the idea that the main staircase would be ideal, as it is basically a set of switchbacks within the castle, with a straight drop from the fifth to the first floor in between the flights. The landings on each level provide the width for something to pass through easily and a place where we could load and unload the contents of the box. This would allow us to simply stack books near the main staircase on each floor." I took in a deep breath after the rambling I had just done. "But we cannot do that," I finished lamely.

"Why not?" both Penny and Benjamin queried.

"Is it not obvious? We cannot use the main staircase as such. That is used by nobility, for guests and dignitaries, not servants."

"And servants are not meant to be seen," Penny added, a dejected note in her usually upbeat voice.

I cringed. I had not meant to put her in her place, and I regretted saying anything.

"I am sorry, Penny," I told her over my shoulder. To Benjamin, I said, "It is not a good idea. It will never work."

"Why can't it?"

"I just told you why."

"But if it made your job easier, would it not be worth it? Not to mention, other servants could use it and smooth out their chores as well. As for the nobility, some of them are so fussy that we would be doing them a service by keeping them on their toes."

I hesitated, then shook my head, even though he could not see it. "No, I do not think it will be worth it and I would rather you drop it. Please."

Considering the stubbornness he had shown today, I figured he would keep badgering me, but he surprised me yet again by keeping quiet.

Later that afternoon, I knelt in a forest of literature. It had an almost magical quality to it.

In the middle of the many stacks of books we had planted, I made myself useful, sorting and organizing them into various collections. I kept referring to the mental map I had of the vast library, of all the categories, and subcategories, as well as their location in the room. I had insisted that we needed to take the time to organize the books, so we could carry on in an orderly manner, which did not suit the free-spirited Penny's personality at all. She wanted to pick up random books and then find their spots in the room. When I pointed out that it would take longer if we were zigging and zagging all over the place, she sighed but thankfully had given in. Clearly she did not appreciate the fine-tuned art of proceeding in a calm, precise manner. Perhaps she would figure it out as she got older. I had hope for her.

"I need a break. I'll be right back," Penny announced, pushing herself to her feet.

I waved to her without glancing up, urging her to not dally too much. She mumbled something under her breath, most likely a complaint of some sort, as she left the area.

Shifting, I winced a bit as the heels of my boots dug into the backs of my thighs. I would most definitely regret being in this position for so long when I returned to my feet.

Glancing at the faded cover of a volume, I leaned a bit toward a smaller pile, placing the book solidly on the top. Mathematics. Another book went into the geography section, and yet another into the popular grouping of political science.

A soft scuff of a footstep behind me interrupted my concentration. I raised my eyebrows. *Penny must have truly taken my advice to heart about not dallying too long*, I thought to myself, impressed.

"Back already?" I called over my shoulder. "Good. I believe we are just about ready to start putting things back."

"How invigorating."

My heart dropped like a felled tree. *Rasmussen*. I knew his voice, even after only hearing it once.

Hastily, I twisted around, and upon seeing him much too close, I scrambled to my feet. I stumbled back a few steps as he advanced, knocking over masses of carefully sorted books. My mind spun and bucked like an unbroken colt, my only thought *escape, escape, escape*. I jumped out of the ring of books where I had been working and hissed in pain upon landing. My knees ached from being on hard wood for so long, but that was not the worst part: my calves and feet were prickling and tingling. Every movement felt like I was walking on fresh bee stings, driving stingers further into the flesh.

Ignoring the agony, I lurched backwards, toward the middle of the room. Chuckling quietly, menacingly, Rasmussen mirrored my movements.

Escape, escape, escape.

The frantic word jogged my fear-addled brain and I began to look around for a way to flee, though I doubted my ability to outrun this man. Even with feet that had full feeling, I probably would not have made it either.

"What do you want?" I rasped desperately.

He put a hand to his ear, leaning forward. "Pardon? I couldn't quite hear that. A puny mouse is louder than you. Speak up!"

His voice had been nearly friendly until the last part, and then it had morphed into something dark and foreboding. Icy fingers of fear squeezed my lungs.

"What do you want?" I repeated, my voice only slightly louder than the first time I had tried. I backed into something hard, hitting my hip, and I jumped at the unexpected contact. It was a large circular table in an opening in the room. I rounded the edge until it separated Rasmussen and I. He made a scoffing sound as he gazed upon my paltry barrier.

"What do I want?" he echoed. "Oh, I want so many things. But first, I want you to fully appreciate my statements from our first meeting. You see, I haven't forgotten your face and you can bet that I am just as determined to show you what happens to those who get in my way."

Rasmussen prowled to the right and I matched him step for step, going in the opposite direction. My heart thundered in my ears. My hands shook.

Escape, escape, escape.

He laughed lowly again, going to the left this time, cackling more as I reversed directions, nearly tripping. We could only keep up this horrific dance for so long before it came to an end. I only hoped Penny would not return in time to see whatever would happen next. She would most assuredly be his next victim.

Bile rose in my throat and I darted frantic looks around the vicinity, looking for a weapon.

Escape, escape, escape!

More than fifteen paces away to the left, a firepoker rested in a rack next to an unlit fireplace. Rasmussen would most likely be on me before I could grasp it, but what else could I do? It was my only chance! I tensed, hands cold, mentally preparing myself to fly. My body responded sluggishly, fear dousing my response time.

Rasmussen's stance changed as well. He knew I was preparing to make a run for it! My stomach tightened. I had to still try! Before I could begin my hopeless flight, I sensed movement to my right. Dread filled me. Did he bring someone else with him, to ensure I could not take flight? But Rasmussen made a growling sound deep in his throat as he turned to face whoever it was.

"Get moving," he snapped. "Ain't nothing for you to see here."

"I beg to differ. There is much to see here," a low rumble of a voice responded. "I see a young woman preparing to run as if the devil himself were chasing her. And I see you. Question is, are you the devil or simply one of his lackeys?"

A pinprick of hope flared. Perhaps all would be well. I kept my body ready to run, ready to take full advantage of this divine-sent distraction, but turned my head in order to catch a glimpse of my possible rescuer.

A servant stood in between two bookshelves, arms crossed. He was about equal distance from the two of us, turning the grouping into a triangle of tension. With closely-cropped hair the color of wheat, a muscular build and a square jaw, his was a face I had never seen before at the castle. I would have remembered, not only because I recalled every face I had ever seen, but because of the ragged scar on his right cheek. I winced upon seeing it, even though it looked years old. Where had he gotten it?

Rasmussen's angry retort yanked me back into reality, into the charged atmosphere.

"What's it to you? Mind your own business!"

"I will not," came the calm response from the stranger. "I'm making this my business. Now, run back to the cesspool you oozed out of and be quick about it."

Rasmussen's chin jutted out. "And what if I don't? Are you going to make me?"

"Yes." The firm finality in the one-word answer seemed to suck all sound out of the room.

I held my breath. I knew without a shadow of a doubt that this stranger could handle himself. I did not know how I knew, but I could feel it in my gut. The men glared each other down, neither one budging. Then it happened: Rasmussen backed down first. He backed up a step, swore at me, but then left the room in a hurry, though he tried not to look like he was running away. He shouted something about not forgetting this, but he was going away!

The air I had been holding in rushed out of me like a flash flood, and I gripped the edge of the table, leaning on it, jitters leaving me feeling weak.

"Are you all right?" the stranger asked. The ominous tone of voice was gone. I nodded. "Thank you," I responded breathlessly. "Thank you."

"You're welcome. I saw him enter the library with the look of a fox about to assault a hen house and figured he was up to no good. Turns out I was right."

I faced him fully, taking him in. He was younger than I had first guessed. He had a strong face, its planes etched from what I guessed was years of difficulty. My eyes took in the scar again, and I winced once more. He saw it and his dark eyes glinted.

"Ask it," he suddenly demanded.

"What?" I asked, shocked at the unexpected demand.

"The question on your lips. Everyone asks it, so get it out of your system."

I thought quickly, taken aback by his abruptness. I had many questions, and settled on the one that nagged at me the most.

"How old were you when you got your scar?"

A myriad of emotions flickered across his face, too quick for me to interpret any of them. He was silent so long that I did not expect him to answer, but he did. "Thirteen."

I closed my eyes at the answer. "Much too young," I murmured. Without knowing what I was doing, I pressed a hand to my heart, curled my fingers into my palm, and slowly thrust the hand toward him, splaying the palm and fingers as I pushed outward. He likely did not understand the movement. In my culture, it meant, *I see your pain; I feel your pain and wish for healing.* It was a gesture used in times of grief, of remembered pain, and on memorial days from those who wished to comfort the grieving, but did not have the words to express their intent.

I opened my eyes, surprised at myself. Where had that urge come from? I had not done that in years, had not felt the need to do so, even through all the turmoil life had thrown my way.

"Thank you," said the stranger quietly. It seemed he could infer what the gesture was meant to signify and was moved by it.

"You are welcome."

He let a few more moments pass, then turned to go. Then he paused, and turned back. He seemed to be stewing over what to say, brow furrowed, then he stared deep into my eyes, piercing me to the core.

"What is your name?" he asked.

Instinctively, I curtsied. "Naya Gavi."

He bowed deeply from the waist, almost too deeply to bow to a mere servant. "I'm Creed Whitaker. Let me know if that weasel comes skulking back and I'll take care of him for you."

For the first time since Rasmussen's appearance, I felt safe. My shoulders relaxed and my heart thudded a little more slowly.

I smiled. "Thank you again, Creed. I am happy to have met you."

He returned the smile, lips lifting ever so slightly. Then he turned and left. I stared after him, feeling grateful to the tips of my toes for the kindness of a stranger.

Chapter Fourteen
Forgiveness Extended

Benjamin

ON THE FIRST true day of spring, the day that had no lingering chill lurking in the shadows, I managed to convince Fitzroy to accompany me on a stroll along the top of the castle ramparts, going in a slow circle. His demanding feline meandered behind us somewhere, occasionally trailing us, at other times watching the birds that flitted around the parapets. Fitzroy squinted in the sun, grumbling about a growing headache. Considering he had complained about the pace and fussed over the possibility of his cat throwing herself off the castle walls, I was running short on patience. Tersely, I insisted that this would be good for him.

"Besides," I informed him, "you are starting to resemble an albino, minus the pink eyes."

"Thanks," he deadpanned. "Just what everyone wants to hear."

I clapped him on the shoulder. "You're welcome."

We continued at a relaxing pace, which irked me, but I doubted I would be able to persuade Fitzy to move at a more efficient gait, so I kept my mouth shut. Up ahead, two guards rounded a corner, in step with one another, hands on the hilts of their swords, heads swiveling back and forth. I lifted a hand in greeting as they drew closer, which they responded to by nodding their heads at me. Then their eyes fell on my cousin as we came within arms length of one another. Their facial expressions didn't change, but I could sense something in the air, a subtle shift in energy. They passed, and Fitzy let out a tense breath. *So I wasn't imagining it*, I thought triumphantly.

I glanced over my shoulder at the retreating backs of the guards, lowered my voice, and asked, "What was that about?"

Fitzy, facing forward, didn't look at me. "I don't know what you're talking about."

"Please," I retorted, drawing out the word. "You know exactly what I'm talking about."

Fitzy suddenly turned into me, glaring. He put a finger to his lips, looked around and then snatched the unsuspecting Mimsy into his arms as she meandered between us. He jerked his head, gesturing for me to follow him. I watched him hustle away, wanting to call after him that he was acting oddly, but sighed instead. It seemed to be my lot in life to follow extended members of my family at a distance to unknown destinations.

I realized very quickly that we were en route to the library. Not surprising that he'd seek shelter in a room swollen with books. He led me to an isolated corner, plopped down in a seat, and began to stroke Mimsy, who wriggled and yowled until he let her go. In high dudgeon, she strutted away. He watched her go, but kept quiet.

I couldn't take it anymore. I leaned toward him, pointing at him. "That was the second time I noticed something since being here. The first was in your study the day we reconnected. Now this. Tell me about it."

Fitzy let out a deep sigh, deflating a little into the overstuffed chair. His face was awash with an expression I had never seen on him before: self-doubt. I straightened in my seat. This was important.

"The guards..." He grimaced, cutting himself off, looking out the window.

"The guards?" I prompted.

"They all...they don't think too highly of me."

"Why?" I asked, thoroughly confused.

Fitzy pulled his gaze back to mine, a sardonic lift to his eyebrows. "Have you seen me? I'm not exactly an intimidating mass of muscles and authority." He gestured to himself.

I nodded unconsciously in agreement before I could stop myself. I lifted my hands at the narrowed gaze he gave me. "There has to be more than that."

"Oh, believe me, there is. I've never been a serious student of war. I tried, I truly did. I am just no good with weapons." His face darkened. "It didn't help that every lesson ended in comparison to Perry. 'Perry mastered this thrust within a week'. 'Oh, Perry was the best swordsman in the kingdom at your age.'"

Ah, I see, I thought, leaning back. Peregrine Lamar, Crown Prince of Mendlewyn and older brother to Fitzy, was six years my senior. He was Fitzroy's opposite in every way. He had excelled in weapons training, mastering everything his masters had taught him, and currently led the Eagle Division, an elite company of highly-trained men composed of foot soldiers and cavalry. Their reputation was far-reaching and daunting. Perry was a natural leader and charismatic; the man could charm a tree into giving up its bark.

And Fitzy was...well, Fitzy.

"I gave up on that endeavor quickly, turning instead to more scholarly areas. I devoted my time to gaining knowledge, hoping to benefit my country in a different way. I didn't realize how bad things were until the last few years. Mind you, the men in my father's guard are never openly disdainful or critical, but I can feel the lack of respect radiating from them. And who can blame them, when they have Perry to compare me to? I'm just the useless, studious prince. Not worth anyone's time."

He spoke, in a voice filled with bitterness, as though quoting someone verbatim. I grimaced, not sure what else to do. We sat there in an uncomfortable silence until I cleared my throat.

"I could teach you a few things while I'm here, get you started on the basics of the sword, spear, hand-to-hand combat," I offered.

He tapped his fingers on the armrest of the chair, deeply thinking. Then he shook his head. "Thanks for the offer, but it wouldn't matter. My reputation among the guardsmen is already in tatters. I'm sure that trying now would only add to the contempt. I doubt there's a way for me to gain their respect."

"We could train in secret."

"No, Benjamin. That opportunity is as dead as our ancestors. Just drop it." He huffed out a humorless laugh, then ended with, "I'll give Perry one point in his favor: the people love him. It's a good thing he is to be king. I'm sure if I were the one in line to become the next monarch, the people would be up in arms."

Fitzy's mood didn't improve much after that conversation. I wasn't too concerned until it became obvious that he didn't even want to read or comb through some dusty manual for interesting tidbits of information. I knew what the situation called for—a distraction—but how to do it? I wracked my mind as I forced him from the library. There had to be something that would take his mind off the dismal conversation we'd had.

On out way out, I spotted the red-haired serving girl who had been a part of the duo lugging books up and down from the upper levels of the castle a few days before. *What were their names?* I moaned to myself. Just as I found the right names, Naya, the older one, appeared and then I knew exactly what to do to pull Fitzy out of his blue devils. Lifting a hand in a wave to the two of them, which they returned with varying degrees of enthusiasm, I gripped my cousin's sleeve.

"I have the perfect distraction for you, Fitzy."

"I don't need a distraction."

"Sure you do. Now, I have this project that I believe you would improve tenfold..."

As we returned to his study, I explained what I knew about Naya's idea for the pulley system on the main staircase, and with each detail I shared with him, the more Fitzy returned to himself. He began to spout theories, ask rhetorical questions, and generally took the reins from me, exactly as I had wanted. He even paused on the stairs as we ascended, leaning out over the drop, analyzing the empty space that ran between them. I could see the blacksmith bellows of his mind begin to swell and gust, feeding the fire of intellect inside him.

Fitzy immediately began to scrawl complicated equations and other such nonsense across a piece of parchment as soon as we got to his study. Pleased, I bade him farewell, which he didn't hear, and left, satisfied with my successful plan.

With nothing else to do, I headed toward my bedchamber, planning on changing into loose-fitting clothes to go and train for a few hours. However, the first thing my eyes landed on was the jar of pain-relieving cream that Aunt Ahmelia had given me several days ago. My thigh had been almost back to normal this morning as Uncle and I had gone about our run. I had no more need of it and I remembered Aunt's request that I return it once my leg had healed. I thought for a moment, then snatched it up and left the room.

A mousy little maid opened the door when I knocked at the entrance to my aunt and uncle's bedchambers. She curtsied upon seeing me, then opened the door wider when I told her of my business. She informed me that my aunt was in the next room, and began to drift away. I nearly left the jar with her to give to her lady, but forced myself to move into the room instead, trailing after the maid. I would place it into Aunt Ahmelia's hands, say a quick 'thank you', and leave.

A faint tinkling touched my senses as I entered the sitting room. The further I moved into the room, the more the sound became a melody, and an enchanting one at that. We crossed through into the main room and I felt like I had stepped into another ethereal world, the music was so all-encompassing. My eyes of their own accord searched until I found the source.

Aunt Ahmelia perched upon a chair in a beam of sunlight, delicate fingers plucking at a harp. She played with an expertise that I had only seen from professional musicians in concert halls—a way my mother had tried to 'culture' me. Yawn. Both the maid and I had come to a stop several feet away, neither one of us wanting to interrupt the music.

Eventually, the song slowed to a finish, with the final notes trilling into the air until they faded. With the silence, it seemed Aunt Ahmelia came back into this reality, and she jumped a little when she spotted the two of us watching her. She smiled bashfully, rose, and made her way toward us. She thanked the maid, who disappeared, and turned to face me.

"Hello, Benjamin," she greeted. "I was not expecting you today. Come, sit. Tea should be on its way."

My first reaction was to deny her request, as I had only come to return the ointment and leave, but instead I found myself following her to a cozy collection of chairs, with a low table in the center.

"I see you have come to return my ointment," she stated into the quiet stillness of the air.

I lifted the jar, and handed it to her. "Thank you, Aunt. It worked wonders."

She smiled as she tucked it under her chair. "I'm glad it was beneficial. It always provides the relief I need for my aching joints, for which I am grateful."

I nodded, lifting my lips in what I hoped was an inviting smile. I didn't know how to continue this conversation, and I had a suspicion that it was going to turn into a strained one at any second.

A soft knock announced the arrival of a tea tray, piled high with goodies, all of them looking rather delicious. Aunt Ahmelia deftly poured two cups of tea, then filled her plate with treats. She gestured with her chin for me to do likewise, then raised her dainty cup to her lips, blowing gently on the surface of the liquid. I loaded the tiny plate with one sampling of each of the items that had been brought in, then lifted my cup as well, trying to not fidget. I forever felt clumsy with fragile china in my large, calloused hands.

Aunt Ahmelia sipped on her tea as she studied me, tilting her head to one side. "How are you settling in to castle life?"

"I'm doing well, thank you. I appreciate that I have the afternoons and evenings free. I honestly wasn't anticipating that."

"Ah yes," she responded smoothly. "Not quite the prison you thought it would be, eh?" She eyed me over the rim of her cup, a slight sparkle in her tawny eyes.

For a minute, I sat in stunned silence. Then, after I could practically hear my mother screaming at me to do everything in my power to salvage the situation, I hastily set my cup down, spilling some of the steaming liquid over the edge. I wiped my stinging fingers off with a napkin, not letting myself wince.

"Aunt," I began, but then I hesitated. How did one go about apologizing for being an oaf? "I just wanted to apologize for my behavior my first day here. It was disrespectful and beyond rude. You were only trying to be kind by inviting me to dinner and I was unforgivably ill-mannered. You didn't deserve that and I'm sorry."

The sparkle had drained away from her eyes, and she watched me seriously. I wanted to squirm or pace, but I forced myself to remain where I was, to make direct eye contact while she pierced my soul with her sharp gaze. She didn't say anything for some time, then slowly nodded, a small smile appearing on her lips.

"I forgive you, Benjamin. I can't imagine how frustrating that first day was to you."

"Thank you, Aunt Ahmelia."

"Now that we have that out of the way, try the little yellow pastry there. That is a delicacy back in Swerth."

I needed no further urging. I popped it in my mouth and began to chew, and then my jaw froze mid-chomp. An explosion of sweet custard took me by surprise and I hurriedly began to chomp again. Reading the look on my face,

Aunt Ahmelia chuckled and nodded in agreement. She urged me to try each and every one of the treats from the tray. I couldn't complain, as all were quite scrumptious.

"I had no idea you were a sugar fanatic, Aunt."

She grinned. "How can I claim Swerthian heritage and be anything but one?"

I grinned in return, going in for seconds, as another knock sounded. I didn't give the servant bearing a silver tray with the daily post more than a passing glance. But I did take notice of Aunt Ahmelia's agitated huff. I glanced up to see her scowling at the letters in her hands, a very unqueenly thing to do.

"Aunt?" I asked upon seeing her looking so flustered. "Are you all right?"

"I'm frustrated with my imbecile of a brother," she said, her accent a bit more pronounced with her annoyance.

I choked back a laugh. "Which one, the king or the high priest?" Both were hilarious options.

She sniffed. "The king."

My, my, I thought, more than a little curious. "What has he done?"

"It's what he hasn't done, Benjamin," she shot back. "He hasn't responded to my last three letters. I have half a mind to march over there and demand he answers them. It's not my fault our diplomat is as dim as a wet wick."

I paused with another pastry halfway to my mouth. "What happened with the diplomat?"

She very nearly rolled her eyes. "He was found in the bedchamber of my brother's second-in-command a few months back; he was trying to seduce the man's wife. It has caused quite the scandal, as you can imagine. The diplomat was promptly recalled, but the second-in-command has since thrown a tantrum and he has my brother's ear. Henri has chosen to distance himself and his court from anything Lewyn. He has even barred the replacement diplomat from entering his castle. Now he has refused to return my correspondence. It's all rather childish."

She remained frustrated for all of ten ticks before she sighed, rolled her shoulders back, and smiled winningly at me. "Enough of annoying siblings. We have pastries to devour!"

CHAPTER FIFTEEN
SONGS AND SUMMONS

Naya

"DID HE TRULY turn tail and run?" Penny demanded, legs tucked under her as she leaned forward on her cot, eyes wide. "Just like that?"

I nodded, tying the twine at the end of my braid before tossing it over my shoulder. "Just like that. Rasmussen left as quickly as he had appeared and my rescuer had not even moved from where he had been standing. It was something to behold."

Penny flopped back onto her cot, letting out a deep whoosh of air. "Thank goodness he arrived when he did." She bit her lip. "Is it bad that I'm almost disappointed to have missed seeing Rasmussen run off like a frightened sheep?"

"I am not sure," I responded. "It was satisfying, but leading up to it was terrifying. I would not have wanted you to experience that."

Just then, the door to our room swung open and Betsy slipped inside. She immediately untied her apron strings, tossed it onto the stool in her corner of the room, and let out a long breath. Her shoes followed shortly, kicked off near her cot, and she plopped down on her bed, working to undo the pins from her hair.

"Girls," she said by way of greeting. "How was your day?"

We returned her greeting; then, as if she could not help it, Penny launched into a retelling about how a dashing hero saved me from the sinister Rasmussen. Her words got faster and faster until Betsy held up a hand, insisting she stop for air. While Penny took in a deep breath, Betsy turned concerned blue eyes toward me. "Are you all right, Naya? Is what she is saying true?"

"It did happen like how she reported and I am fine."

My words did not lessen the worry in her gaze. In fact, it seemed to only grow. I shifted, preparing to push myself to my feet to go and comfort her, but Penny spoke again, drawing our attention back to her.

"So who was it that saved you, Naya?" she asked eagerly.

"His name is Creed. He is newly employed here."

"Creed?" they both repeated in unison. Their twin expressions of pondering were almost comical.

"Yes, Creed. I have not seen him around the castle before today."

"What does he look like?" This question was from Penny.

"Medium height, blond hair, brown eyes. Very muscular build," I stated.

They both gasped. Betsy froze in removing the last of her pins. I glanced back and forth between them, my curiosity rising. "What is it?"

"Does he have a gruesome scar on his right cheek?" Betsy questioned slowly.

"Yes," I responded, confusion replacing my interest as they both seemed to deflate a little. "Why does the fact that he has a scar seem to upset you two so much?"

There was a beat of silence before Penny answered. "Well…it's just that we didn't realize who it was that rescued you until you described him."

I waited for more. "And?"

"And I assumed it had been someone else," she finished, an odd look on her face.

It clicked in my mind. "You mean someone more handsome."

The guilty and sheepish looks they cast my way told me I was spot on. I shook my head at them, slid under my blanket and propped my head on my hand, lying on my side so I could still converse with them. "Why does it matter if he is handsome or not? What difference does it make?"

For some reason, their superficiality bothered me. A stranger had saved me from a blackguard with no prompting, and they could not get past his physical flaws. My sense of right versus wrong was on high alert.

Betsy was the first to respond. "You're right. It doesn't matter," she stated, pulling her knees up to her chest, wrapping her arms around them. "Besides, just because someone is fair of face doesn't mean they're honorable." There was a slight edge of bitterness in her tone.

"But just imagine," Penny cried out before I could pursue my curiosity on Betsy's statement. "You are about to suffer a terrible fate—but wait—an attractive man swoops in at the last second, fists flying, meting out justice with each swing!"

I rolled my eyes. "There was nothing romantic about it, Penny. Just the opposite, in fact."

"Someone has been listening to the minstrels in the royals' dining hall and has taken everything to heart, I see," Betsy murmured in a teasing tone.

"I have not!"

"I agree with Betsy. They have filled your mind with nonsense."

For a moment, it looked like she was about to fling her pillow across the room at one of us, but could not decide who was the most worthy target. She settled for strangling the poor pillow, sending us both a scowl. I glanced at Betsy to see her reaction to the drama in the corner. She was already looking in my direction and when our eyes met, she widened hers significantly, then rolled them until she was looking up at the ceiling, crossing them slightly. It was so comical and unexpected that I could not help but laugh. Betsy joined in, then I heard Penny begin to giggle too; she never could remain grumpy or unhappy for long.

"You two are the worst," Penny gasped between laughs. "Absolute worst!"

Soon we were all propped on our sides, facing the middle of the room. The candles were slowly consumed by flame as we laughed, teased, and talked about anything and everything under the sun.

I could not remember a moment that I had fallen asleep so far past my usual time while smiling.

I was on my own in the library; Penny had left to help with the midday meal. How strange that I used to long for isolation and now, when I was alone, I wanted company almost desperately. I found myself wishing for someone to come into the library so I would not feel as though I had to remain on guard until Penny returned.

Enough of this! This is your safe place. This whole castle is your safe haven. You cannot let someone steal that peace from you. Never again!

With the mental encouragement, I pulled my shoulders back and lifted my chin. I pushed the cart stacked high with books forward; they were the last of the books that Penny and I had collected at the beginning of the week. I forced myself to move smoothly as I returned the volumes to their proper places.

Eventually, I began to hum to myself. I started with tunes from my childhood, lullabies and silly songs. Then I began to softly sing some of the newer songs I had collected. The combined efforts of focusing on the music in my mind and organizing the books had me calming down quickly, much to my relief. I finished the last strains of a song, then jumped into another one, a little louder this time.

I had just finished the chorus and was about to launch into the final verse, which started out with the masculine part, when a rich baritone filled the air around me, stealing the words I was about to sing. I spun around, and let out a gasp when I saw Benjamin leaning a shoulder against the bookshelf nearby. A quick glance up showed a grin spreading across his face. I blushed deeply, embarrassment like thick fog rising up inside me.

"I cannot believe my ears."

"Hello, sir," I mumbled, curtsying hurriedly.

"Oh, no, don't you get all stiffly proper on me now. Especially not after I heard that song coming from your lips!"

Please, let the floor open up and swallow me whole!

"Just where did you hear such a tune? If the castle started blurting poetry, I wouldn't be more surprised than I was a few moments ago."

Anytime now, floor!

He crossed his arms over his chest and rocked back on his heels. Clearly he was not going to leave the thing alone, dratted boy. And apparently the floor was not going to give into my silent pleadings either. Could this day get any worse?

I wiped my hands on my apron. "I worked in a tavern a few years ago up north. I labored late into the night most often. That is where I learned them."

He made a sound of surprise. "*Them?*"

I closed my eyes, regretting that slip of the tongue immediately.

"You mean you know more? Oh my, this day has gotten so much better."

"That is debatable," I muttered, turning back to my chores.

"How many do you know?"

I hesitated, then shrugged. "I do not know how many."

There was a pause, and then he quoted the last part of the song I had been singing. My blush returned as he started laughing even as he was finishing the words.

His chuckle sounded rusty, as if he did not laugh much. But as he kept on it, it grew and rumbled out of him, an infectious sound. Before I could catch myself, I began to giggle. To my ears, it sounded even more rusty than his beginning one. It sounded something like a squeaky door hinge, so foreign and loud. The sound only served to make Benjamin laugh harder, which in turn, made my giggle morph into something closer to a husky chortle.

Soon I had to grip a shelf to keep myself upright. Even so, I doubled over, blood rushing to my face. My laughs soon turned to the soundless variety. Benjamin's belly laugh filled the space around us.

Eventually, we composed ourselves, wiping away tears of mirth. I straightened, trying to reclaim some sense of dignity but what was the point? I had already been caught singing a bawdy tavern song, and had laughed with more enthusiasm than a drunkard on holiday. How could I recover from this display? Would it be easier to simply just fade away?

"I am sorry," I mumbled, rubbing my sore side with a hand.

Benjamin, who had returned to his casual leaning, stood up straight. "Why are you apologizing?"

Where do I even start? "For one, you overheard me singing an extremely inappropriate song. And then you witnessed my unprofessional outburst, and for that, I am sorry."

Out of the corner of my eye, I saw him shake his head. "Apparently you have forgotten that I too knew the lyrics to that song, so I'm not exactly naive when it comes to this sort of thing. And I'd hardly call a good bout of laughter an 'outburst', even if it did drift into the realm of hysteria for a moment."

I opened my mouth to retort, then, as I processed his response, closed it. He had made a good point. I murmured a thanks, then abruptly turned to put a book in its spot on the shelf to my left. I wanted to return to work, yet at the same time wanted to continue this odd sort of conversation. Apparently, my sudden movement communicated the first desire, as Benjamin began to back away down the aisle.

"Well, I will leave you to your work. Have you seen Fitzy in this maze? He told me to meet him here, but forgot to tell me where."

I paused with my foot on the bottom-most rung of the rolling ladder and bit my lip, thinking deeply. "I would try the history section, and if he is not there, check the philosophy section next."

He nodded, turned to walk away, then quickly spun back. "Do you know 'One-Legged Maggie'?"

I covered my face with a book and he chuckled. He began to whistle the tune to that particularly rowdy ditty as he left. I lowered the book, staring at the space he had occupied, sorting through a myriad of thoughts and feelings. Once more, I realized I had misjudged him. He was much different than any other member of the nobility I had interacted with. He had not scolded me for singing while working, nor balked at the genre of song. And he had teased me. I did not know how I felt about that in particular, but I had not been expecting it.

Returning to my chores, I mused over the interaction, alternatively cringing and fighting a smile at the memory of the release that had come with the rush of laughter. Of all the things I had imagined to happen today, laughing over the improper lyrics of tavern songs to the point of tears with a member of the nobility had not been in the realm of possibilities.

Analyzing the memories helped pass the time, and soon I tucked the last tome into its designated pocket. I took a step back, rested my hands on my hips, and nodded in satisfaction. I pushed the cart back into the open area in the center of the library, and glanced around. I still had several hours left in the work day, but nothing to do. I mentally reviewed the list of tasks for tomorrow, weighing my options. Should I sneak away to a corner and pick up where I had left off in that adventure novel I had been reading? Or should I start on the tasks for tomorrow? I sighed. With Penny due back anytime, I figured I had better keep working. Besides, she might squeal in excitement when she found out we were working ahead, which would help her have a longer half-day off at the end of the week; I found her obvious enjoyment of the little things endearing.

Deciding to start the process of cleaning all the rugs, I knew I needed help moving the furniture, and moved toward the entrance to wave down someone in passing in the hopes they could assist me. Opening the door, I held my breath and peeked out, checking both directions before stepping out into the hallway. Turning left, I hurried down the hall.

I passed several men and women with their arms full of various items and dismissed them. I rounded a corner and spotted a familiar figure up ahead. I hesitated for a moment before calling out his name. He slowed but did not halt, and glanced back over his shoulder. He stopped upon seeing me, then began to move at a fast clip down the hall toward me, expression alert.

"What is it?" Creed demanded when he got within speaking distance. His fists tightened at his sides, and his eyes flicked behind me.

It dawned on me that he was tense because he assumed I was in trouble, that Rasmussen had made another appearance and I felt abashed for alarming him.

"I am not in any danger. I-I wanted to ask you a favor," I fumbled, wincing at the stammer in my voice.

Creed studied me, then folded his arms across his chest. He did not appear to relax much, but his eyes had lost the sharp intensity of a few seconds before. He waited for me to continue and I wiped my hands on my apron front. Hastily, I explained my need for someone to assist me in moving furniture off of several rugs in the library. Creed silently thought it over, then nodded. He motioned for me to lead the way back and fell into step beside me.

"Thank you," I said on a rush of breath, relieved to have his help.

"You're welcome."

"I am not pulling you away from other duties, am I?" I asked, suddenly unsure.

He shook his head. "You are actually saving me from cleaning up after the midday meal, so I should be the one thanking you."

"Oh no, did Miss Sue order you to help? Perhaps you should go after all. You do not want to get on her bad side."

"I'm not too worried. She can't enforce orders if she can't find me, can she now?"

I eyed him. "All right. I will try not to keep you too long."

Once we entered the library, I pointed to the first rug, detailing the process. He took my instructions in stride, and we moved in tandem, sliding or lifting items off of the rug before rolling the massive carpet up. We repeated the process again and again.

As we worked, I stole furtive glances up at Creed's face, remembering the conversation with my roommates from a few nights previous. Their obvious distaste in regard to his looks still baffled me. Why did it matter if he was not classically handsome? I found I did not mind his rugged, scarred appearance.

Realizing the course of my thoughts, I blushed deeply, snatching my eyes away before he caught me staring and refocused on my work. *Enough of this silliness*, I scolded myself. *You have a job to do, one that does not involve admiring a man you barely know!*

Setting down the side of the ottoman I was helping Creed move, I started for the end table at Creed's prompting. He hefted the armchair beside it on his own and I followed, using my arms to keep the ornamental vase on the surface from sliding off. As I set it down next to the armchair, I caught a glimpse of a corner of a piece of paper peeking out from the shadowy interior. No, another envelope. I had no doubt that was what it was.

Straightaway, I felt a mixture of trepidation and an unhealthy amount of curiosity fight for dominance inside me. I clearly recalled the ominous words from the last letter. Would this one be the same? Dare I even open it? The last had no name, neither the sender or the intended recipient. Was it even worth trying to check? The curious side of me whispered to simply see if there was a name, while the other side snapped at me to put it back, to leave it alone as one would give a poisonous viper a wide berth.

Before I could overthink it, I snatched it up. Once more, there was nothing beyond the snake symbol in the corner. I opened it, scanning for a recipient like last time. There was nothing but a few short lines in the same untidy hand.

The field is ready for scourging. Await further Instructions.
Our time is nigh

Puzzled, I reread it. There was no mention of birds or cages yet this felt just as foreboding as the last. What did it mean? What was the 'field'?

I felt the air stir behind me and I jumped. Turning, I found Creed standing close to me, attention fixed on the paper I held. Ashamed at being caught, I started to speak, but he snatched the letter out of my hands, as well as the envelope, ignoring me. Taken aback, both by his sudden movement and the fact that he was clearly reading the letter, I stared. Aside from myself and Penny, whose grandfather had been an educator, I had not come across any other servants who could read. It was quite rare. Who was this man?

Creed's attention shifted from the letter to the envelope, and then to me and I felt the full force of his intense gaze. There were no emotions present in either his eyes or face, but I felt as though I were being evaluated, and whether I passed or failed was of extreme consequence.

All at once, he stated, "I must go." He turned and strode away, taking the letter with him.

Sheer anxiety rose up inside me as he disappeared from view. I felt sure I was in trouble. I wrung my hands and paced for a few moments. Worries wound their way up from deep inside my belly until they encircled my throat like a noose. I should not have touched that envelope. I should have pretended I had not seen it and moved on.

I began to automatically organize some figurines on a nearby shelf, barely registering what I was doing. I organized the colorful pieces by height, then weight, and then finally by color, until my nerves had soothed. A quick look at the waterclock showed me almost a quarter of an hour had passed. I began to unwind. Nothing was wrong. I would be fine. I could breathe.

I almost believed it too until a messenger slipped between two shelves and stopped before me. The feeling of dread resurfaced as he cleared his throat.

"Miss, you have a summons from the king. Come with me at once."

If ever I needed the castle floor to swallow me whole, it was now.

CHAPTER SIXTEEN

INTERROGATION

Benjamin

"FAREWELL FOR NOW," I called back into the room as I closed the door. I heard a half-hearted mumble from Fitzy as he slumped over his desk, intent on his studies, and smirked. He'd probably forget I had left in an hour or so and wonder when I had disappeared.

I began to wend my way along the route toward my bedchamber, intent on changing into riding clothes to take advantage of the warm weather. One never knew how long favorable weather would linger this early in spring, and I meant to go on a long ride on Joker.

Up ahead, I spotted Naya. Her dark hair and features made her stand out, and I found myself fighting a grin as I remembered her utter mortification at being discovered singing tavern songs this morning. Something so unexpected from such an unlikely source had been comical in the extreme. It had stuck with me all morning, and into the afternoon, making me restless to know what else hid behind that meek exterior.

As our paths brought us into speaking distance, I had planned on whistling the tune to one of the songs she had been singing to see if she would blush again. That is, that had been my plan until I had been able to see her clearly for the first time. Her eyes were slightly glazed over, wide and staring, and she looked like she was close to vomiting. In short, she looked absolutely terrified.

A rush of heat filled my chest, expanding my lungs. Without thinking, I stepped in front of her. She jerked to attention, eyes refocusing on my face for a split second before she swiftly averted them.

"What's wrong?" I ground out, jaw tight.

"Nothing," she whispered back.

"I don't believe that for a moment. What has happened? Has someone hurt you?" The thought made me furious and I found myself taking a deep breath in through my nose and out through my mouth.

"No one has hurt me. I am fine." She tried to step around me, but I moved in front of her again, determined to find out what—or who—had made her look so frightened.

Someone cleared their throat, and I spun around. A scrawny messenger stood nearby, and he looked nervous but determined. He glanced in Naya's direction, and I realized he must be leading her somewhere. Perhaps that was why she was so anxious.

"State your business," I snapped at him.

The man swallowed. "The king has requested her presence."

"Why?"

"I'm not privy to the king's motivations, my lord."

I grunted, studying him, then motioned for him to continue. I joined Naya as she trailed after him.

She glanced at me out of the corner of her eye. "What are you doing?" she whispered.

"I'm coming with you."

"That is not necessary, but thank you."

"You can't get rid of me that easily. I'm coming," I said firmly.

She remained silent, though her shoulders remained tense. I tried to think of something to say to ease her stress, but couldn't come up with anything. It was a taut silence that accompanied us to my uncle's office.

Unlike all the other times I had been there, the little office minion was not at his post. The messenger marched through the adjoining door into the study and we followed. The secretary stood to one side within. Uncle James paced behind his chair, turning as the door shut behind us. He appeared properly confused and a bit irritated to see me.

"Benjamin," he acknowledged. "What are you doing here?"

"I saw a friend in distress, being led here, and decided to come along to see what was happening. To help if I could."

Uncle James blew out a frustrated breath. "How solicitous. Everything is fine, and frankly, this is none of your business. If you would leave, that would be marvelous."

"I'm staying," I responded flatly.

A flash of anger flickered across his face before he breathed in deeply. I watched one of his lessons in action and a few repetitions of the breathing technique brought him back into control. Grudgingly, I had to admit I was impressed with his ability to control his temper, for showing me the benefits of our lessons. However, most of my admiration faded at his next words.

"I'm afraid that is impossible. You must leave now. Go."

Oh, now it was more than just wanting to protect a friend. Now, I wanted to win. I drew in a deep breath, prepared to do battle, when the side door banged against the wall as a man barreled through. Dressed in serving attire, I found myself dismissing him until I peered closer and saw the scar on his right cheek. I *knew* this man. It was the man that had stared me down! I had seen him coming out of my uncle's office a few weeks ago. He had changed his appearance, but it was most definitely him. Confusion and suspicion flooded my mind. Who was this man? What was he doing here, in disguise?

The impostor clutched a piece of paper in his hand. "Sire, before we begin, I feel the need to say that I don't believe this young woman has—"

He cut himself off upon seeing me. His teeth clacked together audibly, almost as if he were trying to ingest the words he had already spoken. He didn't look precisely guilty, but I could tell he remembered me. I felt triumphant and pointed a finger at his scarred face.

"You," I spat. "I remember you."

"Benjamin, leave now," Uncle tried again, weariness heavy in his voice.

"You might have been successful in getting me to depart before this lug's appearance, Uncle, but not now. I saw him several weeks back, and he wasn't a servant then. What is going on?"

Uncle James hesitated, glancing between the newcomer, his secretary, Naya, and the messenger, whose eyes bulged out at the strain rippling through the air. Uncle first dismissed the messenger, telling him to not divulge anything he heard or saw in this room, then asked the impostor to shut the door behind the departing figure. Then, he gripped the back of his chair and bowed his head. The echo of the door shutting rang around the room as we all waited for him to speak. He raised his head, meeting the stranger's eyes. They seemed to be silently communicating. I couldn't handle it anymore and coughed into my fist. They broke eye contact and both swiveled their focus onto me.

"What is going on?" I asked again, emphasizing each word.

Uncle James cursed lowly. "If you are going to stubbornly go against my demands, I want to hear nothing from you. Do you understand? Not a word. You're intruding in something you know nothing about, but I can think of no way to make you unsee Creed's presence now. Do I have your word?"

I was so pleased to know the impostor's name that I didn't answer immediately. At the narrowed look my uncle gave me, I quickly agreed, giving him my word. He sighed, rubbing his eyes with his thumb and forefinger, then asked his secretary to get ready to take notes. To Creed, he held out his hand for the letter and as he took it, he invited Naya to take a seat in front of his desk. She lurched forward like a marionette on a string, lowering herself down, eyes focused downward. She hadn't uttered a sound since entering into the study and I detected a slight trembling in her upper body. The poor girl was still frightened out of her wits.

As soon as the secretary returned, quill poised to transcribe, Uncle James began to speak.

"What is your name?"

"Naya Gavi, your majesty," came the barely perceptible response.

"How long have you worked in my home?"

"Just over two years, sire."

He came around the desk, arms folded. He looked stern and serious. "Where do you hail from?"

"Whojia, sire. Near the western border."

"How did you come to be here in Mendlewyn?"

"A missionary couple took me in, brought me to this country and helped me create a better life for myself."

"How long ago?"

"Seven years, sire."

He paused, studying her. He went on for the next quarter of an hour, questioning her about her past work history, the education she had received in the care of the missionary couple, why she departed from their company, and many other questions. For my part, I wondered over the reason for this interrogation, for that was exactly what this was. It took everything in me not to blurt out questions of my own, to find out why he was so interested in her background, what this was all about. But I knew that I'd be thrust from this meeting as soon as I spoke up and I was desperate to remain.

"Can you read, Naya?" Uncle James continued, tugging on his beard.

"Yes, sire."

"Did you read this letter?" He held up the paper that he had taken from Creed.

Naya didn't respond for a long moment. She, like me, probably felt the change in the air. *This* was what they truly wanted to know, and her answer would change the dynamics of this situation.

"Y-yes, sire," she finally mumbled.

"Why?" Uncle James said quickly, before she had finished her answer.

"To find out if there was a name inside, to see if I could get it to the rightful owner."

"Was that your only motivation? To find out who it belonged to?"

"Yes, sire."

He weighed her words again. He stared hard at her down-turned head. He glanced at his secretary, then Creed. They gave no verbal or visual cue as to their thoughts or opinions.

"Naya, do you harbor any ill feelings towards me or my country?"

"No!" she cried, horrified. "I mean, no, sire."

"Do you associate with anyone who harbors any hatred toward me or my country?"

I missed her response as my mind tumbled end over end. Just what was in that letter? I had assumed that Uncle James was upset to find out that someone had been reading private letters, but his line of questioning exposed a deeper level of intrigue. This sounded far more grave. I pulled my mind back in from my speculating to listen in on the conversation again.

"Have there been any more letters beyond this one in the library?"

"There have been two others."

"Did you read them as well?"

"I did not read the first one that I found. I read the second one."

Creed rapped his knuckles on the tabletop. "I'm assuming you can't remember what the other one said. Can you remember how often these letters appear?"

"About every two weeks," Naya responded. "And I actually can remember what the last one said." Her voice seemed to get smaller as she completed the sentence.

Naya's words tumbled around in my mind, sounding familiar. I remembered a conversation I'd had with Fitzy shortly after he'd introduced me to Naya. Among the long-winded, one-sided conversation, I remember him raving about Naya's mind, saying something about how she had the most impressive memory of anyone he'd ever met. He'd gone on to tell me a story about how he'd returned a book before he was finished with it, and regretted it immediately. Thinking he'd have to hunt for days to find it again, he had mentioned the title to Naya, who had straightaway taken him to the exact spot where the book had been. Just like that. He said he'd often quiz her on where different books or trinkets were in the library, and as long as no one else had tampered with them, she could find them with stunning accuracy.

Uncle James was the first to speak after that declaration. "Are you sure about that? It has been a few weeks."

Quickly, I shot my hand in the air as if I were a boy in the classroom. Creed saw my hand and promptly ignored me. Uncle James nearly rolled his eyes and I thought for a moment he would disregard me as well. He finally sighed and nodded at me.

"If she says she remembers the note, believe her," I stated simply. "According to Fitzy, she has an astounding memory."

Slowly, cautiously, Naya turned her head to peer over her shoulder at me. I waited for her to meet my eyes to smile at her, but her eyes never reached mine. They stopped at my chin and went no higher. Movement in front of her had her swiveling back, while I pondered over her not looking me in the face. Now that I thought about it, she had never actually looked me in the eye before. That would need further thinking, but not at this critical moment.

"The first one that I read was just as vague as this one," Naya was saying. "It said, '*A wild bird was never meant to be caged. Remember your purpose. It would be a shame to see her wings clipped.*'"

The secretary scribbled as she spoke. Uncle James handed the second letter over to the man as well, and he hurriedly copied the contents down. Then Uncle James asked her where she had found the letter. As soon as Naya gave a detailed explanation, Creed hustled out of the office with the original paper, his purpose to return the letter to where it had been found as quickly as possible.

Once the door shut behind him, Uncle James looked back and forth between Naya and I. He suddenly looked very much middle-aged; he seemed more weary, his shoulders stooped, and his eyes held a sense of something near sadness. It was the most unguarded I had ever seen him and it alarmed me.

Uncle James straightened, then spoke. "One more thing to do. Will you two swear fealty to the crown of Mendlewyn? To me?"

Completely rattled, I gaped at my uncle. What was he saying? I had never in my life expected my uncle—no, not just my uncle, my *king*—to ask me to swear fealty to him. On the heels of that last thought, another one crept into my mind: what was going on that he felt the need to ask his own nephew to make an oath of loyalty to him? Without my consent, a feeling of dread swelled in my chest, into my lungs, leaving me cold.

"I need your answers," Uncle James demanded. "Now preferably. Will you give me an oath of your loyalty to Mendlewyn, and to your monarch?"

"Yes," I answered automatically. "My allegiance is to you."

As soon as the words left my mouth, I couldn't help but wonder just what I was getting myself into.

CHAPTER SEVENTEEN
A PLOT UNCOVERED

Naya

MY HEART SLOWED nearly to a standstill as eyes fell on me; I did not have to look up to know it. I could feel three separate gazes on me as plainly as if there were a trio of flames sprouting up on my person. I was barely keeping my head above the chaotic waves of this whole situation and now this.

I was moments away from making what I expected was a life-altering decision, the weight of which was settling in my chest. All because I had ignored an inner voice telling me to leave the mysterious letters alone.

Breathe in.
Breathe out.
Breathe in.
Breathe out.

The simple breathing exercise, my usual reaction in tense moments, was not working. Every breath came as a ragged pant, as if I were trying to draw in air through a thick blanket. It did not help matters that my lungs felt like they were slowly being compressed through a clothes-wringer. The combined effect of the two led to quicker, more ragged breaths. *Oh no, not now. Not here.* I had not had a bout of hysteria—my Nanni Venna's term for them—in months. The last thing I wanted was an audience to my distress if this episode progressed like all the others.

Think, think, think, Naya, I coached myself. I forced myself to keep breathing deeply through the tension in my torso. As I did so, I flicked my eyes around the room, seeking visual distractions. I worked through my senses: hearing, sight, touch, smell, and taste. I first found five things I could hear. A distant bird call, a shout from outside the room, a squeak of a floorboard as someone shifted their weight from foot to foot, footfalls above us, and finally a distant dog howling. I moved on, searching for four things I could see. The gleam of sweat on the secretary's forehead, Creed's hands clenching and relaxing at his sides, an ink stain on his majesty's sleeve, dust clinging to a half-formed cobweb high in the corner of the room.

I worked through the rest of the senses, until I found one thing I could taste. I spotted a partially eaten biscuit on the king's desk, and imagined the taste of it. Now, I was no longer spiraling; I was more in control. As soon as I finished with the calming exercise, I felt the last of the clothes-wringer feeling fade. I took in a mercifully deep breath and felt my mind clear. I was able to finally cast my mind over the dilemma I had been presented with.

The king had asked me to swear fealty to him and the kingdom of Mendlewyn. He demanded it. Just what was behind the letters I had found? It had to have been of utmost importance if this was the reaction to it. What was I to do?

"Miss Gavi," the king intoned. "I hate to rush you but I need your answer now. Plans have to move forward and your answer is vital to their direction."

I swallowed. "If I may, your majesty, may I ask what this is about? Is there anything you can tell me?" At his silence, I quickly added, "I just want to know what I am getting into."

He exhaled heavily. "Without your oath, I can't go too in depth, but what I can tell you is that it's of national consequence. The future of Mendlewyn lies in the balance."

If anything, that nearly brought on another bout of hysteria.

It was nearly too much to take in. Anxiety gripped me, but I found myself nodding slowly. I found myself swearing fealty to the king and crown.

King James let out a long, tense breath. "Thank you. This office is not nearly secure enough. Here's what we're going to do…"

Half an hour later, tea tray in hand, I lifted a trembling hand to rap on the doors to the king's personal chambers. The king himself opened the door nearly before I had finished knocking, as if he had waited anxiously on the other side, ready to answer it at the first knock.

He waved me inside, eyes flickering down the hall, then in the opposite direction. He led me further inside and I spotted the secretary and Creed waiting.

I briefly made eye contact with Creed, then looked away quickly, distrust brewing. I felt foolish that I had taken him at face value, had assumed he was a servant when he was clearly anything but. Then again, why should I feel upset? I barely knew the man!

"Where is that boy?" the king muttered. "Did he take a detour to the Highlands?"

"Shall I fetch him?" Creed asked idly.

"No, thank you."

Just then, an impatient knock rang out before Benjamin entered without waiting for anyone to answer the door.

"I still don't understand this whole charade, Uncle," were his first words as he drew closer to our grouping.

I found myself agreeing with him. As soon as I had given the king my oath, he had immediately canceled his upcoming meetings by feigning a headache, leaving his secretary to carry out his orders. He then sent us all off with instructions to meet in his chambers a half hour later. Staggered so we arrived at varying times, we each had viable excuses for being in the king's quarters. Creed had been sent to the physician for a draft of headache medicine. I had been sent to the kitchens to fetch tea, with special instructions to have healing herbs mixed into it. While we had been attending to his 'headache', his secretary had accompanied his employer to his chambers, and Benjamin had come with a book tucked under his arm, appearing to all that he was prepared to study with his mentor.

"You don't have to understand it. I just appreciate you all followed directions. Come with me."

He led us to his wardrobe, opening the doors wide. He reached an arm deep inside. I could hear his fingers running across wood; a sliding sound reached my ears. I watched in fascination as he parted the hanging clothing and stepped inside the large furnishing. He disappeared! I managed to pick my jaw up off the floor, stepping closer, trying to see through the clothing.

His secretary followed close behind, barely having to duck through. Creed glanced at Benjamin and me—eyes lingering longer on me—before he shrugged and vanished after the duo. Benjamin approached the wardrobe, stooping to peer through the opening and the passageway beyond. He shook his head.

"You saw that, right?" he asked me.

"Yes," I mumbled. "They stepped through the wardrobe."

Benjamin straightened, hands on hips. "Well, there's no time like the present," he declared, stepping up into the wardrobe. As he folded his powerful build into the gap, I heard him mutter to himself, "Of all the things I thought I'd be doing today, clambering through my uncle's closet was not one of them."

Soon, the swaying of clothes was all that marked his passage. I hesitated a few moments, wanting to quit the room, yet knowing it was impossible. I bit my lip and moved forward. I had to agree again with Benjamin: I never thought I would be climbing through a king's wardrobe. I dropped down on the other side, and hurried to the left, as the secretary was waiting close by and moved toward me. He stuck his upper body back through the hole, closed the wardrobe doors, then slid the wood panel back in place.

Once the hatch was closed, the king waved to us to continue to follow him. Soon we were circling up a set of narrow stairs that hugged the wall. We reached a landing and filed into a perfectly round room with an aged table that fit the room's dimensions flawlessly. King James motioned for us to be seated, then remained on his feet, pacing around the perimeter of the room.

"I fear," the king began, "there are enemies to the crown working within the very walls of this castle. I have suspected it for years, have felt it creeping up on me, but have never found any evidence of it until recently.

"We have discovered a face, so to speak, behind this threat. A radical organization known as the Red Fang Movement, or simply Red Fang, has been growing in numbers since a failed extermination of its leaders decades ago. This group, among many things, desires the destruction of the nobility and everything they represent. They seek to destroy the ruling class, to give power back to the people and I fear they will stop at nothing to see their ends met."

I swallowed heavily. King James's voice rang with deadly earnestness. My mind reeled. Radical organizations? Destruction of the nobility? I could not bring myself to quite believe all that was being discussed; it sounded too fantastical to be genuine, yet the serious expressions of the king and his associates told me it was quite real.

"How did you discover this information, Uncle?" Benjamin interjected.

King James cleared his throat, looking to his secretary. "McMannon?"

The man nodded, then spoke up. "From a trusted source, one which, for their own protection, will not be revealed to you at this time."

Benjamin processed this information, then asked, "And what does he have to do with this? Whatever your name is."

I glanced up quickly to see him flick a hand in Creed's direction. I shifted my gaze to Creed's face, wondering how he would react to the thick layer of dismissal I heard in Benjamin's voice. Creed blinked, entirely unruffled. Despite my newfound suspicion, I felt myself in awe of his calm.

"Creed is my…man-of-all-trades, if you will. If a situation requires a certain set of skills, I call upon him," King James explained.

"I don't think you can get more vague with that answer," Benjamin huffed.

The king did not miss a beat at the interruption. "Once we suspected that the threat was not just outside the capital, but within Castle Dartmoor, I needed a man I trusted on the inside."

Creed took over. "I needed a role that would allow me access in nearly every area of the castle, and so I became a servant. I needed to see without being seen, move seamlessly among staff and resident alike."

King James paused in his pacing, facing us. "Creed has been invaluable. With his help behind the scenes, he has confirmed that a member of my House of Lords is somehow caught up in these nefarious activities. We don't know the extent of it but we're closer than we've ever been to finding out."

"Who is the guilty lord?" Benjamin asked.

"Lord Randolph Donovan," McMannon responded.

I frowned. I knew Lord Donovan. I briefly thought back to the ragged and worn man I had seen at the door to his personal rooms a week or so back, and reviewed the memory with a new lens. Perhaps he was so worn down because of the stress of betraying his country. Yet he had always struck me as a kind soul. But what did I know of the character of men?

I focused back on the conversation when I heard the deep rumble of Creed's voice once again. "Your majesty, now that these two are relatively caught up with the internal conflicts going on here, what will happen going forward? Will they take an active role or be sworn to secrecy and that will be it?"

King James was silent. He did not start pacing again, but stewed. When he spoke again, his voice was thoughtful. "You bring up a fair point, Creed, as always. We still don't know the range of those plotting against us, how many there are, in what position. We need more information. We need more eyes and ears. *Trusted* eyes and ears. I feel, though, that I need to warn the two of you. As I have stated, we don't know much, only that enemies are close, breathing down our necks. This is dangerous work, with no promise of a happy ending. Are you willing to risk everything, your lives, if necessary?"

I dimly registered Benjamin's hearty agreement, given almost immediately after his uncle had finished his speech. I was not shocked to hear it. He, a strong, capable young man, likely trained from birth how to fight and how to command—had the confidence to step forward into risk. But me? I had my doubts, not only about this perilous task, but about myself. I was no hero. Other than my impressive memory, I had no outstanding skills to my name, no great strengths. I was just *me*.

Yet I felt the same stirrings of panic that I had felt each time I was nearing the end of my stay at the various homes over the years. The panic of not knowing whether I would have another roof over my head before the sun set on the morrow. When the fevers raged through my childhood village, claiming all of my family members and leaving me behind, I had been forced to seek out my father's last remaining sibling, a sister days away in a city choked to the borders with humanity. In my Nanni Venna's home, after enduring years of rejection and neglect, without warning I had been sent to pack my meager belongings and told never to return.

I had almost found my place with the Whitman's, the missionary couple who had taken me in and cared for me while I learned Lewyn—the universal language—and other skills. But, once again, there was no place for me there. I had not been able to endure the dank tavern for longer than two years, and though I had left willingly, I had still felt the anxiety as I prepared to depart. It was the same feeling now, as I reviewed the information I had been given. Only now, danger threatened this new home, an unknown scourge. I was on a precipice, staring into the void.

Realizing I had been woolgathering for far too long, I lifted my head. "I want to help," I said, unable to keep the wobble out of my voice. "I cannot in good conscience walk away when I know the castle and its occupants—the whole country—are in danger. I do not know how I can help, but I want to be of service to you."

The men nodded, then conversation continued. Various ideas of different tasks that Benjamin and I could undertake were brought up. My memory seemed my only asset to this group, to compile information, to be a glorified clay tablet where they could store all their clues.

After a time, the meeting wrapped up. We were told to leave as we had arrived, staggered, and in different directions. We all stepped back through the wardrobe into the king's chambers to wait. The secretary, McMannon, slipped out first. King James spoke with Benjamin, their low voices not quite reaching where I stood. I watched as Creed moved toward the door, enough time having gone by from when McMannon had departed.

Before he slipped away, I called out to Creed, my pulse thrumming in my throat. I had to know the answer to a question that had been burning in my mind since I found out who he truly was. He silently waited.

"When you rescued me, were you just following your orders to the king? Keeping the peace as you searched for the people behind this?"

He looked me in the eye, then shook his head slowly. "No," he said. "I acted the way I did because I saw someone in trouble. I was not acting out of duty to my king."

I studied his face, searching for signs of deceit. Instead, I saw an earnestness that was reassuring. I nodded once, then debated on leaving, but he spoke before I could move.

"Should you need my help with a certain low life, I hope you won't hesitate to seek me out." Again, the gravity in his expression was comforting.

"Of course," I responded.

"Good."

With that, he walked away, leaving me behind, and I was warm with the knowledge that I still had a protector.

CHAPTER EIGHTEEN
THE ETERNAL BINDING

Benjamin

TRY AS I might, I could not bring myself to focus on what Uncle James was saying. I'm sure it was something along the lines of *there is great uncertainty afoot, and you'll need all your wits about you.* Saints, he could have been singing the national anthem backwards in a falsetto for all I knew. I found I didn't really care.

What I did care about was that Naya had kept Creed back from leaving, and the two of them were standing quite close to one another. Too close. I felt my eyes narrow. Clearly they knew one another. Their conversation was serious and hasty too, as Creed walked away from Naya shortly after they had started talking. He drew close to my uncle and me, and I forced myself to not shoot him a withering glare. Creed shook hands with my uncle and left.

I watched the door shut behind him, then returned my gaze to Naya. She too, had followed his departure with her eyes. She wore a thoughtful look, her face soft as she pondered something.

I didn't like it. I didn't like it at all.

I tried to make eye contact with her before I quit the room, but she carefully avoided looking me in the face. Finally, biting my tongue to keep from saying something I would or would not regret later, I left the room, stomping away down the hall.

The image of Naya standing so comfortably next to Creed battled for dominance with the knowledge that the seemingly perfect atmosphere of Dartmoor Castle overlaid dangers unseen. That, and the nagging thought of the mystery behind why Naya refused to look me in the eye.

Disgusting, I reprimanded myself, shaking my head. *Some action finally comes your way, and here you are, worrying like a ninny over a girl not making eye contact with you. Pull yourself together, man!*

I pushed all thoughts of girls out of my mind with finality. Or so I thought. I spotted Fitzy trotting down the stairs ahead of me, and called for him to wait.

He paused and before he could get a word in, I blurted, "Why won't Naya look me in the eye?"

Fitzy raised an eyebrow. "Hello to you too. Oh, my day? My day has been great, thank you for asking—for caring." He shook a finger at me. "Benjamin, it is a sad day when I have to be the one to give you pointers on social niceties."

I fought the urge to roll my eyes. "Just answer the question, you crumb."

Instead of answering, he started moving back down the stairs. I watched him for a moment, then grumbled under my breath as I followed close behind him. Soon we passed the landing to his personal study, then the one that led to the library, and I forgot my question as I realized he was leaving the castle. Saints above.

"Fitzy?" I called, lengthening my stride until I was level with him.

"Yes?"

"Tell me something only I would know."

He eyed me, then faced forward once more. "You once ate an entire plate of nipped sweets and then proceeded to vomit into a nearby vase. You blamed it on Gertie."

I grinned. "I sure did. Her revenge was nasty, but it was worth it." I slugged him in the shoulder. "You passed."

He grimaced as he rubbed his shoulder. "Passed what?" he griped.

"The test determining whether or not you're an impostor."

"Why would you think I was an impostor?"

"It's simple, really. You're clearly leaving the castle, and there's not a fire, so I had to make sure you were, well, you."

I couldn't be sure, but I swore I saw him roll his eyes before continuing on. I fell into step beside him. "So where are we going?"

"What makes you think you're coming along?"

"First off, you didn't answer my question. And secondly, I must know what has caused you to emerge from your study into the real world."

He ignored the second part of my sentence entirely. "It just so happens that I'm going to visit with someone who will be able to answer your question better than I can."

I gasped in mock horror. "You, visiting someone? I may need to reconsider your impostor status."

He rolled his eyes heavenward, shaking his head. He led me through the windy streets of Dartmoor, the pathways becoming narrower and narrower the longer we walked. I found myself growing increasingly curious as he took turn after turn. I doubted we were going anywhere seedy—this was Fitzy we were talking about, after all—but I would never have guessed he would go anywhere beyond a stone's throw from the castle.

The reality of where he was taking me soon dawned on me and I smothered a groan. "Are you serious, Fitzy? A schoolhouse?"

"I never invited you, Benjamin."

"Do you ever do anything besides *learning*?"

"I have been debating on taking up horseshoes, but only if a certain, pesky cousin of mine agrees to squat behind the stake for which I will be aiming."

I spun to face him, loping backwards. "And potentially ruin a face like this? No thank you."

"I won't be aiming for your face."

I grimaced. "How heartless of you, Fitzy."

I followed him through the door of a sagging building with unwashed windows and a depressing sign that read 'The Newbury School for Underprivileged Boys'. Musty corridors greeted us as we stepped inside. Fitzy moved forward with ease, apparently familiar with the place. Muffled voices rang out from the various rooms we passed. Our footsteps echoed dully as we made our way down the hallway until we reached a faded red door.

Fitzy leaned in toward the door, listening. He stepped back, whispering that he was wrapping up. *Who was wrapping up*, I wanted to ask but I held my tongue. He remained quiet and shushed me when I tried to drum up a conversation. Eventually, the screeching of chairs across hardwood floors and raised voices of young men filtered out to where we waited. The door opened and a dozen boys filed out in clusters, eyeing us as they passed.

Once the room was cleared, Fitzy entered, striding confidently toward the lectern. I followed a bit more hesitantly. A man had his back to us, returning books to the enormous bookshelf that took up most of the back wall. Curiously, it was only half full, its empty shelves like the gaps in a grinning skull's maw. Fitzy called a greeting, the man turned, and I had to use all my mother's admonitions in decorum to keep from guffawing out loud. The man, with a head as bald as a cue ball—and just as shiny—had the largest, bushiest pair of eyebrows I had ever seen before in my life. If that wasn't a sight, then the fact that they were bright orange would have been the mule's bray.

The man spotted my cousin and a welcoming smile grew quickly over his round face. He set the remaining books he held down on his desk as he passed, arms extended wide to either side as though Fitzy were a long lost friend in need of a warm embrace. Instead, he clasped Fitzy's hand with both of his, pumping it up and down enthusiastically.

"Your highness, it is always an honor to see you!" he cried. He was about to continue speaking when he caught sight of me. Those caterpillar eyebrows shot up. "Who is this?"

Fitzy, almost as if he'd forgotten I was there, stumbled a bit through the introduction. Professor Stephanus, a name nearly as ridiculous as the man himself, took my hand in the same manner as he had Fitzy. I half expected the man to dislocate my elbow, so vigorous was the handshake.

"It is a pleasure to meet you, my lord," he greeted as he released me.

"The pleasure is all mine."

With that, he refocused on Fitzy. "I was not expecting you so soon, highness. I have not had the journal in my possession for a week, and I jotted that note off to you the day after it arrived. I must say, I'm pleased you came so soon."

"Like I mentioned before, Professor Stephanus, this journal is pivotal to my research. I will be forever grateful to you for finding it and notifying me of its existence. This could be the answer to all my lingering questions." I could practically feel my cousin's excitement.

"Allow me to retrieve it for you." With that, the bald man whisked out of the main room, disappearing through a door to the far right of the room.

"What's going on?" I asked Fitzy in a low tone.

Fitzy shifted awkwardly, then dodged the question. "When he gets back, you can ask him your question. I assure you you'll get your answer."

I narrowed my eyes and he quickly turned his back on me. Before I could question him further, I heard footsteps and Fitzy spun toward the door the odd little fellow had ducked through. He emerged, carrying a small item that he handled as though it were fine china. A waterproof sheepskin covering wrapped around the object. Baldy placed it in my cousin's outstretched hands, watching him as he folded back the protective wrapping.

To me it looked like nothing special, just a dog-eared journal that seemed like it was a forceful cough away from being turned to dust. Yet Fitzy was in awe. He thanked the rotund man profusely, asking when he ought to return it. When the professor informed Fitzy he could keep it, I thought my cousin would keel over and die right there.

It soon looked like Fitzy, caught up as he was in admiring the journal, would walk right out the door and leave me behind. Remembering his assurance that this man could answer my question, I cleared my throat.

"Do you know much about Whojia and its citizens?"

Professor Stephanus straightened, looking intrigued. "Why, yes, I do, as a matter of fact. I lived and taught there for two years about a decade ago. What would you like to know?"

"I have recently become acquainted with a Whojian, and I find her…confusing."

"Elaborate, my lord."

"Well, sir, she doesn't ever make eye contact with me. She's quite shy, but I've seen her look other people in the eye, but never me. I find it odd."

Professor Stephanus rocked back onto his heels, smiling widely. "Oh, that's simple. Have you ever heard of the Eternal Binding?"

"No."

"Well, in Whojia, there is this practice that has been around for hundreds of years. Those of the lower classes keep their eyes lowered when around those of higher social rank. It goes beyond a mere sign of respect, however. You see, they believe that to make eye contact with gentry for more than a second binds their soul to that person for all eternity, hence the name. That person essentially becomes their master and they their slave."

That made sense. I reviewed all of my past encounters with Naya with this new information in mind. It explained her skittishness during our first few interactions, her discomfort with me and never looking me full in the face. The more I pondered the reasons for her hesitancy, the more ridiculous it sounded. I expressed this sentiment to Lord Stephanus who frowned deeply.

"It may very well be ridiculous to you, but it isn't to them. They truly believe it, despite the select noblemen's quest to end such superstitions. Just because someone else's culture or beliefs seem odd to you doesn't give you the right to belittle and mock them."

Instantly, I felt anger surge at his rebuke. But before I could snap back, Uncle James's words came to me: *Smell the rainstorm. Blow it away.* We'd practiced the breathing exercise after every running session, with the intent to make it instinctive. Without needing to think too much about it, I closed my eyes and breathed in deeply through my nose, then out through my mouth, imagining a rainstorm in detail. A few repetitions and my rushing pulse began to ease. It had worked, confound it!

"You're right. I apologize."

I was even able to thank the man properly and bid him farewell, something Fitzy was no doubt grateful for.

Soon we were outside the rundown schoolhouse. I was still thinking over my progress in my anger management. I almost felt the urge to sigh in defeat, because my uncle's hairbrained ideas seemed to actually have merit.

As we moved back up the street, I glanced over at Fitzy, who had tucked the journal under an arm. He appeared to be fighting a grin.

"So what is it about that journal that has you and Professor Whatsit so excited?"

"It's Professor Stephanus, and this journal contains the writings of the last known member of the notorious mercenary group that nearly overthrew our many great grandfather Xavier III. The author had been a life-long, devoted member to the cause until—"

Nearly overwhelmed at the words flying from his mouth like a horse at full gallop, I interrupted him, saying, "Whoa, easy there. I honestly was just asking to be polite, but you're going to give me a headache. Let's change the subject."

Fitzy's mouth hung open for a second or two before he closed it. He faced forward, the fingers of his opposite hand gripping the book, his face twisting in unreadable lines before it cleared.

"Did you hear? Perry is coming home for a week."

I hooted, clapping, and rubbing my hands together in excited glee. "Ah, Perfect Perry. What daring deeds do you think he has done while away this time?"

"I bet he's brokered peace with the Yukands."

"I wouldn't be surprised if he's wooed every gently bred young lady from here to Grandwich. Too bad they don't know how boring he is."

We continued to list increasingly impossible, and highly imaginative accomplishments Perfect Perry could have done in his months-long absence until we got back to the castle. Fitzy made his excuses as soon as we made it to the stairs.

"But what about our chess game?" We had made plans to play this afternoon a few days ago.

He turned back around, not quite meeting my eye. He tapped the journal with his fingers with emphasis.

I huffed a laugh. "Of course. You've got an important meeting with a new friend." I scoffed again. "Why continue with plans you've made when you can read a new book?"

Fitzy's smile didn't reach his eyes. "I'll see you later."

With that, he hurried up the stairs. I was left at the bottom, watching him leave.

Chapter Nineteen

Seeking Deceit

Naya

I COULD NOT quite believe I was bold enough to do it. But when push comes to shove, as they say…

I poked my head into another room, scanned it, then moved on. I felt my palms grow more clammy with each room I searched. I tried to count my footsteps as a way to distract myself. *One, two, three, four, five…* I reached thirty and started over again.

Here I was, shirking my duties as I tried to find Creed; the man was proving remarkably good at remaining out of sight.

I had to find him. Four days had passed since I had sworn fealty to the monarch of Mendlewyn, my adopted country. Four days since I had been made aware that there was a plot to tear down the ruling class, to destroy the nobility and the realm in the process. Four days, and no word from the king or his secretary. I felt the weight of the threat we faced, but had been left to worry and wait.

I had been willing to brush it off, to believe that my orders were coming, until just half an hour before I had set off on my search. But then Benjamin had entered the library with his cousin, eventually drifting over to where I had been dusting objects. With a furtive glance over either shoulder, he leaned in toward me.

"I have my mission," he had whispered in a voice almost too low for even me to hear him.

Shocked, I had listened as he had described his duty to befriend Lord Donovan at the next feast night in order to investigate him. Benjamin had asked if I were to be helping at the feast to gather information as well. With conflicting emotions, I had told him that I had not received any orders yet. Once again, I felt like I had been overlooked.

Hoping I would find the man quickly, I poked my head into the last room on the third floor and nearly sighed in relief. Creed crouched before the fireplace, cleaning it. I took in a deep breath and stepped inside, shutting the door behind me.

Creed rose to his feet and I waved at him to remain as he was. He sank back down and watched my approach. I could read nothing in his watchful gaze. I was second and third guessing myself and this idea to search him out. But what else was I to do? He was the only person out of the group dedicated to fighting this battle that I remotely trusted. Now that I knew the reasons for his deception, I felt no sting of betrayal.

"Good afternoon," he greeted. "May I help you with something?"

I jumped, realizing I had been staring at him while deep in thought.

"Sorry," I mumbled. "I did not know what else to do. I had to talk to someone."

He glanced toward the door, beckoned me closer and extended a small hatchet toward me.

"Prepare some kindling while we talk," he instructed as I knelt next to him. Then, in a near whisper, he asked, "I'm assuming this is about the project that we discussed four days ago. Am I correct?"

I nodded, eyes directed toward the length of wood I held. I swiftly began to slice off thin slivers of wood, creating a pile.

Creed did not push me to speak. He simply waited while I shaped my words into something coherent.

"I understand that plans are moving forward," I started. I bit my lip and forced myself to continue. "They are continuing without me. I know they are. I want to assist. What can I do to prove that I can help? *Is* there anything I can do? What Benjamin said in the meeting is true; my memory is nearly perfect. I can memorize those letters and any others that we find. That would eliminate the need to copy the contents down on paper. I can eavesdrop on people, memorize conversations. Anything to be of assistance." I was nearly pleading, but if that was what it took for someone to listen to me, then I could withstand a bit of humiliation.

Creed kept up the appearance of tidying the fireplace. He was silent for a long while until he had finished his work. Then he mutely communicated for me to start arranging the kindling within the hearth. He took over with the hatchet.

I waited, feeling my gut twist a little more each passing second.

"All right. When can you start?"

I could not have heard him right. No attempts to placate me, no patronizing or irritation because of my anxiety. I let out a whoosh of air. He was taking me seriously.

"Right now," I declared. "Today."

He nodded once. "I admire your enthusiasm. But first, I need to ask a few questions."

I raised my chin. "I will do my best."

He cracked a smile. "I expect nothing less. Who has ink stains under the fingernails of their right hand?"

For a moment, I did not understand, but then I began to sort through my memories, focusing on the right hands in particular.

"The king's secretary, McMannon."

"Who has a severe lisp?"

"Guinevere, the scullery maid."

"Good. Lastly, who has too short sleeves on their uniform?"

I furrowed my brow. This was tricky. *Or maybe not.*

Confidently, I said, "No one. Mrs. Cox would never allow someone to have ill-fitting clothing working under her." Mrs. Cox, the housekeeper, was a busy-body and meticulous to an unhealthy amount. She made Miss Sue look like a laze-about.

Again, there was that half smile. "Nicely done. You have proven to me you have the needed observational skills. This wouldn't have worked if you couldn't see the tiny details." The smile vanished as quickly as it had come. "But I feel the need to warn you. This is not a task for the faint of heart. This is the kind of mission that gets in your blood, tenses you up until you can't see anything beyond the untruths. It takes a lot out of you to be actively looking for deception in those around you, in your friends and acquaintances. It can affect your sleep, your eating habits. And once this mission is over, you may still be weighing people's words, sifting through each word and action, searching for lies. It isn't something you can just shut off after days and weeks on end. Do you have what it takes to maintain your calm under the strain of these conditions I have laid out?"

When he put it that way, doubts swarmed. I was not a coward, but neither was I brave. Did I have what it took to spy on my fellow servants? To analyze everyone around me? In truth, I could not say. All I knew was that I could not wait around and do nothing while my newfound home was destroyed. The peace I felt here, the desire to do everything I could to ensure it remained that way, was forefront in my mind. Could I be brave, to protect this safe haven that I had found?

I squared my shoulders, nodding firmly. "Yes, I have what it takes. I can do this."

"Good. Now let's put that memory of yours to good use..."

The next half hour flew by in a haze of instructions and warnings. I would be reporting directly to Creed with any suspicious behaviors, such as shifty actions and words, or obvious lies. I was only—and Creed made sure to emphasize this point—to observe and report back. I was not to engage in conversation with anyone under suspicion, but that he would do the honors in a way that would not make them nervous. I would only be observing, utilizing my sharp memory as a way to store information.

Once he was sure I knew my instructions and he had answered all of my questions, Creed thanked me for my willingness to do more. He extended a hand to me and, without hesitation, I took it. His hand, massive in comparison to mine, was rough with callouses. I thought I could feel some scars on the palm as well; there were several on the knuckles and back of his hand. This man was a fighter, of that I was certain. How had I ever mistaken him for a servant?

"Thank you for giving me a chance to help," I said, shaking his hand, then letting go.

He studied me. "You're welcome," he responded. "Will you promise me something, Naya?"

Nervous at the seriousness in his tone, I twisted the edge of my apron in my hands. "If it is within my power, I will promise it."

He looked me solidly in the eye, then stated, "Promise me that if I tell you to back away from this matter, you will."

I paused. More than any of the cautions he and the others had spoken, this request chilled me. The earnestness in which he held himself as he waited for my answer told me he was deadly serious.

Swallowing as best I could with a suddenly dry throat, I whispered, "I promise."

Conversations flowed around me, a cacophony of sound. Laughter, teasing remarks, excited exclamations, anecdotes and whispers all meshed and mixed together in the dining hall. I let them all filter in through my consciousness. I remained alert, eyes skimming over the faces of those already seated. I watched people conversing, the way they hid smiles, shifted in their seats. Who played with their hair as they flirted, who laughed too loudly. I took note of everything, down to the kind of jewelry people wore—if it was too pricey for servants to own—to the tattoos I saw peeking out of the sleeves of some of the men. My head pounded as I attempted to take everything in. I dreaded the prospect of having to sort through it all later. The last two nights had been long ones as I searched for untruths in between the lines of offhand conversations. It was pulling me apart.

Already I knew exactly what Creed had been talking about, the strain and uneasiness that came with hunting for lies and half-truths. It rested like a vulture on my shoulders, digging its claws into my flesh, a constant reminder that there were enemies lurking somewhere around me and I was trying to root them out. Once I had shifted my mind into that mode, it was truly hard to shut it down. I was constantly analyzing inane conversations, trying to unearth any hidden agendas. It was utterly exhausting.

Sighing, I shut my eyes and massaged my temples. I needed a break, someone to talk with to ease the body-wide tension. Unfortunately, Penny and Betsy were not present, having been assigned to a later lunch rotation for today. Faced with the idea of eating alone again, I could not stand the thought. The past month and a half of sitting with friends had spoiled me. I craved the camaraderie, the sense of belonging that I had been seeking my whole life. I glanced around the room, hoping to find a friendly face.

My eyes ran over Creed, who was in a far corner, and I felt the urge to go and sit by him. I debated all through the line on whether or not I should approach him. We had not spoken since our secret meeting in the empty room days earlier. I had nothing to report to him, but what harm could there be in talking?

I approached Creed, who was busy tucking into his meal.

"May I sit here?" I asked.

He looked up from his plate, an expression of surprise sliding across his features. He opened his mouth to speak, but nothing came out. Another moment passed, then I felt doubt settle in. I began to back away.

"Forget I asked," I murmured. Were we not supposed to interact now that we were monitoring those around us?

"No, no," he said hurriedly. "Sit." He motioned to the empty bench across from him and after I got comfortable, he picked his fork back up. "I apologize. You surprised me. As you can see, there's not a lot of people shoving their way to sit near me."

I had noticed the wide gap around where he sat. It was one of the reasons why I had decided to sit by him. But I was not about to say that to him.

We sat in comfortable silence, eating our separate lunches. After a while, I noticed he had piled all of his carrots in one section of his plate.

"Do you not like carrots?" I asked him.

He glanced down at his plate and shook his head. "I don't. Never have. I never could convince myself to eat something orange."

The answer was so unexpected and odd I found myself laughing. He cracked a small smile.

"Don't mock. Food aversions are no laughing matter."

I pressed my lips together to stop another laugh from escaping. "All right, you make a good point. I promise to not mock any of your food aversions ever again." I raised one hand as if I were swearing an oath.

He bowed his head, all too serious. "I thank you."

A few minutes go by and then he shifts in his seat. "What about you?"

Puzzled, I cock my head to the side. "What about me?"

"Do you have any foods you don't like?" he clarified. "So I can promise not to mock your food aversions."

I think for a moment. "Pickles," I finally threw out. "Pickled anything, really."

"Oh?"

"Yes. Pickled eggs, pickled beets, pickled pig's feet."

Creed pulled a face. "Naya," he complained. "I'm eating here."

I laughed again. "Sorry."

"I'll forgive you, this one time."

"Thank you."

"Nothing pickled for you, then."

"Correct," I said.

"Have you really had to eat pickled pig's feet before?"

I nodded, crinkling my nose at the memory. "It was at my grandfather's sixtieth birthday celebration. My father forced me to eat it and I was sick the rest of the night. I have studiously avoided anything pickled since."

"Was that hard to do?"

"Oh, yes. We Whojians take pickling quite seriously. Everything is pickled back home; it is almost a matter of national pride."

He laughed out loud at that quip. I could not help but notice how the scarring on his right cheek affected his smile, causing a warp that made the whole expression crooked. It was actually quite endearing.

He shook his head. "You're funny."

Taken aback, I blushed and dropped my eyes to my plate. No one had ever told me I was funny before.

We returned to companionable silence. It was nearing the end of the midday meal when I felt the emotions in the room change. It was subtle, nearly nonexistent, but I could sense it. I swiveled my head around, searching for the source of the change. To my dismay, I found myself the focus of nearly a dozen people. Some whipped their gazes away when I made eye contact, while others brazenly kept right on staring. Lucinda and Hattie were among the last group. The twin looks of smug vindictiveness made me queasy.

"Are you seeing what I am seeing?" I whispered to Creed.

"Yes," he replied in an equally soft tone. "The stares are continuing to multiply."

"*Lovely.*"

Just then Betsy and Penny rushed into the room. They seemed to be searching frantically for someone. Penny spotted me, snatched Betsy's arm and thrust her chin in my direction. They hurried over to us.

"There you are!" Betsy whisper-hissed. "We came as soon as we heard."

"I don't believe it. I can't believe it. Horrible, horrible man!" Penny added.

My heart thudded dully. "What did you hear?"

Betsy glanced around, saw several people watching us with rapt attention, and made a rude gesture, telling them to scuttle off. She refocused on me, gripping my hand.

"I have it on good authority that Rasmussen has been whispering things about you."

Creed leaned forward. "What things?"

It spoke of the direness of the situation that Betsy and Penny did not even blink at Creed's presence.

"It's awful!" Penny cried, hands at her mouth.

"Shush!" Betsy scolded. Turning back to me, she lowered her voice. "He has been telling everyone that will listen that you are a loose woman, among other things which I will not repeat."

My face and neck heated with shame. I fought the urge to slide under the table, but to do so would be an admittance of guilt. Instead, I shut my eyes, fighting the wave of sickness that rose inside me. Cruel, disgusting man. He was ruining me, not in actuality, but in reputation. To some, it made no difference. I doubted I could recover from this.

I blinked rapidly, forcing back the tears that wanted to surface. That would also be a sign of guilt to my eager audience. I refused to feed the flames of the gossip-mongers around me. I took in deep breaths until a semblance of calm came over me. I may never recover from this, but I had survived worse. I would keep my head up, be strong. I would never let Rasmussen see the damage he had caused.

I caught a glimpse of a dark look that passed behind Creed's eyes. "Creed," I said lowly. "Just let it go. The people whose opinions I care about know the truth and that is all that matters. Please, just move on."

He threw down his napkin, rising from his seat. "This may not be a physical threat, but make no mistake: this is an attack. An attack on your character, and a cowardly one at that. I can't let it go, Naya."

On that declaration, he marched off. I watched him leave. I knew without a shadow of a doubt that Rasmussen was about to pay for his slanderous comments.

CHAPTER TWENTY
A FEAST OF LIES

Benjamin

I HAD THE morning free, which was a first. A messenger had rapped lightly on my door this morning as I had been dressing for my usual run with Uncle James. He had handed me a slip of paper, which had informed me Uncle James was indisposed and that our run had been canceled. At a loss of what to do, I had debated on sleeping in. Old Benjamin would have jumped on the opportunity. But I found the idea distasteful and had started out on a walk.

On that walk, I had crossed paths with the Lively brothers, who were just returning to the barracks from being on duty. They were congenial, greeting me respectfully. We chatted for a few minutes, and I walked away with an invite to an afternoon training session with the brothers. I had jumped on the idea, needing movement after nearly two months of routine morning exercise. We made plans to meet up in a quarter hour after Clark and Anthony changed.

I quickened my step, en route to the private training room where I had fought my uncle on my first day of mental training.

From down the corridor I heard raised voices, and quickened my stride. I turned the corner in time to see Creed forcefully shove Rasmussen up against the wall, a taut forearm across his throat.

"I had pegged you as a toadstool from the start, but I didn't know you were a spineless newt as well!" Creed growled before thrusting a knee into the outer part of Rasmussen's thigh, causing the man to hiss in pain and shy away from further strikes to come.

"Whoa," I called, hurrying to break them apart. As much as I detested Rasmussen, I didn't particularly want to see him murdered, for that's what it seemed Creed was itching to do.

I yanked on the back of Creed's uniform, pulling him back. "What's going on here?" I asked him.

Creed shook off my grip. Without taking his eyes off of Rasmussen, he spat,

"He's been spreading lies about Naya. I'm putting him in his place."

Rasmussen sneered. "Are you sure they're lies? I'm sure the little light-skirt would be more than willing to prove you wrong." His voice dripped with innuendo.

Rage was hot and immediate. I spun away, doing all I could to draw strength from my mantra. Remarkably, Creed was still standing where I'd left him, fuming.

"Are you going to rip his head off or will I?" I seethed.

"We can take turns," was his response.

He invaded Rasmussen's personal space, going nose to nose with him. Despite his bluster, Rasmussen swallowed convulsively, thoroughly intimidated.

"You are going to retract your falsities forthwith. If you don't, a knee to the thigh will be the least of your concerns. Am I clear?"

Rasmussen attempted to smirk until Creed, with the speed of a viper, gripped his face with a scarred hand, squeezing until the tendons in said hand looked ready to burst forth from the skin.

"Am—I—clear?" he said in a tone so menacing I felt a twinge of nervousness for Rasmussen. "Blink once for yes."

Rasmussen's eyes fluttered. Creed released him and wiped his palm on the front of his jacket, as if touching Rasmussen were repulsive. I didn't blame the man.

"Leave. Now," Creed commanded.

Rasmussen started to reach for his lower face then stopped, clenching his fists. He huffed a few times before retreating. It appeared he was trying to swagger, but his quick stride undermined the act, making it look like he was running away.

Creed and I watched him go, both of us glaring at his back until he was out of sight. Creed then let out a puff of air of his own and turned to face me.

"I don't know whether to thank or curse you for holding me back," he said abruptly. "He deserved a thorough beating."

I crossed my arms. "Would you forgive me if I told you I regret stopping you from delivering that thrashing?"

He thought for a moment. "Perhaps."

"Can I be there to participate in the annihilation if he doesn't follow through?"

"Only if you provide refreshments."

We both chuckled. It died off quickly. I was torn between asking for more details about the lies Rasmussen had told and also not wanting to know. I decided against asking for more information, as I couldn't guarantee I could keep my temper in check.

"Good day," Creed said, starting to walk away.

"Save some derring-do for the rest of us, will you?" I called after him.

He lifted a hand in response, but didn't comment further. I shook my head. I didn't like the man, doubted I could fully trust him, but, in his defense of Naya, I found I could respect him. Just a little bit.

I resumed my trek to the training room.

The following day, after our usual run, Uncle James settled his horse into a slow walk for the return journey and I followed suit.

"Are you ready for the feast tonight?" he asked.

The feast, where I would undertake my first jaunt into clandestine work, where I would actively interact with a suspected traitor, Lord Donovan. My end goal was to befriend the man with the intent to uncover his secrets.

Determined to do my part to unravel the plans of enemies of the state, I knew I had to move forward with the plans, yet I chafed at the subterfuge I would have to enact. Starting a friendship in order to ferret out information went against my personal beliefs. I was no saint, but I prided myself on being frank in my dealings with others.

I pulled myself back to the present and nodded at my uncle. "As ready as I can be. I'm just going to start a conversation, right?"

"With the hope that it'll be enough to further the relationship, yes," Uncle James agreed.

"Any ideas on how I go about that? I figure leading with, 'How goes it? I'm only here talking to you to catch you in the act of treason' is not the best way to begin."

Uncle James didn't laugh as I had hoped he would. Instead, he looked at me seriously. "I sense you have misgivings about this whole arrangement. Are you having second thoughts?"

He was too perceptive by half, blast the man.

"I have always hated duplicity. I feel like the world's biggest hypocrite going into this interaction knowing I'm there to lie and deceive. I don't know how to move past it."

Uncle James sighed wearily. "I'm sorry about all of this—that you're involved," he began.

I interrupted him. "I nosed my way into this, remember?"

He laughed. "Right. How could I forget?" He sobered. "I can send Creed in your place if you truly don't want to go against your personal beliefs."

"No," I said immediately. "Creed has his identity set as a servant. Keep him where he is. I can do this." *I only hope I'm not starting down a slippery slope*, I added silently.

He apologized again, truly looking weighed down by life. Then he seemed to draw himself up, rebuilding his internal sustaining walls around him. He turned the conversation to my ongoing lessons.

"How have things been for you in regard to handling your temper?"

I pondered a moment, then honestly said, "I have seen improvements. Twice I've used the combination of the mental imagery of the storm and breathing exercise with stellar results." I paused. "That's great and all, but it still overpowers me sometimes, Uncle. It can be extremely frustrating. It feels like I'm taking one step forward, then I stumble two steps back."

"So what I'm hearing is you make progress, then you backslide a little. Is that correct?"

"Yes!" I exclaimed. "For example, I stopped myself from telling off a stranger with the breathing exercise last week. But then, this morning, I lashed out at my valet for nicking my ear when he was trimming my hair this morning. The man ended up shaking so badly I had to take over for him; he had to sit down to regain his equilibrium."

"What you're describing, Benjamin, is completely normal," Uncle James said after a short bit of silence. "Think about when you started weapons training. How old were you?"

"Four."

"Were you able to pick up the sword, dagger, what have you, just like that?" he asked, snapping his fingers.

I smiled wryly, remembering my family's stories about my tears and tantrums at the beginning. "Of course not. We can't all be Perry."

He grinned. "Exactly. You weren't perfect with weapons your first week, month or even year. You're still improving. Why did you expect to ace these exercises in only two months?"

I thought carefully over Uncle James's words for the rest of the ride, drawing comfort from his reassurances.

"What do you mean you're not sitting at the head table with us?" Fitzy asked incredulously. "You always sit up there."

I glanced around at the lords and ladies gradually settling in their seats up and down the massive table. I spotted Lord Donovan enter the hall with two young girls on either arm. Both girls shared his coloring and height.

I quickly looked back at Fitzy, gesturing with my head in the direction of Lord Donovan and his daughters. "You know me. Can't pass up an opportunity to flirt."

Fitzy looked dubious. It was a lame lie and lamely delivered. I hurriedly excused myself before he could poke holes into it. Yet another deception for the night. I just hoped Fitzy wouldn't hound me later on.

A few strides from my spot, directly across from Lord Donovan and his family, I saw Perry entering the room, heading for the elevated table where his parents and brother were to dine. I had not expected to see him; he had been due to arrive later in the week. He made eye contact with me and a grin climbed his cheeks. He extended a hand to me as he drew near.

"Benjamin!" He laughed. "It's good to see you. What has it been, four years since I last saw you?"

I gripped his hand in return. "Something like that. You're here early."

He placed his hands on his hips, confidence radiating from him. "Yes, we were able to get away sooner than I expected. Better to be early than late, eh?"

"I would say so. How long will you be home?"

"It depends. Could be two weeks, could be a month. If the situation at the south border escalates, my division will most likely be sent to regain control. Who knows at this point."

I frowned. "The border is still in chaos? I hadn't heard that."

He nodded seriously. "This is quite unusual. There haven't been problems with The People since my father took the throne. It's a shame it's happening now."

I stepped closer, leaning towards him. "I've heard rumors and I can't get a straight answer out of your father. What is going on down there?"

"Raids by The People. Mostly at night, with disastrous results. Homes burnt. Livestock scattered or slaughtered. It's a miracle no one has gotten killed." He scowled. "Yet."

Just then the master of ceremonies announced dinner and asked for everyone to take their seats. Perry slapped my shoulder, bid me farewell, and trotted up to the head table, where he greeted his family and took his place next to Fitzy.

I slid into my chair, but my mind was hundreds of miles away, at the southern border. Once again, I felt dismayed. I had paid enough attention to my tutors to know that The People, the inhabitants of the scorched wastelands that took up a vast swath of land in the south, were utterly uninterested in association with outsiders. They kept themselves to themselves, neither friendly nor hostile to us, their northern neighbors. Why would they now decide to antagonize us? It didn't sit well with me.

I shook off the unease, deciding to turn my thoughts to the best way to begin a conversation with Lord Donovan.

"Excuse me," a musical voice interrupted my deep musings.

I looked across the table into the eyes of the older daughter of Lord Donovan.

She smiled widely. "I do not believe we have yet been introduced. I hope you will forgive me for my forwardness for initiating this. There are so few young people who attend these feasts," she said by way of explanation. She continued, "I'm Constance Donovan, and this is my younger sister, Caroline. My father, Lord Randolph Donovan."

I greeted them, silently thanking Constance for her boldness; I didn't have to think of a way to start a conversation. I chatted with the daughters for a few minutes before I focused on Lord Donovan.

"Lord Donovan, I hear you're a hunter, and a good one at that," I said, taking a sip of watered down wine.

The second course was just being laid out. Lord Donovan waited for the servants to clear his plate before smiling in my direction.

"You heard correctly, young man. Are you a hunting enthusiast?"

I was not, but that did not serve my purpose, so I told my first lie of the night through a smile. "Yes, I am."

The rest of the meal passed amiably, with the topics ranging from hunting to swordsmanship to the raising of effective hunting dogs. I found myself liking the man. He spoke well and treated his daughters with kindness, engaging them in conversation when he and I fell quiet. It made this whole charade even worse.

Towards the end of the night, I asked if he had mounted any of his prized kills.

"Yes, I have. I have a few here within the castle, in my personal rooms. Would you like to come and see them?"

I agreed eagerly, acting the part of an excited new friend and fellow hunter. I allowed my gaze to drift up to the head table, where I found my uncle watching me steadily. I nodded minutely and he mirrored my action. I had fulfilled my duty for the night.

All that was left to do was find something to hang him with.

CHAPTER TWENTY-ONE
INKY GUILT

Naya

"IT WAS A bust," Benjamin declared. "Sure, I spent time in his personal rooms, but there was never an opportunity to search, as he never left me alone to do so."

Creed and King James leaned back in their chairs, frustration and displeasure evident in their expressions. McMannon simply sighed. We were once again in the round room behind the wardrobe. Benjamin, who had succeeded in gaining an invite to Lord Donovan's rooms, had met with the man last evening, three days after the feast.

"Was there anything suspicious in the room or on his person?" Creed asked. "Anything at all?"

Benjamin turned the question over in his mind. "No, not at all," he replied, then paused. "Aside from an interesting tattoo on the inside of his right wrist."

King James perked up. "A tattoo? Was it the Red Fang emblem?" He lifted a paper with the rearing snake on it.

Benjamin appeared a little sheepish. "No, it wasn't. It was a tattoo with celestial bodies: a flaming sun with a crescent moon and stars in the middle. I can't shake the feeling that it might mean something. Especially since I only caught a glimpse of it, and when he saw me looking, he tugged his sleeve down over it, like he wanted to hide it."

The other men pondered it.

"I guess it would be too much to ask for the man to have the emblem of the radical group on his person," Benjamin said to the room in general.

There were mumbles of agreement from the men. I stayed quiet, listening. Though Benjamin and Creed acted as though I were welcome, I got the feeling that the king and his secretary did not know what to do with me. They knew of my mental capabilities, but I could not tell if they did not quite fully believe it or if it was because I was not someone that they found competent. Did I inspire no confidence? Being invisible—unremarkable—in the past had been a godsend.

Now I found it frustrating to no end.

The meeting ended quickly, as no one else had anything to report. Even Creed and I had nothing to bring forward. Not one person had caught either of our attentions in the week and a half since the first meeting. It was maddening, the minimal progress. It felt like I was standing at the bottom of a mountain, trying to stop an avalanche with nothing more than a shovel and a pail.

Soon we were disbanding like we had done before, leaving randomly and in different directions. Creed had slipped out, then McMannon had been next, ten minutes later. Now it was time for me to make my escape. I had just started for the door when someone tapped on my shoulder. I turned, wary. Benjamin stood close by, and he leaned towards me.

"Will you be able to talk with me in an hour in the library? I need your help with something," he whispered.

I frowned but nodded. I was immediately curious. Why did he need my aid? Would I even be able to help?

The next hour passed simultaneously in a flash and as slow as molasses. Penny, luckily, was some distance away from me when Benjamin slid through the shelves nearby, looking over his shoulder as he drew near. He greeted me at a normal volume, and then lowered his voice to the barest of whispers.

"Have you ever seen a tattoo like the one I described in the meeting?" he asked.

He certainly does not beat around the bush, I thought wryly. I searched my mind, coming up empty.

"Can you draw it?" I requested.

He scoffed. "I'm no artist, trust me," he complained. "I couldn't draw a cow even if it ran me over."

His confession had me smiling, the mental image of a cow trampling the king's nephew while he earnestly attempted to sketch the animal a humorous one. The more I thought of it, the more trouble I had trying to not laugh. It was a good thing he was so focused, otherwise we might have started laughing again, like last time.

"Well?" he suddenly demanded.

I blinked, remembering he had asked if I knew of the tattoo. I bit my lip, lifting my hands in surrender. "I have never seen it. If I have not personally seen it, then I cannot remember it. I am sorry."

He scuffed the toe of his boot across the hardwood. "It's all right. It was unlikely anyway. It didn't seem like it at the time, but—" He waved a hand in dismissal. "Oh, well."

I still felt guilty. "I wish I could help."

"You can help, by leading me to the geography section, specifically to where the atlases are."

I lifted an eyebrow at the unexpected request but said nothing, beckoning him to follow me. We weaved a bit through shelves, past armchairs and through an arch to a more private area. I stepped to one side to let Benjamin pass, but he sidled up next to me. I edged away as subtly as I could, not wanting to offend but trying to maintain proper distance.

"Is there any particular reason why you needed this section?" I asked, then mentally scolded myself for being impertinent. I was there to serve, not ask intrusive questions. "I mean, is there anything else you need?"

I felt him turn his eyes on me. "Yes, actually. Would you take me to the atlases containing the mountainous regions to the north west?"

I answered by moving down the aisle, squinting as I mentally whisked through the atlas section. I skimmed my fingers over spines until I found what I was looking for. I pulled it from its home, and hefted it over to a table specifically used for unrolling maps to their full width. I flipped page after page until I found an exquisitely detailed map of the north western mountain range.

"Astounding," he murmured. "Fitzy was not kidding when he said you were a genius."

I felt myself squirm from the praise, and murmured, "Genius? Hardly." It was preposterous, the idea.

"No, truly," he insisted. "You have an amazing mind, Naya."

I shifted from foot to foot, feeling tense and awkward.

"You're supposed to say 'thank you' when someone compliments you," he said off-handedly, studying the map.

"Th-thank you." I turned to leave.

"Wait," he called. "Don't you want to know why I asked you to bring me to this section?"

I hesitated. "Yes," I admitted.

"I want to have a backup plan just in case we lose to these fanatics."

"Oh?" I did not appreciate the reminder that we could very well lose.

"I plan on running off to the mountains and becoming a goat herder."

I chuckled, glad he was not being serious after all. "You are funning me."

"No, I'm not! I would become a hermit, living with goats and hiding in the rugged terrain. I'd probably wear one of those hats made from a raccoon pelt." He struck a pose, pantomiming the outline of a hat with a long tail.

I laughed again. That seemed to encourage him. He jaunted around, walking bow-legged and shuffling as if he had a limp. I covered my mouth with a hand, laughing harder. Soon I moved the hand over my eyes, peeking out through the gaps in my fingers at the outrageous display.

He halted his walk. "You could come with me," he suddenly said.

I pulled my chin back. "What? Live with goats? No, thank you. They are stinky creatures."

"But what if things go bad? What will you do?"

A knot of worry began to entangle itself in my stomach. Every day I tried so hard to keep my mind from lurching down the path of 'what if', that to have someone ask me to actively think about the negative possibilities made me queasy.

"I do not want to think it," I replied honestly.

"Why not? In order to be fully prepared, to strategize, you have to think about things like that."

I shook my head. "I am not like you, Benjamin. I crave peace and it makes me scared to think about what could go wrong."

"If these people succeed in their goals, there will be no room for that sort of mindset."

I glanced over his shoulder and straightened. "Shush. Your cousin is coming. Cease talking about this."

He glanced around, then laughed. "Right. Fitzy is close by. Nice try on changing the subject."

Just then, his smile slipped as footsteps sounded close by and the prince's mutters reached us, Benjamin's mouth worked for a few seconds, then he gripped his head with his hands.

"How?" he cried. "How is that possible? Are you psychic? You can see into the future, can't you?"

Shaking my head, I pointed over his shoulder and he turned. Mimsy the cat slid along the bottom of a shelf, tail bobbing.

"Where there is one, the other is close behind," I said.

Benjamin pivoted back to me. "That was sorely disappointing," he declared.

I shrugged. "It was you who jumped to the conclusion of me being a psychic, not me."

"It would have been so much more amazing had you just gone along with it."

I tapped my chin. "Hmm, I *am* seeing something," I said in a serious tone. "I see, I see...I see myself leaving now." I turned my back, lifting a hand to wave as I walked away.

He laughed and gave me a farewell.

"Isn't this wonderful?" Penny exclaimed, raising her face to the spring sun. She tucked an arm through one of my arms, then reached out to Betsy, who took a bit more convincing to link arms with us.

"It is," Betsy allowed.

Penny looked ready to protest Betsy's neutral tone and answer, so I piped up. "This was a good idea, Penny. I am having fun already."

On Penny's other side, Betsy raised an eyebrow, and I lifted a shoulder in a silent defensive move. She cracked a smile and I returned it.

Today, there was a hiring fair in the city market, and the local hawkers and entertainers were taking full advantage of the fact; if the rumors were correct, there would be storytellers, fire-eaters, acrobats and more. I had even heard of a few games that had been set up. It was fortunate we three were able to have our half day off together *and* on such a fun day too.

Linked together as we were, we emerged from a side street into the crush of people flowing toward the main square. On either side of the road, men and women in need of employment stood holding the tools of their trade; a man clutched a hand saw, showing he was a carpenter. A woman displayed a tape measure and a spool of thread, identifying her as a seamstress. I spotted Mrs. Cox questioning a young girl who held a feather duster, signifying she was looking for a job as a maid. Beyond her, I saw Miss Sue talking to another young woman who held a scrubbing brush, and I remembered Miss Sue saying she needed another scullery maid, since her best one had left to have her baby.

Past the stretch that was specifically for the hiring fair was the main square of Dartmoor. It was a vast open space, teeming with people mingling in the early morning sun. Along the outer perimeter were the hawkers, their voices rising and falling in competition with one another. In the middle were the games and entertainers, which drew the most people. Penny, Betsy, and I remained together, starting at the far right of the square.

Betsy and Penny kept spotting friends of theirs in the crowd and waving. Sometimes they would slip over and chat with various people for a few minutes. When that happened, I was left to wait, often on my own if they both saw people they recognized and wanted to speak to. Several times, I saw people watching me out of the corner of their eyes. No one came to speak with me, and I saw a few people whispering to one another while staring. Their expressions were not overly mean, but there was more curiosity than I would have liked.

Creed had returned to the dining hall to escort Penny and I to the library on that rotten day when Rasmussen had spread his falsehoods. On the way, Creed had informed me that the rumors should die down after his *interaction* with the man, as he called it. While I had been concerned about what he had done and if, like before, it would cause worse things to happen, I had thanked Creed and meant it. It was a novel experience to have someone so serious about defending me. I had not had that since my early childhood, when my older brothers had been my fiercest guardians.

I felt the familiar pang of sadness at the memories of their loving protection, among other treasured recollections of them and the rest of my beloved family. The sadness was not nearly as overwhelming as it had been immediately after their deaths, but I still felt it; I suspected I would always feel it. If only the sickness had not been so thorough. If only we had known to stay clear from the homes of our neighbors who had the illness. If only I had remained well longer, to care for everyone a bit more. Perhaps that would have made the difference, prevented at least one death. But no. There was no use dwelling on the past.

I shook myself from the thoughts as Penny returned to my side, linking her arm through mine once more. I looked around, searching for Betsy. I could not see her anywhere.

"Where is Betsy?" I asked.

Penny waved a hand. "Oh, she said she had promised to meet up with a few friends and made me promise to tell you not to worry like an old mother hen."

I grinned. "Is that so?"

Penny's smile was a little bit wicked. "Among other things."

I laughed. Oh, how I loved this girl, this dear friend. She made my heart happy.

Penny chatted on and on as we continued forward, and I could barely get a word in, which was how it usually was. My role was one of listener and I was content.

Betsy returned sometime later and we decided to go and play some games. We pressed through the thick crowds and got in line for the bean bag toss. As we waited, Betsy and Penny began to assess the young men around us, whispering to each other over various physical features and giggling like little girls. I rolled my eyes, but allowed myself to enter into their conversation.

"Oooh," Penny breathed, gesturing to a young man stepping up to the arm-wrestling competition. "He is quite handsome, don't you think?"

Betsy said something in agreement that I did not hear; I found I could not focus on their chatter. I stared intently at the young man as he clasped the hand of his competitor, but not for the same reason as my friends. My attention caught on the tattoo on his inner right wrist.

A tattoo of a flaming sun, with a sliver of moon and stars in the center. Just as Benjamin had described.

Could it be a coincidence? I wanted it to be so, but something in my gut told me I was wrong.

CHAPTER TWENTY-TWO
NO SUCH THING AS COINCIDENCES

Benjamin

"REMIND ME AGAIN why we're here?" Fitzy grumbled as he swept his gaze over the milling crowds, who watched the royal procession with awe and deference.

"You're here because it's required of you."

"Oh, right."

I could almost feel his lack of excitement for being in the thick crowds. I understood the reasoning for him being here, but why was I? As long as I'd be able to leave the procession and be out among the crowd, I'd be fine.

I tried to engage Fitzy further in conversation, but his responses were terse and his focus was not on me. It was on his brother, Peregrine. The man was waving to the crowds, shaking hands with those who were in the front row. I didn't like the look he wore, a mixture of sadness and defeat.

"If he starts kissing babies, I might throw up," I said to Fitzy in a low voice.

He cracked a smile. I was glad to see it.

Twenty minutes later, the parade was officially over and I managed to snag Fitzy's sleeve and pull him into the crowd. He tried to protest, but I reminded him of being a part the stupid procession, and how he should look at this as a reward for his patience.

For nearly an hour, we moved through the crowd, talking and enjoying the experience. I even managed to convince Fitzy to try a game or two. He was not even remotely successful, but I think he had fun, which was the most important part. The man needed a break from being so focused all the time.

Fitzy nudged my shoulder, then pointed. "I see Naya." He began to move away from me.

I followed where he had gestured and, sure enough, I spotted that familiar face. Upon seeing her, my actions from the last time I was with her came to mind. I cringed, remembering my ridiculous shuffling dance I had done. *You bumbling fool!* I scolded myself. Then another thought was quick to follow, saying, *But I made her laugh. That has to count for something, right?* If only I had the power to erase embarrassing memories from other people's minds. And also my own.

Resigning myself to forever having that less-than-stellar moment hanging over me, I followed Fitzy's path toward her. As I was coming to a halt next to my cousin, Penny and a girl with blonde hair that was nearly white appeared out of the crowd to stand on either side of Naya.

The newcomer looked Fitzy and I over with cool blue eyes. Introductions were made and this new girl, Betsy, looked us over critically. I couldn't tell if her findings were positive or not. Then out of nowhere she smiled brightly at us, her straight teeth shining, and then welcomed us. I couldn't quite make sense of her behavior, but I didn't dwell on it long as I was quickly distracted by Naya tugging on my sleeve to get my attention.

Her gray eyes—I wondered if I had ever noticed before that they were gray—settled somewhere around my chin. She leaned in close and I fought the urge to fidget at her nearness.

"I believe I have seen the tattoo you were talking about a few days ago," she said softly.

The intensity of the crowd around us and her quiet voice made it difficult for me to process her words. My mind took a few extra ticks to catch up. The tattoo.

"You saw Lord Donovan?"

She shook her head. "No, I saw a young man from the stables that had the same tattoo. A flaming sun with a crescent moon and stars in the center, right?"

"Yes," I replied. "Are you sure you saw it?"

"Positive."

I frowned. "What does this mean? The man we are investigating and a random worker have the same tattoo. Could it be a coincidence?"

Naya fingered the edge of her skirt. "I want to say that it is, but I cannot dismiss it so lightly."

Unfortunately, neither could I.

"Show him to me."

She sighed, "I lost him in the crowd when you and Prince Fitzroy came over. I apologize."

"Don't worry about it," I said, glancing around at the swarm of humanity. "We know where he works, if nothing else."

She released a pent-up breath. "Yes, we do. Thank you for your calm."

I tossed her a cocky grin. "You're welcome."

She returned it with a small smile, not meeting my gaze. I felt a bit of frustration as I remembered her people's superstition. How was I going to get around that?

"What are you two whispering about?" Penny asked, making both Naya and I jump at the interruption.

All three of our companions were watching us curiously. Fitzy waited for a response while Betsy's eyes were on me, studying me again. Penny looked a little worried as she glanced between Naya and I.

I fumbled for a response. "I…we were just talking about the weather."

Naya shot me a glance, then nodded. "Yes, the weather," she said, continuing our ruse. "I was just saying that I thought summer might make an early appearance this year. What do you all think?"

Penny and Fitzy seemed to take the explanation in stride, but Betsy seemed unconvinced. She didn't say anything, but I could sense her distrust. She was shrewd, I would give her that.

Fitzy and I remained with the girls for the rest of the day. We waited in lines for the majority of the events, and I was the overall champion of the games of skill. Surprisingly, Naya was the next best. As I watched her flick her wrist to send a little ring flying toward her target, I could tell her aim was true just by the angle of it. I shook my head in awe.

First the tavern songs, now this finesse with carnival games, I thought to myself. *Will she never stop surprising me?*

Sleep, the fickle temptress, evaded me like a hunted pheasant in thick brush. Too much had happened earlier in the day—the hiring fair, Naya and her discovery—and my mind would not settle.

It was in this state of sleeplessness that an idea niggled its way into my brain box. I had just been thinking of Naya and her information about the second man with the tattoo. Like her, I couldn't dismiss the connection between Lord Donovan and this new man. Somehow we had to discover the link.

This determination sparked the thought process. The plan formed quickly, with little coaxing on my part. After that, sleep was never an option.

Not surprisingly, the restless night came back to haunt me on the morning run with Uncle James, but he didn't comment on my lagging pace; he had bruises under his eyes that most likely rivaled mine.

Later that morning, my feet, almost of their own accord, carried me to the library, where I found Naya humming under her breath as she worked. She glanced up in surprise when I stopped beside her.

"Naya, I have an idea and I want you to hear me out."

By the raising of her eyebrows, I knew it was one of my more of my inelegant greetings, but she didn't stop me, which was perfect.

Her eyebrows kept raising the longer I went on, and her eyes went wide. Perhaps it wasn't so perfect after all.

Chapter Twenty-Three
An Impulsive Plan

Naya

"JUST SO WE are clear, you are proposing we use the next feast as cover to send me to search through Lord Donovan's rooms?" I asked.

Benjamin nodded.

I immediately shook my head. "No. No, no, no."

"Yes, it'll be perfect! It'll be easy!"

The young man was perfectly mad. There was no way I would be able to sneak into someone's rooms and search through his things! It was already making my lungs tighten.

"All right, Naya." Benjamin sighed. "All right. Let me give you two scenarios. The first is where I use the feast as cover to sneak into Lord Donovan's rooms to comb through his belongings. You're at the feast, keeping an eye on our target. I made it to his door just fine, but there's a problem." He paused, baiting me.

I did not want to, but I took the bait. "What is the problem?"

"I don't have a key to his door."

Drat. "I can get the master key to you before the feast."

He nodded, acknowledging my solution. "I use the master key you have given me. I search the rooms top to bottom. Whether I find something or not isn't the next problem."

I put my hands on my hips. "You know what I think the problem is? Your negativity. Change your outlook, Benjamin. It cannot be healthy to be so negative."

He smiled. "You may be right, but that isn't the point I'm trying to make. Back to the scenario, the next obstacle is that I'm spotted leaving Donovan's rooms. I'm questioned and the ruse is up."

"Clearly, you need to be a better liar."

He crossed his arms. "Now you're just being stubborn."

I crossed my arms in return, then realized I was being stubborn—and arguing with the king's nephew to boot. I was giving him an attitude, being disrespectful and deliberately trying to be difficult. I clasped my hands in front of me.

"You are correct. I am being stubborn. I apologize. Please continue on and I will be more respectful."

"Moving on," he began again, sounding perplexed. "Now we have the second scenario, one with you in the position of searching his rooms, while I remain at the feast to make sure Donovan stays long enough for you to sneak in and out. You have access to the master key. We won't have any difficulties trying to get the key to me, then returning it to its original spot. You'll blend in with your uniform. If someone catches you, it won't be too hard for you to convince them you belong there."

I let out a defeated sigh. "I guess there is no reason to debate further with such sound logic, is there?"

He made what sounded like a half-hearted apology. I accepted it because that was what was required of me. Benjamin then began to eagerly expand on his plan, and I listened with growing nervousness. I could see his ideas were well thought out, it was just…unexpected. And impulsive.

I felt a little better after I made him promise to run his plan by Creed or his uncle before we did anything about it. At least that would ensure another person heard the idea and would be able to check any risky parts.

I moved to another part of the library and Benjamin followed, whistling lightly. I eyed him. He had finished the purpose for his visit, so why had he chosen to remain? I would never ask him outright, as he could interpret it as me wanting to get rid of him, even though a small part of me did.

"There you are," Penny said as she rounded a bookshelf. "I finished the southern corner, as you requested and—"

Her words cut off as she spotted Benjamin next to me. She half-turned, as if she wanted to run, then spun back. Her hands began, seemingly of their own accord, to fix her hair and smooth down the front of her apron.

"Hello," she greeted, dipping into a curtsy.

Benjamin nodded to her. "Hello, Penny. How are you?"

She beamed. "I'm well, thank you. And you?"

He answered her and they chatted for a little while longer. I kept working, sweeping the floors. As I swept, I turned over the possibility of sneaking into Lord Donovan's chambers and tried not to get lost in fretting over what could go wrong. It was a hard-fought battle.

I could only hope, if I had to sneak in, that I would be able to get in and out with no one noticing.

Oh, how I prayed that was the case.

I got word via Creed the next day that there was another meeting with the king. This time around, Creed led me to the door of a deep linen closet down the hall from the king's personal chambers. After checking to make sure the corridor was clear, Creed motioned me inside. There was a false wall at the back of the closet, and a narrow hall on the other side that connected to the staircase leading to the circular meeting room.

Just before we entered the room, Creed knocked in a particular pattern, then paused before walking in. Creed and I were the last to arrive. Benjamin was slumped in a chair, but straightened when we entered. We nodded to one another.

The king must have been anxious to begin, because he started the meeting before we could even take our seats. He explained that this meeting was to discuss the possibility of searching the suspect's rooms. The king gestured for Benjamin to take over.

Benjamin stood, clasped his arms behind him, and addressed the room as a whole. He finished vocalizing his plan with, "I figure the next feast night would be as good as any to sneak in there, considering Lord Donovan will be in the dining hall with his daughters."

"Who will be the one to search the place?" McMannon asked.

Benjamin nodded in my direction. "Naya will," he responded. "She's got the best excuse should someone question her."

The men began to discuss the plan, and I tuned them out, my mind fixating on the phrase *'should someone question her'*. I did not like how many times Benjamin had brought up the possibility of being nabbed. In my home country, we have a saying that goes, *"Pull on Fate's tail enough and you will meet her."* In other words, do not tempt Fate by trying to predict the future, because it just might come true. No one should try to predict the future; it was only known to Him. But the fact that Benjamin kept repeating the risk of being detained over and over kept me from fully calming down. I could not help it. No matter that those in the southern countries thought of us as superstitious, I had seen it happen enough to be wary.

"Naya."

I startled back to reality. Creed had been the one to say my name. I was the center of attention, and I cringed. How long had they been trying to get me to answer?

"Yes?" I asked, feeling like the biggest fool.

"Are you all right? You're looking rather pale."

I summoned up a false smile. "Of course. What was the question?"

The king cleared his throat. "There was no question. We have concluded the meeting and we became concerned when you hadn't moved."

I felt myself flush. I had missed the rest of the meeting? *Oh no, what must they think of me?* I thought with mortification. I wished it was appropriate to slide under the table and melt into a puddle of embarrassment. Instead of slithering out of my seat, I stood, clenching my skirt in my fists and moved to the side as Benjamin slid my chair back into place. I shuffled out the door after the men, trying to recall if I had heard anything after my worries had taken hold; I could not. *Drat.*

While we were waiting to leave, I moved to Creed's side. I felt more comfortable asking him the details of the rest of the meeting; I had a feeling Benjamin would tease me for my lack of focus.

In response to my question, Creed explained that the king agreed that the plan would move forward in five days. Creed would make sure he would be on serving detail to provide support to Benjamin, whereas I would be left to search the chambers alone. I would have an hour and a half from the beginning of the feast to get in and out undetected, leaving no sign of my being there.

At least I know I will be able to remember where everything goes, I thought in an attempt to reassure myself. I still felt trepidation at the responsibility I had taken on.

Old fears like quagmires threatened to entrap me, fueled by my Nanni Venna's voice that I could never shake. It was an awful thing to never be able to escape her scathing lectures, ingrained as they were in my mind.

I am no longer that little girl. I am enough! I matched my rebuttal to the cadence of my footfalls as I left the king's rooms.

The five days leading up to the next feast rushed by, seeming to sneak up on me like a specter.

I had met with Benjamin and Creed separately, going over the plan again and again with the former and seeking reassurance and advice from the latter. I could imagine their frustration with me as I repeated myself and asked questions in different ways, seeking the same answers.

My shift in the library was drawing to a close when Miss Sue waddled in. Penny, who had been telling me a story, darted away upon sighting the woman, snatching up a feather duster and dusting objects that I had already polished. I refrained from correcting her as Miss Sue came to a stop in front of me.

"I hate to do this to you, dearie," the large woman said by way of greeting, "but I need your assistance in the kitchen tonight. Katarina scalded her hand severely preparing lunch today and cannot work for the next fortnight. I need you to take her place."

I froze, apprehension churning in my gut. *No, no, no*, I thought. *This cannot be happening!* How would I be able to do my duty if I was toiling in the kitchen throughout the meal? I scrambled to think of a way out of it, desperate to escape this work detail. Any other day, I would have submitted with a bit of coaxing, but not today. Today was the worst possible day to have this happen to me.

I blurted out the first excuse I could think of. "Miss Sue, I have had a smarting headache since early this morning. I do not think I can last the rest of the day."

"You have been rather quiet and pale today," Penny chimed in unexpectedly from where she stood. Bless the dear girl!

Miss Sue frowned heavily, compassion warring with regret on her face. "I'm sorry, lass, but there's no one else I can spare. Three of my servers are down with a fever and I have to make do with what I have."

I shut my eyes, rubbing in between my eyebrows in thought. I had to get out of this, I just had to! But how? Penny was already stepping in to cover for the sick servers. Betsy would be there too. I had no other friends to call upon.

"I tell you what," Miss Sue went on. "Help me prepare the potatoes for the later courses and I will let you go. It should only take you about half an hour, an hour tops after your shift here. Do we have a deal?"

I hesitated, debating on whether or not to protest further. She was obviously trying to work with me, believing I was truly unwell. I found myself agreeing.

Sick with fear, I finished in the library and filed into the kitchens with a swarm of other servants. Miss Sue caught sight of me and beckoned me over to a corner. She promised me once more that I could rest after preparing the potatoes for the fifth course and gestured for me to sit on an overturned bucket next to another girl; she appeared to have just started to tend to a large basket of peas that needed shelling.

I stared at the mountain of potatoes that I needed to skin. I felt a real headache begin to form as I contemplated how long this would take me. Would I even have time to search the rooms? I gritted my teeth, picked up the knife from the table near me and sat down. I reached out and snatched up my first potato, using the knife in quick, short movements to remove the rough outer layer.

I soon got into a rhythm, peeling faster and faster. I glanced in the corner at the water clock, and felt my heart sink. I was moving too slowly. Twenty minutes had passed and I knew the feast had started five minutes ago. Tearing my gaze from the clock, I pushed myself to work even faster.

A girl who was tending a pot nearby began to watch me. "Slow down," she warned. "If you aren't careful, you might end up with bits of your fingers shaved off! I doubt the royals would enjoy a side of manflesh."

I ignored her, continuing at my feverish pace. I had to finish and finish soon. My hour and a half time limit was dwindling away like dew under a hot summer sun. I forced myself to not watch the clock, knowing it would only add to my growing nausea and anxiety.

At last, I set the knife down, having gone through the whole mound. I shot to my feet, weaving through the crowd to where Miss Sue paced like a general inspecting her troops.

"Done already?" she asked. "Excellent. Do go and have yourself a lie down, dearie. You look like you're about to faint!"

I nodded, wiping my brow and hurrying from the blazing room. A glance at the clock told me I had barely forty-five minutes to get a broom from the supply closet to help with my cover and hurry to Lord Donovan's chambers to inspect the place before leaving again. I had planned to leave with ten minutes to spare, but I knew that was no longer an option. Deciding I had no choice but to rush upstairs, I abandoned the idea of retrieving the broom, hoping I would not regret it later on.

I paused around the corner from the rooms, breathing deeply. My heart threatened to explode from my chest, its elevated pace encouraging my lungs to heave. I could feel an episode coming. *Not now!* I forced the panic down, focusing instead on Creed's advice: *move like you belong and people won't question it.*

Straightening my shoulders, I moved with purpose into the hallway outside the rooms. I kept it up until I had unlocked the door with trembling hands and slipped inside. I blew out a breath, resting for a fleeting moment with my back against the door. I had made it! I could scarcely afford to take a moment to collect myself, but I felt it crucial for the success of the mission; I had to be able to turn the suite over with a clear mind.

Without warning, someone pounded on the other side and I knew I was found out.

Chapter Twenty-Four
The Heckler

Benjamin

I HOPE NAYA is out of the Lord Donovan's rooms, because I don't know how much longer the man will remain at the feast, I thought to myself. The man had been fidgeting all throughout the meal, glancing alternately at the clock, and then at the door, looking ready to bolt; only politeness seemed to have kept him in his seat. He seemed to be anticipating the moment when dessert was to be brought out, one of the only times where you could exit a feast without raising eyebrows; some hoity-toity busybody years back decided that to keep one's figure, you had to skip offered sweets. Therefore it was relatively normal for the ladies of the nobility—and sometimes their husbands as well—to glide from the room as the servants changed courses.

I mentally reviewed ways of detaining him. I quickly dismissed the idea to start pretending to choke on my steak, as that would be too dramatic. Hurling food across the table wouldn't work either. I guess I'd just have to be boring and talk to the man, try and engage him in conversation. I tried to think of the best way to do so.

"Lord Donovan, where is your lovely wife? I'm surprised she has yet to make her appearance in town this year." The woman who had spoken closely resembled a brightly-colored bird with feathers sticking out of her hair, her clothing, everywhere. How she managed to eat without swallowing plumage was beyond me.

Lord Donovan's smile was feeble. "She is at her mother's estate, visiting her in her dotage."

As Birdy continued to ask questions, I couldn't help but overhear Caroline mutter in a tight aside to her sister, "It doesn't make sense. Mama never visits Nana in the spring. That's when Nana is working on her landscapes. She doesn't like her creative time to be disturbed, and Mama knows that. Not to mention she's never gone this long."

"Hush," Constance whispered. "Not now."

Caroline pouted, but didn't go on.

I paid little attention to any of their further conversation, and instead focused on their father, who looked increasingly distressed. I feared he would flout propriety and leave the feast even before the dessert course.

I opened my mouth to strike up a conversation but yet another person interjected. This time, however, the man directed his comment toward me.

"Say, Lamar, didn't you end up disqualified from your local showcase tournament a few months back?" The man seemed to chortle into his goblet, eyes fixed on mine in ruthless expectation.

The tar pit in my soul, more dormant every day, bubbled. I felt my nostrils flare. I deliberately reached forward and took a sip of my water, breathing in slowly. *Smell the rainstorm, blow it away. Smell the rainstorm. Blow it away.*

"You are correct," I replied with forced calm, staring down my attacker. "The judges disqualified me."

His sneer of triumph faded at my even response. So that's what he was trying to do, stir me up into a fit of rage. *Just what I need, in the midst of turmoil brewing in the kingdom.* Well, this crumb was in for a letdown; there was nothing I enjoyed more than proving someone wrong. If he wanted me to explode here in a public place, to make myself a laughingstock, then he would be greatly disappointed. I would follow in my uncle's footsteps, be unmovable, no matter how much this heckler antagonized me.

He tried again. "Weren't you sent here because your father deemed you—how did he put it—a reckless hothead? Unfit for service to king and crown?"

Oh, yah, yah, yah, you muckety-muck, I mocked silently, refusing to give in no matter how much my reckless, hotheaded side—his words, not mine—hollered for me to unleash the beast he so feared. To lash out at hearing my father's words repeated again.

Creed, who was refilling Birdy's goblet, made a good show of not listening when he clearly was.

A few more seconds passed as I breathed deeply, eyes piercing my opponent, not so much as letting an eyebrow twitch. I would show him how mistaken he was.

"What do you have to say to that, *boy*?" the man prodded.

His emphasis on the last word stirred the tar, agitating it. I would have to pound a sandbag for a good long while after this to vent the frustration and anger that was welling within me.

I bit into a roll, chewing thoughtfully, the image of a rainstorm fixed in my mind. I could do this. I would come out victorious.

"I must say—" my hook-nosed foe began, but Lord Donovan cut him off.

"Good heavens, man, do shut up. Quit trying to provoke the young man; obviously it isn't working. Let him eat his meal in peace. That's all anyone ever deserves: to be left alone." He seemed to say this last part to himself.

When my critic drew breath to argue, Lord Donovan cried over top of him, "No, leave him alone! Clearly he's a better man than you, Evans, and if you keep running your mouth, you'll just end up making it more obvious. The past is the past. Let it go."

By now, most of the hall had gone silent; even my extended family at the head of the room focused on this stretch of the table. Lord Donovan appeared to go to great lengths to return to his meal. Entirely trounced, Evans retreated moodily into his wine glass.

As for me, I struggled to maintain order of my swirling thoughts, watching Lord Donovan. I didn't know how to react. My own father had tossed me to the wolves and yet a near stranger hadn't. Did I deserve his support? His defense of me further fueled the guilt that had been taking root inside me. Lord Donovan was a good man, and quite possibly a traitor as well. How could those two things coincide?

I was jerked from my swirling guilt when movement caught my eye. Lord Donovan was making his way up to the head table. He was making his excuses, bowing out of the remainder of the evening. *Boil and blast.* I wiped my mouth with my napkin, gulped down the rest of my water and thrust my chair back from the table. Waving Creed off as he moved to intercept our mark, I exited the dining hall at the closest door, paralleling Donovan as he too left the room. He was making his way to his chambers. I couldn't let him go. There was still nearly half an hour left for the time allotted for Naya to search the place. I had to buy her more time in case she was still in the quarters.

I jogged after him, catching up to him shortly. I called out to him, asking him to wait. Luckily, he did pause.

"I just wanted to thank you for your defense of me back there," I said once we were face to face.

He smiled tightly. "Of course. Now, if you'll excuse me, I'm rather tired and my bed is calling my name." He turned to leave once more.

I gritted my teeth. An idea sprang to mind and I clenched my fists. "Wait."

He halted again, only half-turned away from me.

"Can we talk in the library? I need to tell you the whole story of why I was sent here. Then you can retract your statement if you like."

He hesitated, debating internally. Then he sighed. He motioned for me to lead the way. I went in the opposite direction, mentally hoping Naya was long gone.

CHAPTER TWENTY-FIVE

FOUND OUT

Naya

"I KNOW YOU'RE in there. You might as well come out."

Faintness threatened to overwhelm me; bile rose in my throat, and dread pooled like rainwater in divots in a cobblestone street.

Shakily, I opened the door. An armored-clad chest, broad and tall, blocked most of the doorway. I flicked my eyes up and quickly scanned the face. Instantly his name flooded my mind: *Gregor Leander.* The leader of the men that escorted Benjamin here, who had taken up residence in the castle with the intent of taking his charge back home at the end of the year.

Random facts that the other servants spoke of about the imposing man filtered through my mind: mottled eyes, one half gray and half brown, split down the middle, and the other clear blue, that skewered you to your core. A Yukandian heritage that made the Lewyns he served with naturally dislike him. The man had a no-nonsense attitude and a strict work ethic, which also did no favors for him getting along with his fellow guardsmen.

"Are you a sneak thief? You had better answer me, young lady, and answer me truthfully. I will know if you lie."

I blinked, heart hammering. What was I to do? I was not a sneak thief, but neither did I have entirely altruistic intentions being in here. To tell the truth would be to expose a plot to a stranger, but to lie would be tantamount to chipping away at my own soul.

"I am not a sneak thief, sir," I whispered, then cleared my throat and went on, "Please, you have to believe me."

He crossed his arms over that wide chest. "I don't have to do anything. What are you doing in Lord Donovan's quarters?"

Again, I refrained from answering right away. How was I going to explain myself? *Could* I even tell him anything? I was on a secret mission, one that only a handful of other people knew about. A matter of national security. *Oh stars, what am I going to do?* My poor heart; it had been thundering beyond full speed for what seemed like an eternity. I clasped a hand over the distressed organ, thinking desperately. I did not know what else to do, so I decided to wade in without scrutinizing the riverbed.

"Do you love your country?" I asked suddenly.

Silence. "I do," he answered slowly.

"Are you loyal to the throne? To your king?"

He seemed to draw himself up. "There isn't anything I wouldn't do for him. I would give my very life for him if I needed to." His voice rang with conviction.

That was good enough for me.

"I am searching Lord Donovan's chambers to try to find evidence of treason. I only have scant time left to do so. Will you help me?"

I waited with bated breath. Would he help me? Or would he declare me a lunatic? I sounded like I was howling mad, speaking the whole of it out loud.

"For some reason, I believe you," he said firmly. "What can I do?"

"Keep watch and alert me if you see someone coming, please."

He motioned for me to close the door, explaining he would knock in a specific rhythm should he spot anyone.

I shut the door with a soft click. I spun to face the room, which was as dim as a cave, then hurried to one corner, searching for a candle. I found one and lit it quickly. I began to carefully sweep the room, checking under things, in crevices and behind objects. I lifted his mattress to see if he had stashed something there; I found nothing and moved on. I finished in the main room, then slipped into the little office off the living space. I picked my way through the drawers. Nothing. I felt frustration brew and hurried to the small bookcase.

I set the candle to the side, then grabbed a book, turned it page down and thumbed through it, waiting to see if anything would tumble out from between its pages. Nothing slid free, and I put it back. Five books later, I found what Lord Donovan did not want to come to light. A parchment fell to the floor and I hastily put the book on the table next to the candle, plucking the paper off the ground, turning it toward the light.

A detailed map of Mendlewyn, as well as writing, filled the page. *This is it!* I thought with triumph. I skimmed the page, committing every detail to memory. As the content soaked into my mind, my stomach began to knot. Written on the page was an outline of plans to start a war with The People to the south, and the raids that were on the lips of everyone in the castle were the catalyst to upheaval. Soon, the raids would be on the unsuspecting People, rather than Lewyns.

This was it. I held in my hands the evidence of Lord Donovan's guilt.

CHAPTER TWENTY-SIX

CONFESSION

Benjamin

"I'M GIVING UP a soft, warm, lovely bed right now, remember?" Lord Donovan prodded.

I smiled weakly. "Sorry. Just gathering my thoughts."

It had been several minutes since we had settled in the library. I stared into the fire I had started, watching the flames dance. Without looking at the man opposite me, I began my unpleasant tale.

The day of the yearly exhibition tournament, where young men turning eighteen and looking to join the army had the chance to prove their worth, was cold and rainy. The young men's skills would be put on display for the top generals and captains to see the talent pool and make their selections in advance.

We were nearly at the end of the event when my best friend, who had just been thoroughly bested, lumbered over to me.

"He's cheating, I tell you," Lewis hissed into my ear, cradling his elbow close to his chest.

"Unbelievable," I growled. "How?"

He explained how his last opponent strategically positioned himself to block his actions from the judges. Then he removed a slender, carved piece of wood from his belt and hid it in his fist. The weapon—blunted at one end to not pierce the skin—could still do damage when wielded expertly. When Lewis had swung his sword overhead, the boy had dodged to one side, and jammed the weapon into the gap in his armor, between the forearm and upper arm, and hit the nerve on the back of his elbow. Lewis's forearm had gone numb from the elbow to fingertips, causing him to drop his sword and for the boy to defeat him, moving the cheater up in the competition.

I seethed as I watched the same boy do it over and over again, moving so he hid his underhanded actions, immobilizing his opponent's sword arm.

He was getting away with it! The other boys who he had fought weren't saying anything and the smug little cretin was getting altogether too confident.

That decided it for me. I would take great pleasure in knocking him off of his self-constructed pedestal.

"I know that expression. What are you going to do, Benjamin?" Lewis had asked.

"I'm going to make him wish he'd never picked up a sword."

"I don't like that look in your eyes. Perhaps you should just tell your Pa."

"Where's the enjoyment in that?"

Lewis truly did look nervous. He shook his head as we walked to the next match.

My heart picked up pace and I smirked, excited to be the dealer of well-deserved comeuppance.

"Then what happened?"

Lord Donovan's voice startled me from my pondering. How long had I been lost in my turbulent memories?

"I fought the boy for the championship. When he tried to attack my sword arm like the others, I...I broke his wrist. And his jaw. The judges had to pull me off of him."

Lord Donovan breathed out a soft exclamation and I winced.

Up until the last week or so, I had always looked back on the events of that day with a profound sense that I had done the right thing. Now, nearly two and a half months into the deal I had made with my uncle, I knew that I hadn't been in the right. As much as it pained me to admit it, my father had been right that day.

"Continue with the story, please."

I emptied my lungs. "After they pulled me off of him, I crowed for all to hear that this was what happened to cheaters. I explained what he had been doing. Lewis backed me up. My father, who had been silent up until this point, had emerged from the crowd and sidled up to the judges. They talked quietly, then disqualified the cheater. And then they disqualified me. I was so mad. I ranted and raved about the injustice of it all. I cursed the judges to Holda, threatened them, even.

"My father had dragged me into our carriage, where he threw the entire contents of a flask in my face. It only made me madder. But then he yelled at me to shut up. He went on, after I had quieted, to tell me I was a disgrace to the Lamar family name, that I was a petulant child in need of reprimanding. He also told me he made the judges disqualify me. They were going to let me win, but donate my cash prize as a warning for my aggressive behavior. My father made them disqualify me. He told me if I couldn't be honorable in my actions, then I didn't deserve to have the honor of winning. He then told me he was done dealing with me. He didn't want to see my face for a long time. And he didn't, in the three weeks that it took for his letter to reach Dartmoor and then return, for me to pack up my life."

"Goodness. Did he see you off?"

I slowly shook my head. "No. He had left to oversee training in the west a few days before I departed."

Donovan absorbed all of what I said and I awaited his condemnation. Nearly all who had heard of my actions that day shamed me. Only my mother and Mary hadn't. But I could see how disappointed they had been, though they tried to hide it.

"I imagine that was difficult for you, having your father treat you like excrement; I can't imagine what that was like. I personally cannot fathom being so abrupt with one of my girls, nor denying them my presence for weeks, months now."

I gaped at him. He wasn't going to condemn me? I sank further into my chair, wishing I could sink away from my deception.

"That's a first. No one has been understanding of this whole debacle."

"I can see from the way you told your tale that you don't revel in it. Do you regret your actions?"

"Yes. I should have listened to my friend and told my father instead of taking it into my own hands."

"Then I say you have had enough punishment. You are learning from this. There's no sense in holding you against the fire anymore."

I swallowed. "Thank you."

My guilt churned thickly. Here he was, being kind rather than judgmental and cruel, while I distracted him so my friend could find evidence of treason. What kind of man was I?

"Well, I had better get going. Thank you for telling me your story."

I rose with him, shaking his hand. "Thank you for listening."

I watched the man leave. Now it was truly out of my hands. *Naya, I hope you're long gone.*

CHAPTER TWENTY-SEVEN

CONSEQUENCES

Naya

I WAS STILL in the little office, continuing to comb through Lord Donovan's belongings, when a rapid pattern of knocks burst through my concentration. That was Gregor's signal; someone was on their way here! I gulped, shoved the book I was searching through back onto the shelves, and snuffed the candle.

Panic surged. Through the fright, I mentally scrambled, reviewing the memories of the room as I had walked through it. If Gregor was signaling that someone—and it was highly likely it was Lord Donovan himself—was coming, then I could not leave the way I had come. I knew for a fact that there were no hidden passages leading to this wing, for servants to move unseen. That left the balcony.

Frantically, I ran from the office, dodging furniture in the half-dark, and reached the balcony. As I softly closed the door behind me, I thought I could hear the front door to the suite swish open. *Great goblins, now I am really stuck.* I was trapped on the balcony, four stories up. I resisted the urge to pace or vomit. What was I to do? Could I wait until he fell asleep? No, that left too much of a risk. I flicked my eyes around the balcony, searching both my surroundings and my mind for a solution. I could not stay here long term.

An idea sparked as I looked across to the balcony of the chambers next door. I could possibly… *No. Could I do it?* On feather feet, I crossed the balcony I was on, reaching the edge. I eyed the gap. It was probably four or five feet across. Could I jump it? Hearing scuffling from the rooms behind me, I decided I would have to.

Boosting myself up onto the ledge that came up to my chest, I teetered for a moment. Naturally, my eyes fell to the drop below me. My vision swam at the sight of the dark cobblestones so far below. I yanked my gaze up to the ledge across from me, refocusing on it. I could do it. I had to do it. I widened my stance, squatted, and swung my arms back and forth, working on drawing from my well of courage; it was frighteningly dry.

Finally, I sprang. Wind rustled my skirts as I cleared the gap—almost. I was just a fraction of an inch short! I was so close that my shin scraped the edge. I flung out my arms and caught myself. The jarring impact radiated through my body, but I ignored it, focusing on pulling myself up and over the ledge. It felt like every muscle in my body was straining at once, but I finally managed it. I wanted to lie there and weep for an hour, but forced myself up.

I tried the handle to the door and it was blessedly unlocked. I briefly thought about what I would have done if I had discovered it locked, then shoved that thought from my mind. I had done it. I slipped through the rooms, alert to any sound coming from within the apartment, and let myself out the front door.

I could finally breathe a few minutes later. Now all I had to do was report to the king.

The late-night meeting with the king and the rest who knew of the plot against the country was going well. That is, until I admitted that I had not gotten away without being seen. It seemed the whole room froze after I had revealed that. My heart, which had gotten a much-needed break from stress, began to pick up speed.

"What happened?" the king demanded.

"I-I was caught right after I got inside Lord Donovan's rooms, sire. He forced me to open the door and explain myself."

"Who was it?" both Benjamin and Creed queried, at the same time the king asked, "What did you tell him?"

Figuring it was best to answer the king's question, I whispered, "I told him the truth, sire."

The room went dead silent. I knew right then that I had made a monumental mistake, and I was about to reap the consequences. My lungs felt hollow, like I could not draw enough breath. Sweat broke out across my palms at the same moment they went cold. Memories assaulted me. I had been on the receiving end of scoldings and punishments countless times in my Nanni Venna's home. I was balancing on the line between eighteen and nineteen, yet with the charged feeling in the room, I was sent back a decade. I felt once more like the lost little girl I was back then.

"What do you mean, you told him the truth?" the king hissed.

In my mind, Nanni Venna, in her beautiful, colorful attire that masked a rotting heart and sharp tongue, was standing before me again, condemning me. As the king went on, his voice in the present twisted and mixed with my first tormentor's from long ago, slamming into me.

"Did you fail to understand the stakes we are operating under? The secrecy?"

Idiot child! I explained this to you already. Can't you do anything right?

"You had better have a very good explanation for this, Miss Gavi."

What do you have to say for yourself? No, don't speak. I've changed my mind.

"Well?"

Are you even listening, child? By all things unholy, you aren't even listening!

"Miss Gavi!" the king's voice rang out, snapping me fully back into the presence. "Are you with us?"

I clasped my hands in front of me to conceal their trembling. I fixed my chin to my chest. Best to talk fast and pray I would be let off with only a scolding, nothing more. Remembered switches across my palms flew through the forefront of my mind, the ache of withheld meals I could almost feel scraping at my insides. My body had nearly a perfect memory of the abuses it had suffered all those years ago.

"I told him the truth, sire. I did not know what else to do. I felt it best, that the truth was the quickest way to get back to my task."

I heard a muted curse, then someone started pacing.

"Who was this man you spilled national secrets to?"

I winced at his reprimanding tone. "Gregor Leander, sire."

The reaction was immediate. "Gregor Leander? He was the one you told?" The king's voice was no longer stern and disapproving; a very real thread of relief enveloped his words.

"Yes, sire." I kept the question from my tone.

"Why didn't you lead with that? I know Gregor. He, Damian, and I were playmates growing up. He's one of the best men I know."

If I could have collapsed from the comfort those words brought me, I would have, but I kept my stiff posture. I answered the rest of the questions of my interaction with Gregor, explaining how he had served as lookout for me while I searched the rooms. That brought us back to the map I had found. The king asked me to replicate the map with the enemy movements, as well as what had been in writing. Immediately, I sat down at the king's desk, dipping quill in ink and copying down what I had seen. I worked quickly, listening to the conversations resume around me, all the while fighting tears.

Now that the danger had passed, I felt the familiar threat of emotions. After every encounter with my Nanni, I had found a corner to curl up in and cry in private. *Not yet*, I told myself. *Finish here, then you can have a good old cry.*

Creed was leaving Castle Dartmoor. My hand froze as that fact registered. I listened carefully as the king ordered him to make haste to the southern border and investigate, then forced myself to continue on my task. I listened as Creed explained that he could be gone within the hour. I added the final period as King James expressed his gratitude for Creed's loyalty and wished him luck on his travels. I heard a door shut and wished I had been able to say goodbye to my friend.

The cold of the stones in the hallway soaked through my thin skirts. Sitting on the floor outside the room I shared with Penny and Betsy, I pulled my knees closer to my chest, wiping tears from my cheeks on the sleeve of my dress. The worst of the emotions had come and gone. I could probably pick myself up off the ground and enter my room, but I lacked the energy. I had not cried that hard in such a long time and so had not thought of the weakness that accompanied a bout of tears. I would eventually make my way inside, but not now.

"Why are you sitting on the floor, Naya?" Betsy asked from down the hall a ways.

I jumped, jerking my head in the direction of her voice. How had I not heard her approach? I had not thought my mind had been so far adrift, but apparently so. Then I squinted up at her, wondering where she had been coming from at this hour. I had not seen a clock recently, but I assumed by the growing exhaustion in my mind and limbs that it was sometime long after midnight.

"Where are you coming from?" I asked in a whisper.

She came closer in the rippling light from the hanging lanterns, unclasping her cloak and draping it over her arm. "I was out with friends and lost track of time. What are *you* doing up? And out here?" She got within armslength and her brow furrowed as she looked at me. "Have you been crying? What happened?"

I tried to smile. "What question do you want me to answer first?"

She thought for a second or two. "Why you're out here and not in bed."

"I did not want to disturb you and Penny's rest—or just Penny's, in this case. I thought you had retired long ago."

"Ah," she said with understanding. She moved to my side, swept her cloak from her arm and onto the floor beside me and sat down. She patted the spot next to her and I scooted onto it until our shoulders nearly touched. "Now, tell me what happened."

I took in a deep breath. "I got in trouble. The king yelled at me."

Her eyebrows shot up. "The king? Why?"

I lowered my eyes. "I do not want to say just yet. It is so fresh." *And I already mucked it up by telling one person. I am not making that mistake again!*

"I understand perfectly. You don't have to explain if you're not ready."

We sat shoulder to shoulder for a few minutes without speaking, then she unexpectedly started talking. "The housekeeper at one of my old jobs punished me once because of the way I prepared my lord's tea."

"Why?"

She smirked. "It may be because I put curdled milk in it instead of fresh milk."

I gasped, then could not keep back laughter. "Betsy!" I exclaimed. "You did not!"

"I did too and he deserved it!"

We spent the next hour laughing and talking outside our room until we both could barely keep our eyes open. We stood, preparing to go to bed. Betsy paused with her hand on the doorknob and looked back at me.

"I'm glad Mrs. Cox placed you in my room two years ago, Naya. I'm sorry I haven't told you before."

I beamed. "I forgive you. You are the best roommate I have ever had, after all."

She smiled in return and led the way into the dark room, where Penny breathed deeply in her corner. We got ready for bed in quiet unison, and peace enfolded my battered heart. So much had happened in a day, and I was able to fall asleep faster than I thought, and sleep deeply too. I knew at least one person in this castle thought well of me and was firmly in my corner. It rounded out a miserable day and eased my soul.

CHAPTER TWENTY-EIGHT
MENACE AT THE BORDER

Creed

COVERED HEAD TO toe in dust from the military convoy, I reined in my mount at the ridgeline overlooking the vast expanse of land beyond. About a mile distant was Fort Winthrop, the garrison that straddled the border between Mendlewyn and the desert wasteland that The People called home. The lush spring green petered out some twenty miles in the distance, the vibrant color slowly replaced by dull browns and grays as sagebrush and spindly bushes replaced grasslands; toward the heart of the desert there were rolling sand dunes.

Murmurs of relief from the men around me met my ears and I could sympathize with them to an extent. It was a rushed journey from the capital to the southern border, six days of rough riding and bivouacking. The fort represented rest and a chance to have more than a meal of cold rations for the weary soldiers.

To me, however, the fort held no promise of ease or comfort. I would be unearthing information of the most perilous kind, trying to discover who was behind the attempts to begin a war with our southern neighbors.

I had departed the same night as the meeting where Naya had revealed the information describing the villainous intentions. I narrowed my eyes, trying to bring the map she had drawn to the forefront of my mind. I remembered the pertinent information, but not like Naya. She had drawn the map in stunning detail and all the words that had been on it. I knew without a shadow of a doubt that it had been word for word. If only I had been able to bring her with me; her mind would be an invaluable asset for a mission like this one, but I doubted King James would have sanctioned it, especially after her breaking trust and revealing classified information to an outsider.

Bringing her with me had not been an option, but it would have been the best for her. Rasmussen had been absent for weeks, steering clear of the girl who had thwarted him. But I doubted it was out of a true sense of remorse or the man turning over a new leaf. No, I feared he was biding his time, waiting for the perfect moment to strike. I could only hope that Benjamin was true to his word of being willing and able to take over my place of keeping an eye on her and watching her back.

Shaking off the concerns at home pulling at my thoughts, I nudged my horse into a trot. It was time to get to the bottom of this.

"This is fortuitous timing, your arrival," the captain of the fort, Giles Jepson, stated as he greeted me in his office an hour later.

His aide had found me the moment I had ridden through the gates; I hadn't even dismounted before the man pounced. I had taken a moment to change into a fresh set of clothes and to run wet fingers through my hair. As I had expected, there would be no relaxation for me.

"I'm glad to be of service, captain," I responded evenly. "What can you tell me of these raids?" That said raids were a part of a grander scheme was information I would be keeping to myself for the time being.

The captain described how men in long robes would steal over the border on moonless nights, laying waste to all before them. Innocent families had found themselves displaced as their homes, animals and livelihoods had been stripped from them. He reported how these nocturnal raiders had gradually become bolder in the past weeks, striking on nights where the moon shone high in the sky, then escaping just as quickly as they had arrived.

"And there's more," Captain Jepson said. "We finally caught one."

I shot to my feet. "Where is he? I need to question him immediately."

Captain Jepson rose, circling his desk to lead me out of his office. "He is in our holding room. It's odd…" he trailed off as he led me down the hall.

"What's odd, Captain?"

He paused, facing me again. "The man…He's not one of The People. He's one of ours. He's Lewyn."

Just as I expected, I thought darkly. I nodded to the man, gesturing him to lead on. He opened the last door on the right and allowed me to enter first. Sitting on one side of a table was a wiry young man on the cusp of adulthood; the lad barely had whiskers. He wore a long robe in the style of The People, its hood draped back over his shoulders. His bound hands rested on the tabletop and he stared resolutely at the opposite wall. He didn't flinch as the captain slammed the door behind him.

"He's been totally silent since we captured him. Haven't even gotten his name."

"I'll do my best to get him to talk, Captain."

Approaching the table, I slid the chair to the side, placed my hands on the table and leaned forward. I remained quiet for several minutes, simply staring at my target. He remained impassive, but I saw a hint of sweat form on his brow. Then, without warning, I lunged forward, grasping his bound hands. The boy yelped in surprise as I yanked up his right sleeve, revealing a tattoo that matched Benjamin's description of the one on Lord Donovan's own wrist. I let him go with a shove, then turned to Captain Jepson.

"Now I know everything," I declared. "We're done here."

I left without another word. Captain Jepson exited right behind me, a look of confused shock on his weathered face.

"What is going on? What do you mean you know everything?"

I folded my arms. "I don't actually know everything. He doesn't need to know that, though. I said that to throw him off. We wait a few more minutes and then we go back in. We do this for as long as it takes for him to break."

Captain Jepson looked mildly impressed. Little did he know that I had gleaned a lot of information from that one move. Information that linked Lord Donovan directly to the mischief in the capital.

Dawn was breaking and I lay awake, flat on my back in my tent. I hadn't slept a wink, thinking over the interrogations from last night. I had gone in and out of the room that held the young captive all afternoon, barging in, asking a question, then leaving before he could answer. Other times I would quietly come in, sit down and whistle a tune or eat an apple. Often I would come in, stare at him again, then leave shortly after. Anything I could think of to upend the boy, get in his mind.

All I had learned so far was his name. John. A name that everyone and his mule had, one of the most common names in the kingdom. I felt sure that he was close to spilling all his secrets. I wouldn't be surprised if the next time I went at him was the time he broke.

I sat up, throwing off my blanket. Now would be the perfect time for my next entrance. John, weary from sleeping upright all night, would be pliable before I even began to question him. I dressed quickly, snatching an apple from my pack on my way out of the tent. I set my feet on the path to the main building in the fort.

Pausing outside the interrogation room, I fixed my face in a scowl, knowing my scar wreaked havoc on my mouth with that particular expression; I would utilize every asset I had at my disposal. I opened the door to the holding room, prepared to do battle. Instead, I bit back a curse, rushing inside.

John was sprawled on the floor, a thin red line encircling his throat, his eyes wide in death, horrified and bloodshot. As I reached the table, I heard the creak of a floor board behind me, alerting me to the fact that I was no longer alone in the room. I attempted to spin back the way I had come, but it was too late; a thin garrote slipped around my neck and I was roughly jerked backwards and down. Blackness began to encroach on my vision.

Panic threatened to overtake me, but I fought through it. As the breath was cut off from my lungs, I lifted a leg and kicked away from the wall, shoving myself backwards into my attacker. Using the momentum, I thrust my head backwards; the back of my head smashed into his face and I heard a muffled grunt of pain. Next I immediately snatched my dirk from its sheath at my side, swung the dagger behind me and made contact with my assailant. This time there was a yell.

My attacker released me, and I dropped to a knee, gasping for breath, throat screaming in pain. I panted for a few seconds, letting my vision, which had been fading to black, clear. Only then did I give chase.

CHAPTER TWENTY-NINE
THE ARREST

Benjamin

"THERE YA GO, chum. Now you look dashing," I murmured, finishing with brushing out Joker's coat. "Sorry I have been absent so often these last few months. Thanks for not holding it against me."

Joker swung his head around, side-eyeing me, the whites of his eyes showing prominently. It almost seemed like he was judging me. I made a face at him and he simply faced forward again. I sighed. You could never win with a horse.

Shaking my head, I unsheathed my knife with one hand and pulled out a shiny apple with the other. As soon as my knife bit into the flesh with a crisp slicing sound, Joker's ears twitched and he began to turn around in his stall. Chuckling, I turned my shoulder to intercept him. He snuffled and bumped me, eager for his favorite snack. I fed him the first slice, ate the second, and kept cutting.

Several minutes later, I gave Joker the last slice of apple, rubbed his nose and then left his stall. Just then, a massive horse bounded through the doors, its sides heaving. The hooded rider dismounted swiftly, tossing the reins at an unsuspecting stable lad and rushed out of the building. I felt a sinking in my stomach. I knew who it was just by the way he moved. Creed was back after only eleven days and I doubted he had good news for us.

Breaking into a jog, I followed on his tail. I knew he was on his way to report to Uncle James and there was no way I was going to miss it. I called out his name as he entered the castle and he slowed to a stop, facing me. I drew closer and then my jaw dropped, my feet halting on their own. A thin, angry red line ringed his throat, harsh and stark.

"What happened to you?" I asked, pointing to his neck.

"Ran into a clothesline at full speed." His voice was raspy and feeble, a painful melody of sound.

Balderdash. "Why do I get the feeling you are shamming me?"

"Perhaps it's because you didn't spend your childhood licking rocks." He began moving again and I matched his pace.

Creed unexpectedly turned left into a small drawing room, one that I vaguely knew was there. Brow furrowed, I followed. He commanded me to keep watch and, as I turned back to scan for unwanted eyes, headed for the back left corner. In the time it took me to confirm that no one was coming and to turn around again, Creed had disappeared. The blasted man had left me tottering with my trousers around my ankles!

I grumbled a curse. Glancing back once more and seeing no one, I hastened to the back corner. I spotted a thin gap in between two panels and when I lifted a hand to reach for it, I could detect the barest hint of air flowing out of the space. *A secret passage!* I felt a surge of boyish thrill. Fitzy and I had always suspected there were tunnels and passageways hidden away in his home, and this was further evidence of the truth; Uncle had his secret room behind his chambers and I knew there were more. Once I could tell Fitzy about all of this, he would be just as excited to know he had been right.

Hurriedly, I pried open the panel, slid inside, and found a rope hanging on the other side. I tugged on it, and the panel snicked shut. Perhaps Creed hadn't left me in the dust after all.

The dim passageway was barely wide enough for a single person to pass through; I had to turn sideways to progress further. I reached a set of wooden stairs that wound up into pitch blackness. I put my weight on the first step, testing it.

"It's sound," Creed whispered from a short distance up the stairwell.

I let out a curse. "Warn a man before speaking, Creed! Blast it all, man."

He grunted and I heard his footfalls as he continued upwards. I followed, listening for squeaks or groans of collapsing steps. I heard no such things. Our ascent was smooth and hushed.

"These stairs are well constructed," I observed aloud. "I wonder who is in charge of their maintenance?"

"McMannon and I. We alternate on the upkeep."

"Just how long have you been working for my uncle?"

"Three years."

That was the end of the conversation, our feet thudding up the stairs filling in the silence. If he objected to my continued presence, he didn't say so.

He suddenly spoke up again. "How have things been here? Has Rasmussen been sniffing around?"

"No, he hasn't. I've only seen him briefly here and there, and it was nowhere near Naya."

"Good," he croaked. "Where is she now? Why aren't you with her?"

I bit my tongue to keep my first, snappish response in check, then said, "She's at lunch. It didn't seem prudent for me to linger in the servants' dining hall. Betsy and Penny are with her too, as are dozens of other witnesses."

He grunted. I waited for more, but apparently he'd used up his allotment of words for me; he probably wanted to save his breath for reporting to my uncle. Remembering the ugly welt across his throat, I couldn't blame the man.

We ended up in an empty room, and from the rumble of voices coming through the open door, I knew we were in the small room off of my uncle's office. Creed and I entered Uncle James's office, where McMannon's eyes widened, as I'm sure mine had done, as he got a good look at Creed. Wordlessly, he ducked out, shutting the door behind us; I assumed he would be keeping people from interrupting.

Uncle James rose to his feet, his movements lethargic, as if he were swimming through a bog. He didn't visibly react to Creed's injury, didn't respond at all to our sudden entrance. He seemed to be moving without being fully aware of his surroundings.

"Creed, you've returned earlier than expected," he began, his voice weary. "What do you have to report?"

"Not much, sire. I arrived at Fort Winthrop five days ago, met with Captain Jepson in his office, and was informed that there was a captive raider. I questioned him for the rest of the day, and only got his name. The next morning, I went to start the process again and found the man dead. When I went into the room, I was attacked from behind, in the same manner as the deceased informant. I managed to wound my assailant before he could render me lifeless, and the man fled." Creed closed his eyes momentarily, swallowing heavily. He coughed twice, then opened his eyes and continued, his voice creaky. "I recovered my breath, gave chase but the man vanished. As did Captain Jepson's aide, the one who took me to the informant in the first place. I do not think it a coincidence. I decided it was the best course to return as quickly as possible, before the man returned to finish the job."

"A wise choice," Uncle James acknowledged. "Did you discover anything else besides the captive's name?"

Creed nodded. "I did." He glanced at me. "I found a tattoo. Inside of his right wrist."

Perking up, I pushed away from the wall that I had been leaning against. "Like Lord Donovan's?"

"Like Lord Donovan's," he agreed.

I felt eagerness build within me. I looked to Uncle James. "We need to get Naya in here. She has seen the tattoo on someone else. She'll be able to draw it for us."

Creed and Uncle James turned to me, faces thoughtful. Uncle James didn't ponder for long; he called for McMannon, who came inside his master's office at once. Uncle James tasked him with sending a messenger to find Naya, and the man exited just as quickly. While we waited, Uncle James, Creed and I discussed the implications of such findings. As Creed pointed out, while he hadn't gotten a confession from the prisoner or a description of Lord Donovan, the tattoo was evidence enough that he was directly tied to schemes outside of the capital.

"In addition to that, we know of at least one other man with a wrist tattoo, the one Naya saw at the hiring fair," I said.

The door opened once more and I swiveled to see Naya gliding inside, eyes lowered, looking extremely tense. Considering Uncle had scolded her up and down the last time she had been in his presence, she had every right to be nervous.

"Naya," Uncle James greeted, his voice gentle. He seemed to remember their last interaction as well and was making an effort to not alarm her. "You have seen a copy of Lord Donovan's tattoo, correct?"

"Yes, sire," she replied.

"Can you make a copy?"

"Yes, your majesty." She moved with purpose in the direction of the desk.

Uncle James handed her a quill and piece of paper, then pulled up a chair for her. She sat and began to sketch. I moved closer to peer over her shoulder, watching as the tattoo in question appeared on the parchment bit by bit. I glanced at Uncle James, nodded my approval, and then watched as she added the final touches.

"That is it exactly. Well done," I praised.

Naya didn't respond, merely remained where she was with her hands now folded primly in her lap.

Creed came to stand by my side, eyes studying the intricate design. He too nodded, agreeing that that was the tattoo. He rotated the paper on the desk to face Uncle James, who also took a minute to scrutinize it. He tapped the paper, then looked up at all of us.

"What are the odds that there are more people that have this?" he mused.

Naya lifted a hand. At Uncle James's urging, she spoke up. "I have seen two more people with that tattoo, sire."

This was news to the rest of us. Naya explained that at supper the night before, she had watched as two men at the table next to hers roll up their sleeves in the warm room. The evidence was right there, on their inner wrists. She went on to give details of the men, their names, approximate ages and elaborate descriptions of them. I believed anyone would be able to pick them out of a crowd after she was through.

Uncle James tugged on his beard. "We have enough to arrest Lord Donovan. Let us prepare to take him."

Plans were in motion less than two hours after the impromptu meeting. Preparation moved quickly, with more couriers arriving and departing with messages at ever increasing rapidity. Two letters went to the kitchen and housekeeping; a dispatch was sent to the barracks and a squadron was deployed.

The squad marched through the castle, the din of armor clanging and boots stamping echoing through the corridors. The guards reached an intersection and half of them wheeled off toward the servants' dining hall, where they would arrest the three known spies and turn up the sleeves of the rest of the gathered servants.

I followed the squadron at a distance, heavy with remorse. I didn't want to watch the moment the guards detained Lord Donovan, but I felt it was my duty, as I had been part of the group to bring him to justice. I clamped my jaw tightly, reminding myself that this was for the greater good. This would save lives, and the kingdom would be safe.

Yes, it was what had to happen.

Perhaps if I repeated those truths enough, I would eventually believe them.

All too soon, we reached Lord Donovan's chambers, and the captain of the squadron banged on the door. A few moments later, Caroline opened the door. Her mouth parted and confusion filled her face.

"Is your father present?" the captain barked.

"What is going on? Why are you all here?" she asked fearfully, eyes panning down the line of armed men. "What do you want with my father?"

The man was all heartless professionalism. "Our business is with your father, not you. Now tell me, where is he?"

"I'm right here," Lord Donovan said, stepping up beside his youngest daughter at the threshold. "What is it that you want, captain?"

"Lord Randolph Donovan," the over-zealous man intoned, "you are hereby under arrest for crimes against the crown of Mendlewyn. Come quietly and this will all be over before you know it."

I could see Constance arrive just as the man finished. She filled up the rest of the doorway; she looked from Caroline, who had begun to weep, to the captain and even to me. I forced myself to not look away. I didn't deserve that bit of cowardice.

"What is the meaning of this?" she demanded, trying hard to hide the warble in her voice behind confidence. "Crimes against the crown? That is the most ludicrous thing I have ever heard! Tell them, Papa. Tell them how—"

She abruptly stopped her rant when she saw the look on her father's face. His countenance was awash in resignation, eyes speaking what his mouth could not. He no longer looked like a man of middling age; he appeared closer to seventy.

"No, Papa, it can't be true!" Constance cried, covering her mouth with her hands. She, along with her sister, rushed into her father's arms.

For a long moment, he held the both of them, arms taut. Then he released them, whispering softly. He turned to the captain, arms out in front of him.

Irons were clamped around his wrists and the guards led him away, leaving behind two grieving daughters, standing in the doorway of a place that was no longer home.

CHAPTER THIRTY

A REASON TO CELEBRATE

Naya

THE GUARDSMAN REACHED out, clutched my hand, and yanked up on my sleeve, stretching out the fabric. He did the same to the other arm, then released me. On he went, checking the person to my right in the same manner. I lowered my shirtsleeves, surreptitiously looking around at the dozens of servants crammed into the dining hall. It was the quietest I had ever heard it been since coming to work here.

Two more men and a woman had been found with the same mark as Lord Donovan and had been locked in manacles, taken away promptly. The guards were almost done. Would there be any others found? I did not know.

I locked gazes first with Penny, then Betsy from across the room. They had been cleared and stood waiting like the rest of us. Penny hugged herself, eyes moving from face to face; Betsy looked only mildly concerned. I tried to convey comfort and support to them at a distance, all the while wondering if Lord Donovan was in custody yet.

The guardsmen left the room without glancing back after they were through searching. As soon as the last of guards had cleared the room, murmurs broke out, rising in tempo and volume. Fear, suspicion, and anger laced the air with tension, spilling over and into my chest. I wanted to be anywhere but here, but there were too many bodies in between me and the door.

Penny found me a few minutes later. She gripped my arm, stepping in close so she could be heard over the clamor of the crowd. "What was that about, do you think?"

Before I could speak, Betsy emerged from the press, joining our group in a huddle. "Are you both all right?"

Penny and I informed her that we were fine. Betsy squeezed both of our shoulders, then shuffled off, promising she would return as soon as she could. Penny stuck close by my side until the room began to empty, then she left me to check on her other friends, telling me she would see me later. I followed the wave out of the dining hall, heading for who knows where. It apparently was an unspoken agreement that after the summons and manhandling, we had the rest of the afternoon to ourselves.

Ahead of me, I saw a familiar face. I lifted a hand to wave at Creed. He nodded at me, staying in one place as I had hoped he would. I felt a burning desire to talk to him after his extended absence. In the king's personal study, I had found it too risky to lift my eyes more than once or twice. When I had quickly looked around, I had seen the aftereffects of his near strangulation and had felt a jolt of fear for my friend. In the frenzy to get everyone in place to arrest our suspect, I had not been able to speak to Creed, to ask about how his mission had gone or to find out how he had gotten that ugly bruise.

"Are you all right?" I asked, eyes settling on his throat, which was free of the line; he must have used some cosmetics to cover it up since I had seen him last.

He flashed me a small smile. "I was about to ask you the same thing. Did Benjamin do a decent job of watching out for you?"

I rolled my eyes, fists on hips. "He practically lived in the library! I could only get rid of him at meal times and when I retired for bed. I cannot complain too much, though; if Rasmussen had made an appearance, I would not have been alone."

He nodded. "Good."

I was not going to let him slip away without an explanation of that mark, and whether or not he was well. "How did you get hurt?"

"Someone tried to strangle me from behind."

I grimaced at the thought. "I grieve that you had to experience that. I am so glad you are all right."

"I find I'm pleased to still be among the living."

"I should let you go. Your throat must pain you a great deal, and you have been speaking for a long while. You should go see the physician."

He waved it off. "I will be fine. I've survived worse."

I raised an eyebrow. "You have survived something worse than nearly being strangled to death?"

He laughed, then winced, his chuckle turning into a cough. "That's just something people say."

I laughed now. "That is a silly thing for people to say."

He motioned with his head for us to keep walking. We fell into step with one another.

I glanced around. "Is it done?" I whispered. "Is Lord Donovan in custody?"

He sighed. "Yes. It is over."

I clasped my hands together over my heart, grinning. "It is over." I skipped a step, joy and relief and giddiness all rolling together as one, washing through my soul. "We should celebrate!"

Creed paused for a beat. "That sounds grand altogether. Where should we go?"

I pondered the question for a few seconds as we changed our course from the way to the servants' wing toward the front of the castle. "Oh, I know! There is this small, family-owned eating house near the business district. It has the best northern cuisine I have found since coming to Mendlewyn. It even has some traditional dishes from my home country."

He narrowed one eye. "Is there pickled food in those dishes?"

Laughing had his teasing tone, I proclaimed with feeling, "Thank goodness, no! Nor do they have any orange food."

Creed blew out an exaggerated breath. "Phew. Now that is a relief. I don't think I could have handled it if there was orange food."

We were about to cross over the threshold when Creed paused. He appeared a little bit nervous as he extended an elbow to me. I watched him with curiosity.

"My mother always taught me to properly escort a lady when walking out with her," he explained.

I smiled softly, taking his arm in mine. "Well, we had best not disappoint your mother. Does she live nearby?"

"No, she and my father, along with my siblings, live in the northwest, near Allentown. Close to the Humese-Mendlewyn border."

We strolled arm-and-arm out of the castle courtyard, meandering our way downtown. We spoke in depth of our families, our hometowns and childhoods. I had scarcely spoken so much in years. In fact, I did most of the talking, as Creed's throat was still raw. Yet he did not make me feel as though I were annoying him with my yammering, and kept the flow of words alive with perceptive comments and thoughtful questions at the perfect moments. Our conversation carried us through our meal and a walk down the waterfront. The stars twinkled bright overhead as we started back to Castle Dartmoor.

For the first time in weeks, I found myself relaxing. Peace settled like a blanket around my heart. We were safe. My safe haven was no longer in danger.

I could breathe freely once more.

CHAPTER THIRTY-ONE
A MILESTONE REACHED

Benjamin

FOUR DAYS AFTER Lord Donovan's incarceration, I entered the antechamber of Uncle James's study. McMannon lifted his head, smiled in greeting and informed me that my uncle would only be a few more minutes. Taking the information in stride, I took a seat by the door to wait.

That morning's run had been the best one in the last several weeks; we had both been well rested and eager to get out of the castle. I imagined I could see more of a bounce in my uncle's step and that the dark circles under his eyes were fading somewhat. With Lord Donovan and his cohorts—a total of eight—in the dungeon below us, we could finally return to a sense of normalcy, get back into the mundane day-to-day grind.

Raised voices began to eek out from behind the closed door. I furrowed my brow, listening as best I could. McMannon turned his head, eyes narrowed as if he too were trying to eavesdrop. The voices grew louder and the door, without warning, wrenched open. To my surprise, Fitzy barreled out, hair askew and full of indignation. He stomped to the door, throwing one last comment over his shoulder. "I'm telling you, you're wrong, Father! Why won't anyone listen to me?"

He slammed the door behind him before anyone could answer his frustrated question.

Full of confusion, I stared at the door for a few ticks before looking at my uncle, who had come out of his office after his youngest son. He rubbed a hand down his face.

"What was that all about?" I asked.

Uncle James shook his head. "Never you mind. Fitzroy had some interesting…theories he had to share with me and he didn't appreciate it when I calmly refuted his claims. But enough about that. Come in, come in."

Uncle James thumped my back with his palm as I passed him, settling in my usual chair. He sat down across from me, leaning his forearms onto the desk.

"Now that this whole debacle is behind us, we can focus on the reason why you came here in the first place. Do you realize what is coming up, Benjamin?"

I nodded. "Yes, Uncle. The three month mark of accepting your challenge."

He grinned, rubbing his hands together. "Exactly," he said triumphantly. "Would you say that you have been making progress?"

I bit back a smile at his enthusiasm. I let him wait a few moments, then said with mock regret, "I have made progress."

"And?" he prompted. "Was this oddball correct about the fact that you could begin to control yourself better?"

Rolling my eyes, I shook my head. "You're impossible, you know that, right?"

"Of course." He waited for my response.

"You were correct." I made it seem like he had wrung that answer out of me.

"Fantastic. Do you believe in my methods enough to remain with me for the rest of the year? To continue learning and growing?"

Did I truly have faith in Uncle's process? I reviewed my stay so far. Overall, the tar pit that had always lodged itself in my core had begun to dissipate; I no longer felt like I was a whisker away from erupting on people. I felt more in control, more whole. I was not cured, by any means, but from the many long talks I'd had with Uncle James, I felt sure that it would be a lifelong struggle to remain at the helm. Yet I didn't feel discouraged. I had my uncle's example to look to. He still had to battle his anger, but it didn't make him any less of a man—of a human being. I could do this with my uncle's guidance.

"I want to stay on. I believe in what you are teaching me."

"I am grateful to hear that. I am also honored. We need to reward you on your three-month milestone. What would you say to inviting your family to come and see the progress you have made in person? Letters can only tell so much."

I found myself eager at the thought. "It would be good to see Mother and Mary again." I pulled my mouth to the side. "Gertie too, I suppose. But only if she brings her children."

We shared a laugh. He reached for a fresh sheet of parchment and dipped a quill into his inkwell. "I'll jot off a quick note inviting them to Dartmoor. That should give them enough time to get here in two weeks." He began to scrawl out a message and, focused on his writing, continued speaking. "Will this invitation include your father?"

Huffing out a harsh breath, I slunk down in my chair. Let him take that as my answer. He didn't, of course.

"I know my brother can be stubborn, Benjamin, and a bit cold—"

"A *bit*?"

"But even he can't deny the progress you have made. Believe me, he will see it for himself. He deals with imbeciles everyday and he still gets them in fighting form. I guarantee that he will see your growth, and be proud of you for it."

Remaining slumped, I mulled over what he had said. I didn't want to see my father, not yet, but I also wanted to show him that I wasn't a screw up, that I could overcome this. That I was worthy of respect. There was only one way to show him.

Resolutely, I looked at Uncle James. "Add my father to that list."

After my meeting with Uncle James, I headed toward the library. It was instinct at this point. While Creed had been traveling to the border and left me in charge of Naya's safety, I had become a regular occupant of that tome-filled room; it only made sense that my feet naturally led me there.

It would also be a good thing to see if Fitzy was there. His mood and energy as he had stormed from his father's offices had been in the back of my mind, making me uneasy. I felt the need to check in on him and figured the best place to look was his favorite haunt. Happily, I knew just who to ask to know if he was somewhere within the labyrinth of shelves.

I quickly spotted Naya as I breached the room. As I drew closer, I discovered she was not alone. Penny worked nearby, chattering away. Creed also appeared from between two shelves. I refrained from scowling—but only just.

The man had thanked me for taking his place in protecting Naya upon returning, then had released me from duty, like I was some toady he could order around. I had taken it like a good soldier, but that didn't mean I liked it. That he was near Naya was no surprise.

"Hello," I said to the group as a whole.

They returned my greeting without slowing in their work; even Creed was toiling away. Why was he still here, dressed as a servant? Lord Donovan and his co-conspirators were no longer free. It made little sense for him to continue on in disguise.

I returned my thoughts to my original purpose. "Has my cousin come through here?"

Naya, Penny, and Creed looked back and forth between one another, shaking their heads.

"I have not seen him," Naya said. "He could have come and gone from a different entrance, though."

"We'll watch for him," Penny promised.

I nodded. "Let him know I've been looking for him."

"Will do." That last one came from Creed. His voice was beginning to lose the raspy edge to it.

I thanked them all, then headed for Fitzy's bed chambers, which were also empty. Cluttered, but empty. The last stop on my list of places to look was his tiny study tucked away at the end of the hallway.

I knocked, then tried the handle. It swung open and I grunted. Fitzy never left his study unlocked. *As if someone would want to steal his books and scribbles,* I thought dryly.

Debating on whether to wait or go about my day, I decided to visit Joker, perhaps go on a ride and return in a few hours. That would give him enough time to get back, surely.

Or so I thought.

After a lengthy ride on my mount, I made my way back up to Fitzy's study and found it just the way I had left it, with no sign of my cousin. I frowned deeply. This was not like Fitzy.

Determined to find him, but clueless as to where I should continue to look, I plopped down in a chair to wait.

My head jerking forward as sleep finally claimed me is what, funnily enough, woke me up. I smacked my lips, shifting in the uncomfortable chair, then decided it wasn't worth it to try and fall back asleep. I stood and stretched, yawning widely.

I shambled over to the window, pulling aside a drape to reveal that full darkness had fallen. I had only intended to sleep for a few minutes, an hour into my vigil. *So much for that.*

Just then, the door swung open and Fitzy rushed inside.

"Oi, where have you been?" I complained. "I was looking everywhere for you!"

"Not now, Benjamin," he replied irritably, urgently. He began to dart around the room, snatching up papers and tucking them under his arms or tossing them to the floor in search of others. His movements bordered on panicked.

"Whoa, calm down. What has you in such a tizzy?"

He whirled on me, vexation written in every inch of his face. "My father has arrested an innocent man and I can prove it."

I knew who he was talking about before he finished his sentence.

"Lord Donovan is innocent," he said heavily.

CHAPTER THIRTY-TWO
WHAT THE DARKNESS HIDES

Naya

SLEEP WOULD NOT come. For the life of me, I could not settle my mind. No matter what I tried—counting backwards from one hundred, deep breathing, putting my pillow at the foot of my cot to confuse my brain box—I just could not fall asleep. Sometimes I spent nights like this, alone with my thoughts.

Giving up for the moment on forcing myself into unconsciousness, I sat up, criss-crossing my legs under me. Looking around the dark room, I could barely make out my roommates' sleeping forms. If it was earlier in the night, for I sensed it was quite late, I might consider waking them to talk until I grew tired. But that would be inconsiderate in the extreme.

A sudden memory of my mother bringing me warmed milk filtered through my mind. I smiled wistfully, remembering her soft hands and love-filled eyes.

I threw aside my blankets, snatching up my wrap and tying it at the waist. I searched in the dark until I found a candle and a flint and steel. Once the candle was lit, I ventured out into the dark corridors, bare feet cooling on the stone floors.

I kept a hand in front of the candle flame, helping to keep it alive as I moved. Between my hand blocking the glow of the candle, and the light itself ruining my night vision whenever I looked at it, it was no wonder that I stepped in a pool of something warm and sticky about halfway to the kitchen.

I let out a soft groan of irritation, moving to the side. I imagined another servant who, like me, could not sleep and had made themselves a midnight snack with warmed milk. I could also imagine them tripping over uneven stones and spilling the drink in the dark. But how hard was it to fetch a rag and clean up after yourself? It was rude to leave a mess for someone else to take care of.

Grumbling a little, I bent down to inspect the substance to see what I was up against. I moved my hand to let the light fully shine and felt my limbs turn to ice.

Blood. I had stepped in a pool of blood.

I began to tremble.

A limp hand was only a few feet away, at the edge of the puddle. It was the body of a guard, and behind him lay two more.

I dropped my candle to stifle a scream.

Benjamin

"So let me make certain I have this correct," I said slowly. "Lord Donovan is innocent and we have got to keep looking for the real culprits—emphasis on the plural there—because you have been reading a book that was written by a long-dead conspirator?"

"It's a journal, but that's beside the point. History has an alarming tendency to repeat itself, Benjamin, and if you're not ahead of it, or even aware of the trends, then you'll be swept up in the chaos."

"Let me guess," I deadpanned. "You're the one with the all-knowing information."

He hissed in anger. "Enough with the jokes! This is serious!"

"Sorry. Do go on."

"No, you aren't going to listen to me. No one is!" He let out an inarticulate yell and kicked at a pile of books.

I lifted my hands in a show of surrender. That he had abused books did more to tell me of his seriousness than his words had. I finally managed to convince him to sit down at his desk and take cleansing breaths. He leaned forward, resting his elbows on his knees, hanging his head.

I let him be for a few moments, settling into the corner beside the door. While I gave him space to calm down, I thought over all that he had told me. Could it be true? Could Lord Donovan be innocent and we were missing a larger underlying scheme? I shuddered to even consider it. But why would Fitzy lie about this?

As I was pondering, the door began to creep open, inching wider. I furrowed my brow, watching. Who would be coming in here at this hour? And without knocking? No servant would ever do that. What was going on?

Just then the tip of a sword appeared from behind the door. My muscles went rigid.

Naya

I ran blindly into a wall and pushed off, ignoring the pain in my hands at the harsh contact. I did not care. I had to get away! I had no way of knowing if I was being chased but all I knew was I had to get to safety, had to tell someone.

I rounded a corner, thinking frantically of where I should be located in the castle. I hoped I was near enough to the manservants' sleeping corridors to be heard.

"Creed!" I screamed. "Creed!"

I caught my breath and cried out again.

From both behind and ahead of me, I heard doors opening, followed by angry men's voices. I ignored them all and kept running.

Light began to shine as someone stepped out with a lit lantern, illuminating the scene. "What is the meaning of this?" the man holding it demanded. "Do you know what time it is?"

I rushed past him and up ahead, I saw Creed explode out of his room, boots on his feet, pulling a shirt down over his torso as he whipped his head back and forth. He caught sight of me, and ran in my direction. I crashed into his chest, clinging to him.

"Naya, what is it? What's wrong?" he asked worriedly. "Is it Rasmussen?"

"No," I gasped. "No, it is worse. So much worse!" I fought back a sob.

"Tell me what happened, Naya."

"There are dead men in the corridor. I did not know what else to do—where to go!"

I felt him stiffen. "Wait here," he commanded, then hurried back to his rooms and ducked inside. Moments later he was back in the hall and coming toward me, buckling on a sword belt; a long knife hung on the opposite side as the sword.

"Lead the way to the bodies," he said. To the man who held the lantern, he said, "I'll be needing that light."

Benjamin

I reacted on instinct.

Shooting to my feet, I drew my sword, and charged at the man just as he came fully into view. His eyes widened as he saw me hurtling at him and he swung his weapon wildly. I ducked under his strike and made a thrust of my own. The man barely had time to deflect.

We exchanged several more ringing blows before I slipped inside his guard and struck him in the chest. He went down, crying out in pain, and I kicked his sword away from him, bending to retrieve his dagger. The man would not be getting back up to fight, but I wasn't taking any chances.

As I was returning to my full height, I detected movement out of the corner of my eye and, on full alert, spun to one side. That automatic response ended up saving my life as another man, sword in hand, swung overhead right through the place where I had been standing; that swing had meant to cut me in half.

My spin brought me around to the man's exposed side and I lunged forward as I had practiced and drilled countless times, vanquishing my opponent in a few moves before he could fully square up with me. I took his extra weapon as well, then backed away, lungs heaving, eyes roving for further danger.

"What just happened?" Fitzy asked, voice at a higher pitch.

I looked over my shoulder at him. He was pale, his eyes bulging.

"I think I just saved our lives," I said in response to his question.

On shaky legs, he came toward me, eyes fixated on the dying men. I returned my focus to them, taking in their appearances more closely. They were Castle Dartmoor guards; their uniforms identified them as such. But their uniforms had defaced Mendlewyn flags on the breastplates and they each wore a black arm band with a bright red snake emblem.

The emblem of the Red Fang Movement.

With a rising wave of dread, I gripped Fitzy's shoulder. "We need to find your parents. Now."

Naya

"We should be running away from the bodies, not toward them!" I whispered to Creed as we hurried through the castle.

"I need to investigate this, then report to the king."

I did not like this. Not one bit.

We soon came to the place where I had dropped my candle, and the pool of blood and the fallen men were just as I remembered. I averted my gaze from the sight, allowing Creed to walk among them.

"These men were struck down with little to no warning," Creed said grimly. "Two of them didn't even have a chance to draw their weapons. This one here only managed to pull his sword halfway out of its sheath before he was set upon."

"What does that mean?" I asked, remaining where I was, unwilling to move closer.

The sound of running footsteps from down the passageway cut off any response Creed could have made. He darted in front of me, sword raised.

A shadowy figure came into view and Creed tensed further. "Identify yourself!"

"Gregor Leander."

I breathed a sigh of relief. An ally. A friend.

Creed lowered his sword. "There are bodies over here. Have you any idea what is going on?"

Gregor approached, slightly out of breath. "Unfortunately, I do. Some kind of insurrection is underway, and the castle is under attack from within. Men from my own division turned on me. I had no choice but to flee for my life."

Creed let out an ugly curse. "This is even worse than I could've imagined."

"If we don't get moving, you won't have to imagine the horrors that await us; you'll be living it."

The men began to move back the way Creed and I had originally come.

My mind refused to comprehend what was going on, flooded as it was with panic. Bile rose in my throat. But I did know one thing: there was no way I was being left behind. I followed after the retreating forms of Creed and Gregor, overwrought prayers tumbling heavenward.

I prayed we would be all right. That we would survive this nightmare.

Oh, how I prayed.

Benjamin

The castle was coming alive. Flickering lanterns began to light up everywhere as people ran to and fro, screaming and hollering. Maids, with their hair down and slippers on their feet, moved in packs, crying hysterically. They made me think of Naya, of her friends, Penny and Betsy. Where were they in this bedlam?

The longer we were in the castle, in the center of the pandemonium, the more things went downhill, it seemed.

Gripping the back of Fitzy's shirt with one hand, my sword with the other, I steered him down the hall. We grew ever closer to my uncle's bedchambers. I kept my ears pricked for any noise that might give away another attacker, my eyes alternating between focusing ahead of us and behind. I wished for allies, for more men to fight beside me. There was only so much I could do on my own.

Anger burned steadily as I heard more screams, growing louder and more frenetic as the minutes passed. I felt so helpless. I had to protect my cousin, find my aunt and uncle and get them to safety, but how I wished to be in the fight, to protect these innocent people.

From up ahead I detected the sounds of heavy fighting, which was not a good sign.

"Fitzy," I said, tugging him behind me. "Whatever you do, stay close to me. We're about to enter the fray."

Just as I had feared, the doors to my aunt and uncle's bedchamber were thrown open. I broke into a run, sword at the ready and jumped into the battle, fighting alongside my uncle and two men who were doing their best to protect him. We were up against half a dozen men, who were slowly gaining as one of the guards who had been assisting my uncle sagged to the ground, gravely injured.

Naya

We were nearly to the exit when Gregor, who was in the lead, suddenly waved at us to back up. He crouched down behind a statue, and Creed and I followed his lead. From up ahead, flashes of light and limbs and bloodied swords whirled across our path; a mass of frenzied humanity. It was their chanting that scared me the most.

"*Death to the king! Death to the king! Death to the king!*"

Gregor and Creed made eye contact, faces tight. I knew without them having to say anything what they felt compelled to do: try and save the king.

"We have to get to the king before that mob does!" Gregor said.

Before either man could move, I lifted a hand, looked both ways and then hissed, "Follow me. I know a quicker way up to the family wing."

I could not believe what I was doing. Was I truly rushing headlong into danger, trying to beat an angry mob to their destination?

Ignoring common sense, I led the men to the servants' staircase, wrenching open the door.

Benjamin

Uncle James finished off the last enemy fighter, and he rotated in a full circle, almost as if he thought the lull too good to be true. He stepped over the bodies of the last of his men, the two that had been helping when Fitzy and I had arrived. He lifted his non-dominant arm to inspect a slash in the bicep, pressing his other hand to it. He met my gaze.

"Thank you, Benjamin. Your help came at just the right moment."

"You're welcome, Uncle."

He looked at Fitzy this time, who had flattened himself against a nearby wall. Somehow he had gotten hold of a fire poker. *Good man*, I approved. That was better than nothing.

Still holding his sword, Uncle James moved in the direction of his son. Fitzy started forward too and embraced his father. They exchanged words that I could not hear, and for once I didn't feel the urge to eavesdrop. Instead, I edged toward the doors, listening intently.

Fitzy's voice pulled my gaze back to them though, as he said worriedly, "Where is Mother?"

"I told her to hide. Ahmelia? You can come out now."

There was no answer, no movement. *Oh no.*

"Ahmelia!"

Just then, I heard the speedy approach of several pairs of feet. I raised my sword, preparing to defend the others. I called a warning just as Gregor of all people rushed inside, one hand raised in a show of peace. I lowered my sword and nodded at him. He waved behind him and Naya entered the room, closely followed by Creed, who walked backwards, gripping his weapon in both hands.

"There are enemies en route here, James," Gregor stated. "They're coming to kill you and Ahmelia."

"They may have already partially succeeded, I'm afraid," Aunt Ahmelia said weakly, stepping out of her dressing room leaning heavily on Fitzy. Her elegant hands, so proficient in coaxing beautiful melodies from harp strings, were coated in blood. Her own blood, from a wound in her lower stomach. My throat clenched at the sight and I had to look away.

I heard rather than saw my uncle run across the room, his cry of despair ripping through the air.

Naya

"Sire...we really do need to go now." Creed sounded solemn.

Arms around his wife, I watched as King James lowered her to the ground, supporting her gently. Then he tugged his son down beside them, holding onto both of them. Tears trickled down his cheeks. I found I could not look away, even with my gaze so close to locking with his. His face looked drained, agonized, as if he were the one with the mortal wound, not her.

"The five of you go. Use the passage behind the wardrobe, and take the stairs to the left; they'll lead you to the bottom of the tower. Then go left. The passage will take you under the courtyard, and deep under the moat. There is a hidden entrance on the other side. That should get you some well-needed distance before you have to run."

"No, Father! You must come with us!" Prince Fitzroy demanded.

"You know as well as I do that they are coming for me, for your mother. For you and Benjamin, all of the royal family. They'll stop at nothing until we're all dead. But their thirst for noble blood will be sated for a moment if they find me...and your mother." At this, he swallowed, eyes on his wife in his arms, already looking more gray and weak. He lifted his chin once more, eyes fierce. "Go, Fitzroy. Live. I love you, my boy. I always have."

"I love you too, Father," Prince Fitzroy whispered, voice hoarse, eyes red. He took his mother's limp hand, kissed her forehead and told her he loved her as well.

She could only mouth the words in return.

My beloved queen was dying, her son and husband helpless bystanders.

My heart broke in two.

Benjamin

I made eye contact with Uncle James, and he nodded firmly. In that simple action, I could see his pride in me, his love and also his plea for me to watch out for his son. I nodded resolutely in return. My chest felt like it would cave in on itself.

From out in the hall, I heard chanting. *"Death to the king! Death to the king! Death to the king!"*

"We have to go now!" I hollered, running and grabbing Fitzy by the back of his collar and rushing to the wardrobe, where Creed had the secret door already open. Naya scrambled through first, followed by Gregor. I shoved Fitzy in before me, pushing him through the gap. I watched over my shoulder as Creed closed the wardrobe doors, then the back of the closet.

It was as dark as pitch, but not for long; a lantern was lit and Gregor led the way down the stairs to the ground floor.

Naya

"We're under the courtyard now," Creed murmured. "Any second now, and we'll be under the moat."

My heart in my throat, I clung to the hem of Creed's shirt. Under the moat? How was that possible? What if the tunnel collapsed and water replaced air? I shuddered.

The atmosphere changed, growing damp. I heard water droplets drumming the ground at a regular tempo. My nostrils became overwhelmed with the smell of mildew and rot; my bare toes squished through wet mud.

Several minutes later, Gregor came to a stop. "We've reached a dead-end. Hold on, I see something. The floor slopes up to a wooden door."

"It will open up about a third of the way down the hill, on a pathway leading to the castle," Creed explained. "Once we leave this tunnel, we'll be exposed. We will have to run straight down the hill between the switchbacks. It'll be much faster than veering back and forth down the path. Try to keep up, everyone. We need to hustle to the forest."

Gregor pointed to the lantern Creed held, whispering that it needed to be left behind or extinguished, as it would give us away. Creed nodded, opened the lantern and blew out the candle. Blackness swallowed us.

"On three, we start running downhill," Gregor said.

I gritted my teeth, preparing myself for flight.

"One."

I bounced on my toes, breathing in and out. I heard the door grind open.

"Two."

Dear God, help me keep my feet and my wits about me! Help us survive!

"Three!"

We plunged into the open night air.

CHAPTER THIRTY-THREE

THE MORNING AFTER

Benjamin

IT WAS MY senses that alerted me to the difference in location. Wind tinged with sap wafted across my face. Birdsong above me, a festive sound. A sharp metallic taste settled on my tongue. Light penetrated my eyelids, brighter than I was used to. My mind was waking up more every tick.

I lifted an eyelid and the sight of sunlight filtering through shifting leaves was the first thing I saw. That was decidedly odd. I slowly sat up, and then tried to open the other eye; it wouldn't open. Confused more than anything, I tentatively touched my left eye and felt around the socket, wiping as much as I dared. Dried, flaky blood came away on my fingertips. This led me to move my hand further up, to my forehead and I hissed in pain when I found the source of it. By feel, I could guess it was a cut about two or three inches long, maybe an inch wide. That would definitely be large enough to produce the amount of blood needed to seal my eye shut. When had I gotten that slice?

All at once, memories of the desperate flight the night before—had it only been last night—surged forward and I felt like I had been punched in the lungs; my heart galloped into full speed, blood pounding in my ears.

Lurching to my feet, I realized I had my sword still clutched in my hand. I gaped numbly at the blood-encrusted weapon. That above anything else told me that everything I was remembering was not fictional. It had been all too real.

I looked in all directions, trying to remember where I was, and how I had gotten there. All I could remember was running, through the city below the castle, through the forest.

I heard the faint trickling of flowing water and stumbled toward the sound. It was a small creek, so small I could probably be over it in one large stride. But its current was fast, not stagnant, and I felt I could trust it.

I knelt beside it, my mouth suddenly feeling even more dry. Setting my sword down beside me, within arm's reach, I lowered myself down to the water and slurped water until I felt like my stomach would burst. Then I dunked my head into the creek, screaming underwater at the excruciating pain that ripped through my forehead. I ripped my head up, sputtering. Coughing a few times, I pushed my sopping hair back and scrubbed my face, being more gentle around the wound.

The hair on the back of my neck stood up. I froze. I didn't know how I knew—some sort of sixth sense—but I felt someone behind me. I snatched up my sword, jumped to my feet in one motion, and spun around, a war cry bursting forth from me.

The person screamed as well and fell to the ground, sobbing instantly.

"Caroline?" I asked, lowering my sword.

She kept weeping, curled up into a ball. I sheathed my sword, cleared my throat and crept forward as if I were approaching a wounded animal.

"It's all right, Caroline. It's me, Benjamin."

"Go away," she cried, her voice muffled.

I sighed. I tried to remember how I dealt with my sister Mary when she was slightly hysterical. *Soft voice...already tried that. Chocolate...fresh out of that.* I drew a blank. Sometimes just leaving Mary alone worked best.

"Caroline, I'm going to be right over here, at the creek."

I returned to the water, intent on simply giving the scared girl some space. As I sat there, looking down at my hands, I began to fully notice how filthy they were. There was grime and dirt under my fingernails, blood deep in the creases of my knuckles. Grimacing, I plunged my hands deep into the water, and began to scrub viciously.

While I cleaned my hands, I began to hear movement behind me. Soon, out of the corner of my eye, I saw Caroline crouch by the creek. I didn't acknowledge her, just let her be. I could feel her watching me, but I kept my focus on my hands. She lowered her hands into the water with her hands cupped and began to drink.

She had only taken a few sips when she suddenly went as still as a tree. I quickly searched the area in front of her, looking for a threat. But then I realized she had heard voices. I put a finger to my lips, motioned for her to stay put, and moved in a crouch toward the sound. I would discover who it was, whether we had to run again. *I swear, if I see even one snake emblem, I'm going to go berserk.*

I reached the top of the hill, slithering onto my belly to peer over. At first, I didn't see anything, but then movement far to my left caught my attention. I tensed, squeezing the hilt of my sword. I waited, holding my breath.

Creed. It was Creed! And I spotted Gregor as well, talking to five other men. The Lively brothers were there, along with three other guardsmen who had found us on the road down to Dartmoor and had fought valiantly beside us.

I sighed in relief. I whispered over my shoulder to Caroline that they were friends, that we had nothing to worry about.

She remained where she was, kneeling by the creek in torn and dirty night-clothes, hair disheveled. I didn't push it, instead letting her know that I would be over the hill.

I made sure to call down to the two men below me, so they knew who was coming toward them.

"Benjamin," Gregor replied. "It is good to see you alive. Is Prince Fitzroy with you?"

I halted. "No, he's not." A thread of unease snaked its way through me.

Gregor and Creed looked concerned. "That's not what I wanted to hear," Gregor murmured.

Creed began to walk away, calling out for my cousin in a voice that wasn't too loud. The former guards spread out as well and joined in the calling.

"Caroline Donovan is over that hill, by the creek," I reported to Gregor. "Are the nine of us the only ones who escaped?"

Gregor shook his head. "I don't believe so. I saw several others reach the treeline at about the same time as us. Whether or not we ended up near each other is the real question."

Before too long, Gregor and I were also calling for Fitzy, trying to not bellow his name. We had Creed and the others return, then we stretched ourselves out, remaining line-of-sight with one another, and we began to walk, softly calling for my cousin as we paced away from the creek.

I wasn't sure how long it was before I heard my name go up in response to the calls. I shot my hand up and waved to get Gregor's attention, and he in turn passed the news down the line. They all hurried to my location, eyes intense with focus. I led them in the direction I had heard Fitzy's voice.

Twenty paces later, I saw my cousin. Upon first glance, he appeared unharmed, but as I drew closer, I saw his hands and jolted in panic at the sight of them stained red. A horrible feeling began to take root in my chest; flashes of Aunt Ahmelia's fragile hands also drenched in life-blood flooded my mind.

"Are you injured?" Gregor asked before I could.

Fitzy shook his head. "This isn't my blood."

I doubted he had taken part in the defense of our group so he must have been trying his hand at doctoring.

Fitzy led us up a small incline, where we found a few others.

Constance Donovan sat huddled at the base of a tree. She, like her sister, wore torn and stained night clothes. I was glad to see her here. She, however, narrowed her eyes at me. I deserved that.

"Your sister is with us," I told her.

Her cool look cracked as relief stole over her features. She stood, poised as though she would run to find her sibling. Then she hesitated, glancing over her shoulder. I followed her gaze and saw one more person I hadn't seen upon first glance: Naya. Alarm pulsed through me as I saw her curled in on herself, eyes shut. Her face tightened in pain. My heart sank as I put things together. The blood on Fitzy's hands. *This can't be happening! Please don't let her be dead!*

Just then, her eyes fluttered open and she turned her head to look at Gregor, Creed, and I.

I let out a sigh of relief. "Thank the saints," I mumbled.

I started toward her, along with Creed and Gregor. Constance lifted a hand as if to ward us off.

"Be careful," she said. "Her feet are badly injured."

"I'm a trained physician," Gregor stated, continuing forward.

I stared at him. A trained physician? What a stroke of good fortune.

Constance was about to caution him further when her eyes fixed on something behind me. She let out a sob and knocked me aside as she ran past. I craned my neck to see her sprinting toward her sister, who must have been silently following behind our group. The girls collided with one another, nearly knocking each other over; they stumbled around a bit before regaining their balance. They began to weep in earnest.

Facing forward once more, I watched as Gregor sank down beside Naya, who was sitting up gingerly. Her face was full of worry, her eyes flitting up to Gregor's face, then away, back and forth like a skittish bird trying to land but too wary of predators to do so. She was also trying to hide how much pain she was in.

As Gregor gently spoke with her, reassuring her, I focused on Fitzy. He was watching Gregor and Naya closely, biting his lower lip.

"Are you all right?" I asked.

He didn't answer for a few moments. "I'm uninjured. You, Creed, and Gregor saw to that."

"Good."

A few ticks passed, then he looked me in the eye. "My parents...do you..." He swallowed thickly, then tried again. "Do you think my parents lived through the night?"

I had to look away from the pleading in his gaze. I clamped down on my own emotions, as well as the tide of nausea. Why did he have to ask me that? Why did I have to be the one to say aloud what we both knew?

He waited for my answer.

"I doubt it. Those men wouldn't have left them alive for very long. You know that."

He nodded, his eyes staring off at nothing. "You're right. Of course you're right. I do know that." He blinked rapidly, then pressed the back of his wrist, the only clean part of his hand, into one eye, then the other. "If that's the case, then Perry must be gone too. Your parents. Your sisters. And your little—"

"No!" I yelled, cutting him off. "Don't you say it!"

I stalked off. Fury and nausea and a soul-deep ache all fought for dominance inside me. I had acknowledged that my father had most likely been taken down along with my aunt and uncle, but I had been resisting the idea of anyone else. Mother. Mary. Gertrude. The thought of them—Gertie even—being gone felt like I had been crushed by a boulder. But I could not stomach—could not fathom—the thought of my nieces and nephew being caught up in the carnage. Little Yuliya. Ada and Albert. Albert, who was almost four months old. An *infant*.

"No, no, no," I muttered, pacing in a tight circle.

The tar pit was roiling and sizzling. I wanted to scream. To lash out and destroy and rage against the inhumanity of it all.

Instead, I fought for control, breathing deeply, the image of a rainstorm so real in my mind I thought it would come into existence.

Clarity came, followed by a hollow sense of calm.

It couldn't have happened. I refused to believe it.

Chapter Thirty-Four

Beginning Anew

Naya

I DREAMED I was walking on hot coals.

At first, I was fine, treading normally. But then the heat and pain began to catch up to me and I tried to outrun them. All at once a howl, so real and terrifying, sounded from somewhere behind me in the ashy atmosphere and I knew that the demon Malmaw was coming. I ran faster. No matter how fast I pumped my legs, I could not outrun the pain and the howls that drew ever closer.

Why, oh, why could I not stride a little faster? Every step began to burn, rip, tear. Nothing could compare to the fate that awaited me if Malmaw overtook me, though.

I pushed myself harder and harder, but my feet began to smoke, then caught fire.

With a cry of fear and pain, I awoke, gasping. I scooted backwards, using hands and feet to push myself away from…from *nothing*. It had been a dream, nothing more.

But the pain in my feet was not a dream. It was quite real, radiating deep into my flesh. I sat there panting for a few minutes, trying to adjust to reality, looking over my shoulder, searching for a half-man, half-bestial figure. I saw nothing, but I dragged three hooked fingers over my chest to cleanse myself of the pall the nightmare cast.

With that fear mellowed somewhat, I could breathe. And with the calming breaths, the pain in my feet pulsed fiercer and fiercer.

I pulled a knee up to my chest, gripped the side of my foot, and twisted it until I could see the flat part, and I sucked in a breath at the sight. My skin was a mass of bruises, cuts and scrapes. The only reason why I could identify them as feet was because they were attached to my lower legs.

The sound of the crunching of dry undergrowth ricocheted around me. Like a deer that has caught a hunter's scent, I froze. *Please, let it be a falling branch or a squirrel*, I pleaded.

A footstep.

I was helpless! I could not move fast enough away, could not run. I shut my eyes in some childish hope that if I could not see whoever was coming, then they could not see me.

"Hello? Is someone there?" came a hushed, decidedly female voice.

I nearly gagged on the relief that surged up from deep inside me. "I am over here." I half-turned as much as I could from my sitting position, watching the approach of none other than Constance Donovan.

She was a sight; her hair was in wild waves, leaves and twigs sprinkled throughout. Her clothes, muddied and torn, were in tatters, her slippers now nearly black from dirt and grime.

At least she has slippers, I thought bitterly, thinking of my lacerated feet.

She paused in her passage, studying me as intently as I did her. I averted my eyes quickly.

"I recognize you. You're a servant in his majesty's castle, right?"

I was, I thought morosely.

Pieces of shattered memories floated across the tapestry of my mind: screams and the taste of ash on my tongue; the streets of Dartmoor flooded with a crush of people; crashing through a shadowy forest.

I blinked a few times, pressing the weight of those memories down. "Yes," I said, answering her question. "I was a servant there."

"I'm Constance Donovan. And you are?"

So polite, so formal, even after so devastating a night. Still, she probably was so discombobulated that all she knew what to do was to fall back on the veneer of politeness she had grown up with.

"Naya Gavi, ma'am," I responded. "I would curtsy but…" I gestured to my feet.

She came around, crouching to inspect my feet. She let out a cry and clapped a hand over her mouth.

"My good heavens," she whispered. "Your poor feet."

"What's wrong with her feet?"

The sudden male timbre coming from our left made us both squeal with fear. Constance tripped backwards over a rock, landing hard on her rump.

Prince Fitzroy stepped out from a cluster of bushes, hands extended. He apologized profusely, helping her to her feet. Then he focused on me.

"Naya, I'm so glad to see you alive but what's this about your feet?"

Once more, I pointed to them, and he too gasped at the ugly sight. No surprise there. But it was a huge surprise when he began to try and help me. He removed a handkerchief from his pocket, grasped the top of my foot, and pressed the cloth into the ball of my foot. I bit down on my lips to prevent a sob escaping.

Constance reached out, took my hand, and squeezed it comfortingly. The unexpected touch and the kindness behind the gesture made tears surface, for another reason entirely.

"Fitzroy!"

We all froze at the faint call. A few moments later, we heard it again. Who was it? Was it friend or foe? What could we do? They sounded close.

I rocked back onto my side, curling in on myself. My hands became sweaty. Discovery was nigh, for better or for worse. If it was enemies closing in, I would rather fade into the background. Or better yet, play possum. I shut my eyes tightly, covering my ears in the process.

Minutes passed in a warped sort of silence. I sensed movement, peeked, and found myself the focus of several people all at once. I glanced from face to face. Gregor was there. Benjamin too. Creed appeared as well. I sat up, watching them all.

There was talk of a physician and Gregor knelt by me, asking permission to look more closely at my injuries. I nodded.

Gregor had me roll over onto my stomach, lift my feet toward him and stay still. He did not speak for several minutes, his cold fingers gently touching different areas.

"No! Don't you say it!" Benjamin bellowed.

I tried to turn my upper body, as much as I could while being flat on the ground, to see what had happened, but Gregor ordered me to remain as I was.

"There are several cuts on both feet that need stitching. Benjamin, you said there was a creek back there, right?"

"Yes." He sounded as though he was barely in control of himself.

To me, he said, "I need to clean your feet first, then stitch you up."

He lifted me from the ground, and ordered Benjamin to lead us to the brook.

Feet wrapped securely in fresh bandages, flesh still smarting from being stitched back together, I sat against a tree trunk listening to the conversation swirling around me. Penny and Betsy huddled near me.

The relief I had felt when I had seen my dear friends emerge from the foliage, exhausted and frightened, had been nearly overwhelming. They had survived the night—were whole. The pain in my heart lessened with their presence.

I let my eyes drift over the gathered group of people from so many varying backgrounds. Fourteen of us in all. Fourteen that had escaped into the dark depths of the forest. It was a depressingly small number.

"We have to fight!" declared a young man by the name of Quinn. The former guard had a hodgepodge selection of armor—a breastplate and a forearm guard, no chain mail. It bespoke his frantic flight from the castle. He must have been asleep when the attack had started.

Benjamin and the other young guards, four others, all agreed wholeheartedly with his exclamation, lifting swords.

Gregor shook his head. "The people that pulled this off must have hundreds—if not thousands—to back them up. You're suggesting we take them on with eight fighters?"

Arguing broke out and I wanted to cover my ears. The topic filled me with fear but I could not fully focus on the situation at hand. I had another worry on my mind—my injured feet. Gregor had instructed me to keep my feet clean and dry, to let the stitches do their job. That meant I needed to stay off my feet for the next two weeks. Two weeks! How was I supposed to contribute to this group if I could not stand, let alone walk?

I had learned early in my life that if I had a purpose, I would be more welcome wherever I went. If I was helpful, if people needed me, I would not be abandoned as quickly. I was still left behind or asked to leave eventually, but having a duty extended my stay. That being said, I was seeing the end of my association with these people. Why would they keep me around if I could not help?

A piercing whistle cut through the arguing, silencing it. Creed dropped his hand, moving to stand in the middle of the group. He turned in a circle, looking at everyone one at a time.

"We don't have the numbers to win right now, that is true. We are alone in the forest, slapdash at best. But we have a whole country of people that we can rally behind us."

"Why would they rally behind us?" Prince Fitzroy asked.

Creed huffed out a laugh. "Perfect timing for that question. They'll rally behind us because of *you*. As far as we know, you're the heir to the throne. You are the reason we have a chance of winning. When the people know you live, you will give them hope."

Prince Fitzroy swayed, then sat down heavily.

"Evil triumphs when the good people of this world stand down without a word," Creed went on. "We have to fight back. The courage of a few may be all that we need to start the landslide of change, the start of a new world."

"I'm with you," Clark, another guard, stated.

Voices rang out from around the circle, rising up in agreement. All chimed in their willingness to help. I kept silent.

Plans for where we would go began to form. Creed had a cabin some distance from here, in the deepest part of the forest. That seemed as good a place for a headquarters as any.

At the same time, the men began to take stock of our supplies. Three small canteens, from the guards who had been on duty last night, would have to suffice.

Gregor had his medicine bag.

Creed came over and sat down beside me. "I couldn't help but notice that you remained quiet when everyone was pitching their voices in to help," he said.

I bit my lip, avoiding his perceptive gaze. "I… I do not expect you all to take me with you."

"Excuse me?" he asked, shock filling his voice.

"I cannot walk. I have to stay off my feet. I will not be able to contribute to your cause, not for another two weeks. Why would you allow me to stay with you? It does not make sense."

Beside me, he rested his forearms on his knees, and dropped his head, clearly thinking deeply. "You're suggesting we leave you behind?"

"It is the wisest course for you all."

"Well, it's not happening. To leave you behind is unthinkable. Gregor, come over here." When the stoic man stopped next to us, Creed jerked a thumb in my direction. "Naya here suggests we leave her behind, because of her feet. What is your professional opinion on that?"

Gregor crossed his arms. "Absolutely not. If infection were to set in, I would need to be close by to help combat it. We will take care of you until you heal. Now, if you will excuse me. Several more minor injuries have come to my attention." He left without another word.

"There we go," Creed said, pushing himself to his feet. "You're coming with us. That's final."

I cringed. "You are mad at me," I said hesitantly.

He threw his hands up. "Of course I'm mad at you! To even suggest that we—that I—leave you behind is frankly insulting! I'll carry you all the way to my cabin myself if I have to."

With that, he left me sitting there, staring after him. I felt warm inside with the knowledge that I was not being abandoned.

The fourteen of us were hiking in the direction of Creed's cabin before the sun was high in the sky. We were all stretched out in a long chain, quietly following Creed as he took us on a winding path through the thick forest.

I was currently being carried by Benjamin, the first to volunteer to carry me on our trip. The eight men would switch off carrying me every hour or so, making sure my feet never touched the ground. I felt guilty but also ridiculously happy at remaining with the group.

We had a long way to go to get to our new home. I had a feeling that it was going to be an even longer wait to find some semblance of calm, a sense of safety and peace.

It was fourteen against all odds. Heaven help us.

EPILOGUE

My dear daughters,

If you are reading this, then it has happened: I have been arrested, tried, and executed for crimes against the crown and kingdom. Treason. This must have come as a great shock to you dear girls. Allow me to explain as best I can.

For the past six months, I have been the patsy for a secretive, cunning group of rebels by the name of Red Fang or the Red Fang Movement. I became their lamb fattened for sacrificial slaughter, if you will.

Over the past few months, they forced me to vote a certain way in Lords, to cast aspersions against our king when I have nothing but the highest respect for him. They even used my tattoo against me, having selected a few people in their organization to obtain identical marks with the intent to make it look as though I were at the helm of this organization.

Dear girls, the reason I did not resist, did not fight with all the breath in me, was because they have your mother.

Your mother didn't go to visit your Nana in the fall, as I told you. She had gone to a friend's home a short distance away and instead of returning home a few days later as planned, I received a letter from Red Fang informing me that she was being held at an undisclosed location. There was no ransom, only the demand that I keep quiet and to do exactly as I was told. If I didn't do that, they threatened to send your mother back to me, piece by piece. As proof of their seriousness, they included the tip of your mother's pinky finger.

I was so afraid, for your mother and for you girls, for what they might do to you two, that I complied. I fell in line with their demands. I was the perfect puppet.

Until now.

I risk everything just writing this to you. But the vultures are circling. Evidence of my so-called guilt has been planted and may have already been found. The end is nigh. I can feel it. I cannot rest easy knowing you would end up thinking the worst of me. I seek to answer your questions, to soothe your doubts in me.

I love you both so much. Caroline, never stop singing; your voice makes the birds positively green with envy. Constance, you will be a fantastic diplomat. Don't let the preconceived notions of a few chauvinists keep you from your dreams.

Live as you see fit, girls.

I pray you will, at least, see your mother once more. I also pray for the world you will be living in if these rebels have their way.

With all my love,
    Your father
    R. Donovan

P.S…

The punishment for treason is death. Please, allow me to meet my end as my puppeteer intended. I beg you, keep mum about all I have written. Your lives will be forfeit the moment you breathe any of this to any other soul. Do this for me, please.

TO BE CONTINUED….

ACKNOWLEDGEMENTS

I did it! I just have to say that right off the bat. I never thought I would actually get into the publishing world, let alone the self-publishing route! I did not get here by myself though, and I have so many people who helped me along the way who deserve all the thanks in the world.

I would first like to thank my parents, Troy and Kristi, for being such a wonderful support network, for believing in my work in all its stages. Thank you for showing me the fantastic world of reading from such a young age. And thank you, Dad, for your invaluable edits for this book.

To my husband, Mason, thank you for helping me realize that I could reach for the stars and pursue my dreams. You've helped me gain the confidence to put myself out there and share my story with the world. You are my best friend!

To my dear friend, Rebecca Hunter, thank you for being here from the beginning. You have been the best sounding board and you helped keep the excitement going. Thank you for listening to my crazy rants about made-up characters.

To my little brother Matt, thank you for reading my book and for your positive comments. I don't think you know how important it was for me, right before my release date, so thank you!

To Victoria McCombs, for the absolutely amazing cover art! You made my dreams for my first cover a reality and for that I will be forever grateful.

To proofreader and print formatter, Cheyenne van Langevelde, thank you so much for helping me polish up my manuscript. You were amazing and so easy to work with.

To ebook formatter, Susan L. Markloff, thank you so much for working with me, for taking me on such short notice and for being so efficient.

To Alissa Zavalianos, thank you so much for your priceless guidance as I navigated the self-publishing world! You have been so kind and patient with my innumerable questions.

And, last but not least, YOU, the reader! Thank you for taking a chance on this writer.

ABOUT THE AUTHOR

Stacy Bair Ogden has been writing as long as she can remember, weaving together rich worlds with a wide variety of characters, from kids with superpowers to young adults struggling to overcome self-doubt. When she is not daydreaming about her writing, she dabbles in watercoloring and has her nose in a book more often than not, eagerly devouring the written word that has come to mean so much to her. Stacy lives in the Pacific Northwest with her husband and baby boy.

Instagram: @authorstacybairogden

Made in the USA
Las Vegas, NV
17 November 2023

80980288R10115